Dead Reckoning

Dead Reckoning

A Pirate Voyage with Captain Drake

LAURIE LAWLOR

Simon & Schuster Books for Young Readers

New York   London   Toronto   Sydney

SIMON & SCHUSTER BOOKS FOR YOUNG READERS
An imprint of Simon & Schuster Children's Publishing Division
1230 Avenue of the Americas, New York, New York 10020

SIMON & SCHUSTER BOOKS FOR YOUNG READERS is a trademark of Simon & Schuster, Inc.
Book design by Greg Stadnyk
The text for this book is set in Centaur MT.
Manufactured in the United States of America
10 9 8 7 6 5 4 3 2 1
Map on pages vi-vii © HIP/Scala/Art Resource NY
Library of Congress Cataloging-in-Publication Data
Dead reckoning : a pirate voyage with Captain Drake / Laurie Lawlor.— 1st ed.
p. cm.
Summary: Emmet, a fifteen-year-old orphan, learns hard lessons about survival when he sails from England in 1577 as a servant aboard the Golden Hind—the ship of his cousin, the explorer and pirate Francis Drake—on its three-year circumnavigation of the world.
ISBN 0-689-86577-5
1. Drake, Francis, Sir, 1540?-1596—Juvenile fiction. 2. Pirates—Juvenile fiction. [1. Drake, Francis, Sir, 1540?-1596—Fiction. 2. Pirates—Fiction. 3. Seafaring life—Fiction. 4. Survival—Fiction. 5. Explorers—Fiction. 6. Orphans—Fiction] I. Title.
PZ7.L4189De 2005
[Fic]—dc22   2004021682

FIRST
Ⓕ
EDITION

For my brother and loyal shipmate
Douglas McMasters Thompson

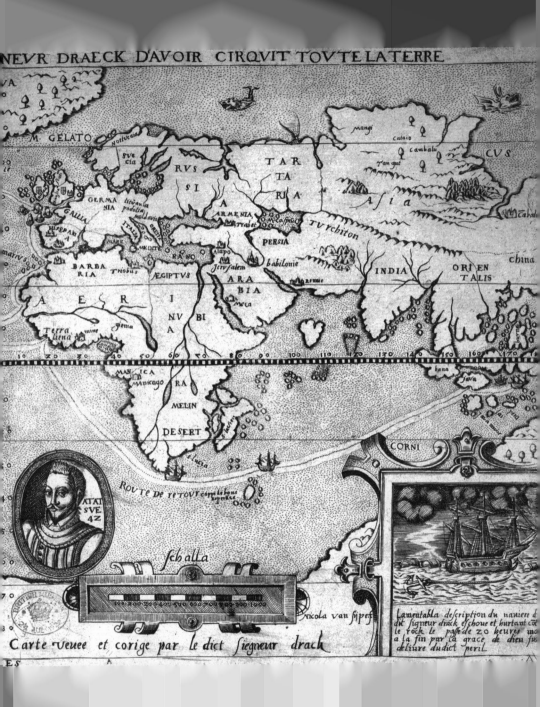

NEVR DRAECK D'AVOIR CIRQVIT TOVTE LA TERRE

M. GELATO · SVECIA · RVSSIA · TARTARIA · Asia · mangi · Cataio · cambalu · CVS · Tangut · Cabalu

GERMANIA · lithuania · podolia · moldavia · GALLIA · ITALIA · HISPANIA · MARE · MEDITERANO · BARBARIA · Triobus · AEGIPTVS · ARMENIA · Arrabet · Meffou · PERSIA · babilonie · TVrchiton · Alapo · Jerusalem · ARABIA · INDIA · ORIENTALIS · china

AERI · NVBIA · meca · Terra hena · mine · gema

MANICA EL Manicago · RA MELIN · DESERT · lena · Java · lucia

CORNI

ROVTE DE RETOVR

schalla

ATATIS SVE 4Z

nicola van super

Carte veuee et corige par le dict sieugneur drach

Lamentabla description du naniere du
dit signeur drack eschoue et hurtant con
le rock le passe de 20 heures ma
a la fin par la grace de dieu fus
deliure dudict peril

Dead Reckoning
A calculation of the ship's place without any observation of the heavenly bodies. A guess made by consulting the log, the time, the direction, the wind, and so on. Such a calculation may suffice for many practical purposes, but must not be fully relied on.

—*E. Cobham Brewer*
Dictionary of Phrase and Fable, *1898*

Chapter One

The cottage shuddered with a loud knock. "Open this door!"

Not another villager! Emmet dipped his quill into a bottle of ink. He studied the V shape on the sleek head of his pet adder. The snake lounged comfortably on the table among piles of books, scummy wooden spoons, apple cores, and greasy pewter plates. *Such a beautiful face,* Emmet thought.

"I know you're in there!" A heavy fist slammed against the wooden door again.

Emmet had never been bitten. Not once. It grieved him to see his neighbors kill every scaly creature they found basking harmlessly among the dry bracken slopes and heather banks on the moor.

Boom! Boom! Boom!

Emmet sighed. He hoped it wasn't Bellamy, the cobbler who'd come last week to have his sick sow cured. *Another botched job.* His teacher, God rest his soul, would have been so disappointed.

"Open up, I tell you!"

"Father Parfoothe is dead!" Emmet shouted. "Go away."

The latch rattled. "Some gentleman come a long way to see you. You want for me to kick down this door?"

Tenderly Emmet scooped up the adder and tucked it inside a

crevice in the cottage's stone wall. If only Father Parfoothe were still here. He would know what to do, what to say. "Patience, sir!" Emmet called. He unlatched the door and opened it just a crack.

The ragged moorman, who had been pounding, darted away from the door, cap in hand. He bowed again and again in the direction of a ruddy-faced man with a red beard, seated on an elegant horse. The stranger wore a splendid blue velvet doublet. Tied beneath the creamy ruff around his neck was a black fur-trimmed cape. On his head he wore a green velvet cap with an embroidered band, and his hands were gloved in fine white leather. He sat very tall in the saddle, and there was something about his expression that was as bold and daring as Satan himself.

Emmet was so stunned by the unexpected arrival of such a fine gentleman, that he stumbled out of the cottage. He barely managed to tug off his cap and bow without tripping over his own feet. "My lordship, how may I be of service?" He felt a rising sense of terror. "I can assure you, sir, that my teacher intended to pay what he owed on his rent. You can tell Lord Russell, if it pleases you, sir, that my master passed away quite suddenly. It was the appearance of the comet that killed him, I think. He has been dead for three weeks, and I've tried to keep his possessions in perfect order, but—" Emmet paused, desperate for words. Sweat started to run down the insides of his arms. He wished he were not such a bad liar and miserable coward. "How can I serve you, sir?"

The man on the horse stared down at him with cold, dark eyes. "You can serve me by ceasing your chatter. Enough of your jawing-tackle!"

"Yes, sir." Emmet had no idea what the stranger was talking about. Terrified, he bowed humbly three times. A nobleman like one of Lord Russell's men could say or do anything he pleased—especially if he found out who Emmet really was, and what his teacher, dead these three weeks, had really been about. Maybe the moorman had told him. Emmet winced. He could already feel the hangman's rope tighten around his neck.

The stranger dismounted. "You do not recognize me?"

Father Parfoothe had instructed Emmet in the ways a person's character depended upon the balance of the humors. Emmet noticed right away the stranger's flushed face—the sign of too much blood. *A sanguine, cheerful personality,* Emmet thought. There was something familiar about the gentleman's booming voice—or was it the prominent nose, the high forehead? Emmet had spent so much time gazing into Father Parfoothe's crystal looking for signs of missing children and runaway lovers, guilty thieves and holy angels, he sometimes confused real people with visions. Had he heard this stranger speak in a dream, perhaps? Or had he drawn him?

"I am sorry, sir, I do not recall who you are," Emmet mumbled. Silently he prayed that the nobleman would not come inside his teacher's cottage. Then he'd know everything. Emmet tried to remember some chant, some charm to keep the stranger from crossing the cottage threshold. As usual in emergencies, Emmet drew a complete blank. He could think of nothing. Not a word.

Without pausing, the stranger pushed past him and marched with a proud limp straight into the cottage. "Are you coming?" he barked from inside the cottage. "I wish a word with you in private. Send that beggar fool away."

Emmet did not need to motion to the lurking moorman, who dashed obediently out of sight. Emmet shuffled inside.

The stranger was already inspecting the books, the charts, the crystal. "Shut the door," he commanded.

Emmet twisted his worn, woolen cap. His eyes darted from the dusty shelf crammed with books with Latin and Greek titles to the unmade bed, the piles of clothing, the heaps of dried pennywort, bay, rue, rosemary, and sage, and the bunches of vervain. Why had he never noticed before how disordered his teacher's one-room cottage had become?

The stranger sniffed. "What is that horrible smell?"

"I . . . I don't know, your lordship," Emmet stammered. "Perhaps the collection of skulls."

"Skulls?"

"Mostly small rodents and birds, sir. Skeletons were a fascination for Father Parfoothe, sir. I can explain—"

"I am not interested in lengthy explanations, Cousin. I am in a hurry. My ship sets sail in less than two weeks."

Emmet gulped. *Cousin?*

"Of course you don't remember me."

Stunned, Emmet glanced at the stranger in fine, rich apparel. He looked old enough to be his father. *Is this some kind of trick?* "Sir," Emmet said slowly, "my family is of humble origin. Except for my grandmother's people, no one's risen above tenant farming, sheep shearing—"

"So you need convincing?" the stranger said, smiling. "I'm your cousin Francis. My father, Edmund, was your father's brother."

Edmund. Edmund. Something unsavory was connected to that name, but try as he might Emmet could not remember what. He cursed his poor memory. "In one ear and out the other," that was what his teacher always said.

"The last time I came to visit our grandmother at Crowndale," the stranger continued, "you were only knee-high. We sat beneath the arbor where she grew grapes. Beyond the apple orchard were beehives. You kept calling to the bees. She seemed to find this amusing."

Emmet was too shocked to speak. Grandmother's house at Crowndale, the grape arbor, the apple orchard. He knew them all so well that when he shut his eyes he could even recall their sweet fragrance. He could hear the sound of the bees and his grandmother's gentle voice. Calling down the bees, she had said, was a sign of his gift. *If she only knew how wrong she'd been.*

"Forgive me, sir," Emmet said quietly. "I have no close relations left alive. Grandmother has been dead for five years. My father died when I was but an infant. My sisters passed away—"

"From the plague," his cousin interrupted. "I've already heard the story. You're all that Grandmother ever talked about. How she took you in as a small baby when your mother lost her mind and nearly dropped you in the fire."

Emmet gripped his cap tighter. With all his might he tried to betray no discomfort. He did not like to be reminded of the way he'd been abandoned by his wretched mother.

"You showed signs of such brilliance," his cousin continued. For a moment something cruel flickered at the corners of his smiling mouth. "Your talents were remarkable, even for such a young child. A promising boy made more promising with the tutoring of that old monk. Like all the other popish infidels, he had nowhere to go after the Crown shut down the abbey. What was that cunning man's name?"

Emmet blushed. *So he knows.* "Father Parfoothe."

"You worked as his scryer, staring into crystals and mirrors. He bade you tell him what you saw, didn't he?"

Emmet shifted uneasily from one foot to the other. No matter how patient his teacher had been, he could not seem to teach Emmet the innumerable rituals for finding lost objects, blessing bleeding wounds, or saying charms for mad dogs, sick horses, thorn pricks, snake bites, scaldings, toothaches, cramps, swellings, and ragings. "Sir," Emmet said at last, "my master harmed no one. He did good service revealing thefts. For his charms he never asked for pay. He sought only truth that is useful and necessary. He gave the people comfort for their pains and illnesses."

"That may be," his cousin said, and yawned. "But all of your master's powers and good works certainly did you no great service. You were supposed to go to the university, but then Grandmother died and all of your inheritance disappeared. A pity." His cousin fingered the heavy gold chain around his neck. "And now what are your prospects?"

"Prospects, sir?"

"Your future. Surely you have thought of it. You can not bury yourself in this horrible hovel forever."

Emmet cleared his throat. "I can teach Latin and Greek and mathematics. I can teach music."

"To whom? From what I've seen, the rats are more intelligent than the children in this starving village."

Emmet dug his toe into the dirty rushes scattered on the floor. It was disconcerting that his cousin knew so much about his life when Emmet knew nearly nothing about him.

"Stand up straight, boy. You remind me of Uncle Robert the way you slouch. Such a pitiful, bookish kind of man. Not the kind you could depend on to reef a bowsprit or haul a clew line with a will."

"Yes, sir," Emmet said, his face flushed with anger.

His cousin grinned as if glad that the insult of Emmet's father had hit its mark. Carelessly he thumbed through some of the sketches on the table. "You draw?"

Emmet nodded, teeth clenched.

"Excellent. And do you also know how to cast a horoscope?"

"No, sir," Emmet replied in a low, careful voice.

"Good. Prophecy is something that should be left strictly to the experts. I've already had my horoscope cast for me by a respected, learned man in London. He told me some important things. He said I must take you with me on my next voyage to North Africa. A trading voyage to Alexandria, Tripoli, and Constantinople."

"Me, sir?" Emmet said in disbelief.

"We'll be taking on a cargo of currants. You'll be my page. So get your things packed. You'll enjoy seeing the world. Why, any hawse-pipe sailor would jump at the chance to be my servant and learn the ways of proper behavior and social manners. At dinner before the officers you'll play the lute and sing. I know you're skilled in music. The cunning man taught you the lute, didn't he?"

Emmet nodded and glanced at the stringed instrument that hung from a peg on the wall. Everything was happening so quickly, he wondered if he were dreaming. *Go to sea as my cousin's servant? Play the lute and sing?* He felt as helpless as he did in nightmares when he was being pursued by wolves with gleaming yellow eyes and could not move a muscle to escape.

"I have special plans for you, kinsman." Using the tips of two gloved fingers his cousin plucked a dusty satchel from atop a heap of dirty clothes. He flung the satchel in Emmet's direction. "I imagine you'll have a few things you'll want to take along. Quill pens, brushes, paints, and parchment. You can record what you see on the voyage. Shrubs, insects, fish, birds. You would like that, wouldn't you?"

Emmet nodded and licked his lips. Father Parfoothe had taken him on numerous collecting expeditions out into the moor to find special herbs and roots, to watch birds, and to study the stars and planets. These adventures always delighted Emmet. Yet in all his life he had never traveled farther away from Tavistock than Blackmoorham. The exotic sound of faraway Alexandria, Tripoli, and Constantinople thrilled him. Perhaps his cousin's arrival was a sign of special providence. *Could this mean that I am ready to try my fortune?*

Without warning, a disturbing thought crossed his mind. "Why, sir?" Emmet asked with all his courage. "Why have you come such a long way to invite me to go with you on the voyage? I don't know how to sail. I can't even swim. Surely there are other servants, other artists better qualified than I am—"

"Nonsense!" his cousin said, and chuckled. "You are kin. I depend on loyalty most of all among the men who serve under my command. What better loyalty can be found than among our own blood ties?" He paused and placed his hand reverently over his heart. "I am a childless man. Helping a lad make his way in the world gives me pleasure. I see this arrangement as a way to repay the deep gratitude I owe our grandmother. May she look down from heaven upon us at this very moment and give us her blessing." His eyes closed for a moment as if he were deep in prayer.

Emmet watched him and felt impressed. Father Parfoothe had

taught Emmet to be wary of the company he kept. "Obey God, do right, and be honorable in all things," he always said. Surely someone like his cousin, someone so full of piety, generosity, and family loyalty, would meet even his teacher's high standards. Emmet felt ashamed that he had questioned his cousin's motives even for a moment.

"Since you are to be my servant," his cousin said, "I need to know something of your name."

"Certainly, sir," Emmet replied. He stuffed his one change of clothing and his art supplies inside the satchel.

"Your Christian name is John. So why are you called Emmet?"

"My teacher gave me the nickname when I was young. It means 'ant.'"

His cousin burst into harsh laughter. "A good name for someone small and insignificant."

Emmet bit his lip. "And what, sir, shall I call you?"

"Captain. Call me Captain Drake. Do not ever call me Cousin on board ship," he said, flicking dirt from his doublet with care. "And don't forget to take the book."

"What book, Captain?"

"You know the one I mean. *The Key of Solomon.*"

Emmet paused. "You are referring perhaps to *Clavicule?* That's in Latin." He pulled the thick volume from the shelf and blew cobwebs from the cover. "This won't be very helpful for navigation, sir. My teacher never used it. As I explained before, he did not dabble in these dark arts. He was a natural philosopher. This, sir, is a book on how to gain wealth, love, and power; it lists principle demons and conjurations to find treasures, curse enemies, and procure love."

"I said take it." Captain Drake's eyes narrowed. He handed Emmet his own satchel. "And the crystal, too."

Emmet fumbled with the book and the crystal, a shining, clear stone no bigger than a large goose egg. He slipped both of these into the captain's satchel. "I'm really not skilled—"

"And don't forget the Mosaical Wand."

Emmet took a deep breath. He was about to tell Captain Drake that this, too, was something he did not know how to work. Father Parfoothe had long, long ago abandoned treasure seeking with the Mosaical Wand. Too dangerous, he said. But there was something so unexpectedly threatening about the captain's glance that Emmet packed the dousing rod made of witch hazel into the satchel with the book and crystal.

Captain Drake took the satchel and cradled it carefully under his arm. With the toe of his elegant boot he swung open the door. "Hurry now. We're going to Plymouth. I have a horse waiting for you. You can ride, can't you?"

Emmet nodded. Something twisted in the pit of his stomach. Perhaps he was making a terrible mistake.

Captain Drake was already out the door and had mounted his horse. He motioned to the swaybacked pony tied to a nearby tree. "Are you coming?"

Emmet grabbed the precious lute that his teacher had given to him the day he died. He slipped the strap over his shoulder so that the stringed instrument hung against his back. On his other shoulder he carried his satchel of personal belongings. He fumbled with the door and latch. What would become of the cottage after he left? There'd be no one to look after his teacher's books of poetry, philosophy, and music, or his moth and butterfly collections. It was terrible to imagine so utterly deserted the place where Emmet had been so happy during much of his life. Carefully he pulled the door shut.

As Emmet turned away he felt surprised to hear loud shouts and angry voices in the distance. Across the field from Tavistock a rowdy crowd appeared to be marching in the direction of Father Parfoothe's cottage. What could they possibly want? Some carried torches and pitchforks. Others carried pikes.

"Bear a hand, boy! Some disappointed customers off port bow. Up keeleg!" Captain Drake announced in a calm, clear voice. "We must be on our way directly, unless you want to walk up Ladder Lane and down Hemp Street."

Emmet stood frozen with terror. *They're coming for me!*

"Up anchor!" Captain Drake barked, louder this time.

Terrified, Emmet rushed to the pony, untied the reins, and swung his leg over its broad back. With shaking hands he slung his satchel across the saddle.

Captain Drake, astride his snorting horse, trotted south along the muddy path toward Plymouth. Emmet bumped and rattled behind him. The lute made a sad thrumming sound with every jolt. His cape flapped wildly as he tried to keep up with the captain.

Only when they were nearly half a mile away did he dare glance back in the direction of his beloved teacher's cottage. Plumes of dark smoke floated skyward. "My adder!" he cried out, even though he knew it was too late.

A cold October wind that smelled of burning thatch blew across the moor. Emmet hunched forward and kicked the pony in the ribs. There was no going back.

Chapter Two

Plymouth bustled with craftsmen, peddlers, and farmers on their way to market. Barefoot children and barking dogs wove through the crowd. Wagons filled with lumber and casks, bales and barrels, trundled along the road through town in what seemed an endless parade.

Never in his life had Emmet seen so many people, so much activity in one place. The din of shouting, sawing, and hammering, and the bellowing of herds of cattle driven to market was nearly deafening. Sleepy Tavistock seemed as far away as the moon. For a moment Emmet forgot about the terror of watching his teacher's cottage set aflame. He forgot he was homeless. He forgot that he could never safely return to the village where he had been born.

In wonder he gazed about the busy seaport town. He sniffed. A salty, fishy, distinctly unfamiliar aroma pervaded the air. The ocean! Somewhere beyond the crowd and jumble of buildings lay the harbor and the great, wide sea. Emmet had never seen the ocean before and was eager to inspect it.

"D'ye hear?" Captain Drake's sharp voice jolted Emmet out of his daydream. "I'm talking to you, boy!"

"Yes, sir," Emmet said in a sheepish voice. "Sorry, sir."

"Go to the *Pelican* directly. I have business in town with my officers. There's not a moment to lose."

Emmet dismounted and handed the reins of the pony to the captain. As he adjusted the lute and satchel over his shoulders, his stomach growled. All that he'd eaten since morning was a stale wedge of cheese. "The Pelican, sir?" he asked hopefully. "Is that a tavern?"

Captain Drake scowled. "For all your brilliance, you're as dull as a mallet."

"Yes, sir," Emmet replied miserably.

"The *Pelican* is my ship. She's being loaded at the dock. Be on your way. Tell Stydye you're my page. He'll inform you of your duties." Captain Drake turned his horse and, with the pony in tow, disappeared among the crowd.

Suddenly Emmet felt very alone and confused. "The *Pelican*. Stydye. The *Pelican*. Stydye," Emmet repeated so that he would not forget. He trudged toward the forest of slender wooden ships' masts that crowded the harbor. Could this be the dock?

Tanned, muscular men shoved past him with bundles balanced on their shoulders. Some sported tattoos on their beefy arms. Others wore bright kerchiefs knotted around their necks. They did not walk like ordinary men. They ambled with a rolling, loose-kneed gait. *These tough, freewheeling wanderers must be sailors,* Emmet decided. They had been out in the great beyond of ocean and faraway lands. They knew things that Emmet could only imagine.

"By your leave, sir," Emmet asked humbly of a sailor toting a long wooden chest, "can you tell me where the—"

"Out of my way, lubber."

"Excuse me, sir," Emmet said to another fellow with light blond hair. "Do you know—"

"No Engleesh. Yah?" The sailor shrugged, then hoisted a coil of rope.

Desperately Emmet searched the crowded dock. What if he never found the *Pelican*? What if he never found Captain Drake again?

An elderly fellow with a grizzled beard hobbled past using a gnarled cane. "Sir," Emmet begged, "do you know where the *Pelican* is?"

The man squinted. He took off his blue cap and scratched his bald head. "Yonder spy the lumpers?"

"Lumpers?" *What strange language is this?* "No, sir."

The old man sighed loudly. "Those fellows hauling hogsheads and bags, barrels and boxes. You see them carrying cargo aboard the galleon?"

Emmet blinked hard. Every ship looked the same to him. "What is a galleon, sir?"

"Haven't got the hayseed out of your hair, have ye?" The old man spit with disgust. "A galleon's got a long beak under the bowsprit, ye see? The crescent profile rises higher at her stern than at her forecastle."

"Sir, please help me!" Emmet pleaded. "I do not understand a word you say, and I was told to find the *Pelican* with all haste."

The old fellow paused as if considering Emmet's plight. "Follow my wake," he ordered, then hobbled along the dock.

Emmet kept close behind him, dodging the other sailors as best he could. "So that's it?" Emmet said in awe when they reached the end of the dock, where the smell of kelp was particularly powerful. Beyond the harbor he glimpsed deep-blue, open water. *The ocean.*

"No, that ain't it, Hayseed," the old man replied impatiently. "The *Pelican* is yonder." He pointed his cane at a nearby ship swarmed with men loading boxes, barrels, and bales. "A fine, fast ship they call her. She has legs. You on her crew?"

"I am a servant to Captain Drake," Emmet said, sounding prouder than he'd meant to. Why did this fellow insist on calling the *Pelican* a she? And how could a ship have legs?

"Drake, is it?" The old man spat. "Then you may return a rich man. Or a dead one."

Emmet gulped. *A rich man or a dead one?* "Sir," he protested politely, "we're bound for North Africa to take on a cargo of currants."

"Currants be damned!" The old man laughed so hard he began to cough.

"What mean you, sir?" Emmet asked in confusion.

"Only what every Dutchman in this harbor already knows. There's not a bit of trade goods being loaded into the hold of the *Pelican*, Hayseed. Just plenty of guns, gunpowder, and longbows."

Emmet bit his lip. "Surely those many barrels might contain trade goods?"

"God's wounds, no!" the old man sputtered. His toothless grin was even more disturbing than his laughter. "Those are the crew's victuals. Salt pork, cod, dried peas, biscuit, beer, and wine."

For several moments Emmet watched as casks of lentils, flour, onions, vinegar, oil, and salt were rolled aboard along a long plank from the dock. There seemed to be a tremendous amount of food being loaded onto the *Pelican.* "How, sir," Emmet demanded, turning to the old man, "are you certain—" He stopped. The man was gone.

Odd, Emmet thought. He rubbed his eyes, then scanned the crowd on the dock. Nowhere did he see a sign of a blue cap. Anxiously he adjusted his satchel and lute. He must keep his wits about him. *Rich or dead, the old man said.* Clearly the crazy, ancient fellow was just trying to frighten him.

With new resolve Emmet crossed the bouncing plank to the *Pelican.* As soon as he stepped aboard, the roll and pitch of the deck caused him to nearly tumble headfirst down an open hatchway into the dark depths of the ship.

"Take care, soger!" a tall, thin fellow shouted and cursed at him.

"Out of my way!" bellowed another hauling a barrel.

Emmet clutched the railing that ran along the sides of the ship. The entire length of the *Pelican* appeared to be no longer than one hundred paces—as big as Grandmother's house set end to end with the byre, where the animals lived. The width of the ship was perhaps twenty paces. At the far end of the ship a fancy door and windows indicated some kind of special lodging area. Emmet wondered how such a small place might fit so many sailors. How would there be room enough for everyone to sleep? Above this compartment, layered like a Christmas pudding, were two more platforms surrounded by railings and connected by ladders.

The sounds and smells around Emmet reminded him of a barnyard. Crammed on deck were makeshift pens containing lowing cattle and squawking chickens. The smell of manure and feed filled the air. A goat tied to a rope nibbled a kerchief. Mildewed sails, tarred rope, and muddy cable were heaped in a confused jumble among barrels and casks.

Three great masts as thick as trees rose from the deck. Each was connected with a web of ropes, horizontal pieces of wood, and bunched-up rolls of canvas. At a dizzying height high overhead Emmet glimpsed a small figure who darted with the dexterity of a spider among a network of ropes and lines. Emmet watched in fascination.

Suddenly the deck lurched. Emmet tried to steady himself by looking down and gasping for fresh air. No good. His dizzy head pounded, his stomach cartwheeled. The cheese rose up in his throat. He rushed to the side of the ship, bent over, and retched.

"Hay-Comber!" someone called in a musical-sounding voice.

Hurriedly, Emmet wiped his mouth with his sleeve. He looked up, horrified.

A barefoot boy had been watching him and laughing. The boy's skin was very black, and he wore ragged breeches and a sleeveless leather jerkin. "Never did I spew first time I come aboard Old Man's ship," proclaimed the boy, who stood a head taller than Emmet. When the boy grinned, his teeth shone white. Dramatically he gestured first to his head, then to his hands. "*Con razon.* Every hair like a yarn rope. Every finger a fish hook."

What language was this? Emmet felt too queasy to ask. He'd never seen someone with such black skin. He'd never heard anyone boast so grandly.

"*¿Cómo se llama usted?*" the boy demanded.

"Pardon?" Emmet replied. He took a deep breath and prayed his stomach would not betray him again.

"No Spanish? *Es lástima.* Your name?"

"I'm called Emmet."

"Diego," he said, and pointed to himself. "You hear of *Cimarrone?* We escape Spanish, live in jungle with Indians. I serve Old Man since Nombre de Dios. You hear of Nombre de Dios? *Mucho oro. Mucho plata.*" Diego rubbed his hands together and winked. "You and me, *opulento, sí?*"

Emmet gazed at Diego in confusion. Emmet's knowledge of neither Greek nor Latin seemed of much use. But then he'd hardly met anyone whose language he understood since he'd come to Plymouth.

"What will be your job?" Diego asked.

"I am a page to Captain Drake."

Diego's eyebrows shot up in surprise. "Old Man tell me nothing about new manservant." He clamped Emmet on the shoulder. "You and me, we share work. *Bueno!*"

Emmet wasn't sure why Diego seemed so pleased they'd both be servants for Captain Drake. Perhaps working for the captain was more than one person could handle.

"Sogering again, eh, Diego?" shouted a fat man with a book under his arm. "Good-for-nothing skulker." The man tried to cuff Diego on the side of the head, but the boy was too fast. He ducked and scrambled out of sight.

"*Pajaro puerco!*" Diego called. "Stydye!"

As soon as Emmet heard that name, he remembered what he was supposed to do next. "Sir?" Emmet said. "I was told by Captain Drake to seek you out."

Wearily, Stydye opened his enormous book. "From the cut of your jib I can see you're no sailor."

Awkwardly Emmet adjusted his lute over his shoulder and hid his ink-stained hands behind his back. "My Christian name is John Drake, sir. I go by Emmet. I'm to be a page for the captain."

"Another Drake," Stydye said with little enthusiasm. He took a quill tucked inside the brim of his hat. He dipped the quill in a stoppered bottle tied to a leather belt around his waist and made a mark inside his book. "Page, is it? For which captain? Which ship? There's more than one."

"Captain Drake, sir." Emmet felt confused. "How many boats are there?"

"They're ships, boy. Not boats. And there are five of them," Stydye said and spat. "The *Pelican*—she's one hundred and fifty tons. Then there's the *Elizabeth* at eighty, the *Marigold* at thirty, the *Swan* at fifty, and the pinnace *Benedict* at seventeen."

"Oh, I see, sir," said Emmet, not wishing to show that he did not know what any of the numbers meant, except that the *Pelican* seemed to be the biggest.

"How old are you?" Stydye demanded.

"Fifteen, sir."

"For fifteen you're no bigger than a sprit-sail sheet knot, nor heavier than a paper of lampblack—and not strong enough to haul a shad off a gridiron!"

Emmet clutched his fists. Even though he did not understand exactly what Stydye meant, he could tell he was being insulted.

"As page you'll do as you're bid," Stydye said. "You'll serve at captain's table, clean dishes after meals, scrub the cabin, wash laundry, empty the chamber pot. Any task the captain requires. Waggishness and idleness will result in a flogging. Think you are strong enough to handle the work?"

"*'Philosophum non facit barba!'*" Emmet muttered.

"Dowse that now," Stydye said darkly, and slammed the book shut. "There'll be no conjure words aboard this ship."

"I was only speaking Latin, sir." Emmet's voice shot into a nervous treble. "'The beard does not define a philosopher.' Just an expression from Plutarch. A figure of speech."

"Beards, is it?" Stydye suspiciously studied the peach-fuzz whiskers on Emmet's face. "It's a long voyage, Johnny. So I'll give you some advice. Sailors can be a danger as great as the sea itself. Knock off the Latin if you want to stay alive."

"Thank you, sir."

"Stow your belongings below. Cook will tell you what to do." Stydye shook his head and walked away. "One hundred eighty common rogues. What a ragged regiment!"

Below? Emmet had no idea where this was. He wished he were back on solid land again. Perhaps he wasn't meant to go to sea. Before he could clamber back across the plank to freedom, someone nabbed him by the collar, stuffed a dead chicken into his arms, and dragged him toward the open hatchway.

"You, page! For the captain's table," a gruff voice said. "Take it below to the galley." The sailor planted a hard kick into Emmet's backside. Emmet lost his balance and nearly went flying down the hatchway ladder. At the last moment he caught his balance, dropped the limp bird, and let go of the strap attached to his lute. The precious instrument crashed against the deck with a loud *thunk* and *twang*.

In horror Emmet stared at the splintered wood. His most precious possession—ruined! Emmet bit his lip and blinked hard to hold back any tears.

"Hurry up now, miserable midget," the man with the boots shouted, "before I—"

"Do what?" interrupted a gentleman in a black velvet cape. He bent over and picked up part of the smashed fret board and turned it over in his long, elegant hands. "Your carelessness has damaged a valuable musical instrument."

"I meant no harm, Captain Doughty, sir," the sailor said, and pulled off his cap. His black hair stood out in spikes. "No harm meant."

"Be gone, Moone, before I tell Captain Drake what you've done." At the very mention of Captain Drake, Moone turned pale and scurried out of sight. "An Italian lute, is it not? A lovely instrument too," Captain Doughty said to Emmet. "Perhaps it can be repaired. My servant is clever. We'll see what we can do."

Emmet felt speechless. "Thank you, thank you, sir. It was my teacher's."

"An educated lad. How unusual," said Captain Doughty. He wore a gleaming earring in one ear. A small, dark moustache had been precisely combed into two points on either side of his wide mouth. "You play?"

"Yes, sir. I am fond of ayres and dance pieces. I have studied Milano and Verdelot."

"You were instructed well. And how came you to be on this ship of bedlam beggars and coney catchers?"

"I am to serve as page, sir. To Captain Drake."

"With some music," Captain Doughty said in a cheerful voice, "perhaps this expedition will not be quite as dull as I feared."

"Yes, sir," Emmet said, retrieving the dead chicken.

"Of course, the blazing star does give one pause about our day of embarkation," Captain Doughty said. Absentmindedly he studied the sky.

There seemed something familiar and reassuring about Captain Doughty's kindly manner, the way he spoke, and the way he paused and listened. Without thinking, Emmet blurted, "Just above the Tropic of Capricorn, sir?"

Captain Doughty gave him a curious look. "Moving above the head of Sagittarius now. The thing glows with a clear white light surrounded by a discolored mane. What else have you noted?"

Emmet paused, choosing his words carefully. "The long tail curls like a sword. At first the star appeared in the west, pointing toward the New World."

"So you have studied stars as well as music?"

"My teacher explained to me how stars and planets possess good and evil aspects," Emmet said with enthusiasm. "They radiate benign or malignant influences on earth, like ripples across the water."

"I presume you've had the opportunity to study the original Latin books."

"*Ars Notoria, Sepher Raziel*—" Suddenly Emmet stopped. *Careful.* He felt a kind of cool wind slice the air and he shivered.

Marching across the deck was the unmistakable form of Captain Drake. Every sailor he passed took a step backward, doffed his cap, and bowed nearly to the ground.

"Good morrow, sir!" Captain Doughty called in a reserved but friendly voice. He touched the tips of his fingers to his brim, but he did not remove his jaunty plumed hat. "I was just speaking with your page. A true find. He is both a musician and a natural philosopher."

Captain Drake glared at Emmet. His steely eyes flashed an

unmistakable warning: *Don't say another word.* Captain Drake cleared his throat. "Boy, don't you have work to do?"

"Yes, sir." Emmet wiped his sweaty palms on his jerkin. He bowed and bowed again, then hurried with the dead chicken down the hatchway ladder into the hold.

Chapter Three

On the lower deck the ceiling stood only five feet high. Grown men hunched forward and bent their knees to make their way through. Emmet ducked to avoid slamming his head against crossbeams in the ceiling. Somewhere in this dank, dark part of the ship that smelled of tar, damp hemp, and rat droppings was the galley or ship's kitchen—the place where the cooking utensils were stored. He had only to find his way forward, a helpful sailor had told him, and he would find the cook.

"Doctor hauls the firebox above deck twice a day to fry sea-pie and choke-dog," the sailor had confided.

Emmet did not feel the least bit hungry after hearing this description of the cook's specialties. But being determined to deliver the captain's chicken, he stumbled along through the semidarkness.

Up ahead he heard something thump. A crowd howled. There was a crash, then a cheer. When Emmet spied a group gathered in a tight circle, he knew there had to be a fight. Eager spectators hunched forward with their hands on their knees. The only illumination came from sunlight filtering through gaps in the planking of the deck overhead.

"Keep at it, Flea!"

"I lay my wager on Sky."

The boy called Flea lay crumpled on the floor, his face bloody and swollen. His right eye had turned nearly purple and bulged shut. He looked no older than Emmet. Sky, perhaps in his early twenties, did not seem a bit worse for wear as he slouched in a slow circle around the fallen boy. Sky was sturdy and broad shouldered, with a fair complexion and scanty beard. He reminded Emmet of the bull-legged fighters who brawled in front of the Tavistock ale house during holidays for the pure joy of fighting.

Flea crawled a bit, then staggered to his feet. He swung wildly with one fist. Sky dodged, then slugged Flea in his soft, fat gut. The boy doubled, reeled backward, and fell against the crowd of gamblers. As soon as Flea tumbled to the floor, Sky leaned over and kicked him again and again. "Teach you to steal from Edwards, soger!" Sky shouted.

"Didn't . . . take . . . the charm," Flea blubbered. He seemed to be trying to protect his stomach from Sky's kicks by turtling into a ball.

"He's down for good!"

"Go at him, Sky!"

The smell of the blood and the sound of the groaning boy being booted to death by a stronger young man made Emmet look away. It wasn't as if he had not seen people die before. He had assisted Father Parfoothe in nursing the sick and maimed many times.

"On your feet, Flea!"

"—five, six, seven, eight—"

Suddenly Emmet felt as if he might puke again. *Why doesn't anyone help him?* Bracing himself with the chicken in one arm and the satchel in the other, he bent forward and butted his way through the howling crowd to try to reach fresh air.

Somebody grabbed his arm before he could escape. "What's your wager, Hay-Comber?" a familiar voice shouted into his ear. It was Diego, carrying a bucket of water and a scrub brush.

Emmet could barely breathe. "What?"

"The box-about. *¿Qué apuesta?*"

"Don't know," Emmet murmured in horrified confusion. *Is it just a game?*

A whistle pierced the darkness. "Tumble up!" a voice shouted. "Enough sogering. There's work to be done!" The men collected their bets and reluctantly drifted away. Diego, too, seemed to have the good sense to vanish. In his hurry, he'd abandoned his bucket of water.

Emmet remained hidden in the shadows of the lower deck. He watched Stydye prod fallen Flea with the toe of his boot. The boy groaned. Stydye shook his head and walked away.

Emmet hesitated. Sometimes Father Parfoothe's blessings had stopped the bleeding and cured broken bones. Sometimes not. Everything, Father Parfoothe always said, depended on faith. "They cannot heal such as do not believe in them."

Emmet looked down at the bedraggled chicken in his fist. He was supposed to take this to the galley. He had work to do. If he were found wanting in his duties, he'd be flogged. And yet he knew that Father Parfoothe would have been ashamed of him if he simply walked away now. *Do right.* Wasn't that what he always said?

Emmet crept closer with the bucket. Flea's hand twitched. He was still breathing. Emmet sighed, untied the boy's dirty kerchief from his neck, and dipped it into Diego's bucket. Almost out of habit, Emmet gently pressed the wet cloth against the boy's battered face. Emmet closed his eyes and silently said three times three a blessing to stop the bleeding. He wasn't sure he remembered correctly the part about the River Jordan waters, wild and rude. Still, it didn't hurt to try, did it?

Flea's one good eye fluttered open. "Leave me alone," he said miserably. "Didn't do nothing."

Emmet leaned over and was about to dip the kerchief into the bucket again when he saw a wavering image of misery and cruelty reflected on the surface of the water. *The face of a thief.* Startled, Emmet looked up. Towering over him was Sky. Emmet felt Sky's iron-hard pinch on the back of his neck.

"Who do you think you are?" Sky demanded in a mocking voice. "Surgeon's mate?"

"I'm nobody, sir," Emmet said in a quavering voice. He wished he were a better, quicker liar. "Not doing anything."

"You got a name, boy?"

"Emmet, sir," he said, flinching with pain. "If it pleases your lordship, I'm on my way to the galley to deliver Captain Drake's chicken." He motioned as best he could to the abandoned mound of feathers on the floor.

"Hasten, boy. My brother doesn't like to wait for his dinner." The pincer grip tightened.

"Please let me go, sir." If Sky knew they were cousins, Emmet was certain he'd be beaten. Emmet closed his eyes and tried to think of some chant to release him from Sky's talonlike grasp. He could not recall one word.

Flea moaned.

Emmet glanced in irritation at Flea, the sprawled boy who had caused him so much trouble. "Butter Box had it coming," Sky murmured. "Stealing a good luck charm from Edwards—that's dangerous business." He laughed, then let go of Emmet's neck. "Why'd you help him?"

Emmet scooped up the chicken and satchel. His heart beat loud enough that he felt sure Sky could hear it. "Nobody else," he mumbled, "would lend a hand."

"It's a good dog nowadays," Sky said with a smirk, "that'll come when he's called, let alone come before it." Suddenly he lunged toward Emmet. "Now clear out of here!" he hooted.

Sky's jeering laughter echoed in Emmet's ears as he scrambled through the darkness toward the galley.

Two months passed. Once the agony of seasickness abated, life aboard the *Pelican* became a blur of new faces and customs. Emmet was not sure that he'd ever understand how to speak so that any of the seventy other men and boys aboard ship could understand him.

He marveled at the differences between his former surroundings and life on ship. Ashore, back in Tavistock, a bull was a farmyard creature. At sea it was a small keg. Ashore, a lizard was an exotic animal. Aboard ship it was a bit of rope with an iron thimble spliced into it. Back home a beating was a form of punishment. At sea it was a way to sail in a crisscross motion. On land a cat's paw was an animal's footprint. Aboard ship it was a kind of wind that moved unexpectedly across the water.

When the bosun's whistle blew in the morning and the next

watch was called, Emmet often awoke from the thin, hay-stuffed pallet where he slept, tucked between two cannons on the crowded lower deck, and wondered where he was. What strange, new wooden world was this? Sometimes he dreamed of Tavistock. Sometimes he dreamed that Father Parfoothe was still alive. Then a harsh voice would bellow in his ear, "Bear a hand!" and shake him hard, and immediately he knew it was the beginning of another confusing day aboard the *Pelican*.

This afternoon Emmet stood very still in the captain's cabin, the private compartment where Captain Drake slept and entertained guests. The cabin was one of two luxurious compartments for officers, located on the main deck at the rear, or stern, of the ship. Sweat trickled down the back of Emmet's neck, inside the stiff ruff collar of his yellow brocade doublet. Whenever the expedition officers were rowed in the longboats from the other ships to attend formal meals on the *Pelican*, Captain Drake insisted that he wear the torturous peascod-belly doublet with the padded and stiffened point in front. "A fashionably dressed page lends the best appearance possible to a gentleman," Captain Drake reminded him. Emmet did as he was told, even though wearing the cursed outfit with the heavily padded shoulders meant that he could barely breathe. Any movement made him sweat uncontrollably.

The four paned windows in the cabin were pushed wide open, but no refreshing breeze entered. Since they'd sailed west from the Verde Islands off the coast of Africa a week ago, the sun scorched them unmercifully. Hot weather made tempers flare. By remaining completely still while Captain Drake and the dozen gentlemen and officers ate, however, Emmet thought he might appear to be invisible. No one could criticize or punish him with a beating if he were not seen, he reasoned. Sometimes the trick worked. Sometimes it didn't.

Emmet glanced around the room at the four younger boys who stood behind the chairs of each of the expedition's four other captains. The other pages did not dress in special clothing or seem to care how they waited on their masters. They wore rumpled linen shirts, sleeveless woolen jerkins, and ordinary woolen breeches covered with dirty aprons. Three leaned against the cabin's ornate carved wall, almost as if asleep. Another picked his nose. Meanwhile a fifth servant carelessly fanned the diners with a large bamboo fan that did nothing but stir the cabin's sour smells of sweat, wine, and boiled beef.

Unlike the other pages, Emmet had been warned not to pare his nails or pick his teeth with a knife while standing at table. Captain Drake forbade him to spit on the floor, lick his fingers, or blow his nose into his hand. He was to remain ramrod straight, with a clean linen napkin draped precisely over his right arm. When called upon, he was to offer perfumed water from the silver urn for the gentlemen's sticky fingers, or refill the gentlemen's goblets with wine kept cool in a copper tub of water.

As usual, Diego had managed to find a comfortable corner out of Captain Drake's sight. Eyes closed, he squatted on his haunches, his back resting against the slanting wall adorned with a brocade wall hanging. Diego's job was to help carefully wash and dry the captain's silver dishes, spoons, and knives when the dinner was finished. Dinner this afternoon was taking a long while to finish. Diego had plenty of time to rest.

The captain's cabin was a tight fit for the dozen or so officers and gentlemen crowded around the biggest, fanciest carved oak table in the fleet. The table, covered with a turkey-work carpet, was now littered with gold-rimmed silver dishes containing bones of boiled capon and fried rabbit, leering heads of turbots, scattered rinds of dainty candied fruit, crusts of white bread, and crumbs of sweet wafers and gingerbread. Flies buzzed around flaccid pools of melted butter and sticky smears from a spice custard pie. Nearly two dozen bottles of fine Portuguese wine had been emptied.

"A toast!" said Captain Wynter, the slight, sallow-faced commander of the *Elizabeth.* This was his seventh glass of wine, and he wobbled dangerously when he tried to lift his arm from the place where he sat at the table on a hard, plain bench.

"To equal companions," Captain Drake said from the head of the table. His ornate raised chair had a fine velvet cushion. He raised his glass and glared at Captain Doughty, whom Emmet had been instructed to seat on an insultingly hard, plain bench below the ornate salt service that stood in the middle of the table.

"And to friendly gentlemen in our enterprise, which Captain Drake and I have jointly planned," said Captain Doughty in a jovial voice. "I commend you in the name of Lord Hatton, my dear friend. After a disastrous beginning, may we have only smooth sailing ahead."

"To smooth sailing!" Captain Wynter managed before hiccupping. "Now that we have a skilled pilot, that is." He lifted his glass toward the glum-looking man with a beard, sitting beside him. Nuño da Silva did not smile or return Captain Wynter's toast.

Captain Drake had insisted that Emmet provide Nuño da Silva, the Portuguese pilot, with a cushion, even though he was a captive aboard the *Pelican*. The fifty-year-old pilot, along with his ship, maps, and charts, had been hijacked by Captain Drake only a week earlier off the coast of Africa. Before setting sail from Cape Verde, numerous arrangements had been made in the fleet. The *Benedict* had been traded for a local fishing boat, and renamed the *Christopher*.

"Your comment about the beginning of the voyage, Captain Doughty, irks me. Must you always belabor the past?" Captain Drake puffed up both cheeks with irritation and let out the air all at once. "What we experienced was only a minor squall."

The hanging silver candleholder that usually swung back and forth barely moved in its place in the middle of the ceiling. The sea was so calm. For several moments no one spoke.

"Enough to drive my *Marigold* into the rocks, sir," said Captain Thomas. "Not to mention the way you were forced to cut the main mast from the *Pelican*. If we had not found safety in Cornwall, we would have never made it back to Plymouth for repairs. Nearly a month wasted. Minor squall, indeed!"

"I told you that the comet boded ill for us to leave in November," Captain Doughty murmured.

"Do you take yourself for a conjurer?" Captain Drake demanded.

Captain Doughty laughed. "Sir, you do not frighten me."

"The most untackled, unballasted, and unvictualized ships I ever saw," Captain Wynter said in a slurred voice to no one in particular. "Not a one ready. That is why we rid ourselves of Stydye, is it not, Captain? A reckless, unprofessional fellow."

"Calling someone a conjurer is a dangerous accusation," announced Francis Fletcher, the *Pelican*'s pious chaplain. The minister never went anywhere without a sponge of vinegar and other confections concealed in an orange peel to keep away pestilent air. Fletcher lifted his goblet and drank his wine with such haste that he began to cough.

Captain Drake reached over and slapped the clergyman so hard on the back he nearly fell to the floor. "More wine, boy!" Captain Drake bellowed at Emmet. "Can't you see the cleric's choking?"

With shaking hands Emmet poured another glass. Fletcher gulped it down quickly. "To the captain-general of the fleet!" Chaplain Fletcher murmured, and held his glass in Captain Drake's direction.

For the first time since the roasted neat's tongue had been served, Captain Drake smiled. It was a thin smile. A calculating smile.

Captain Wynter struggled to his feet. "I want to speak."

"Speak, sir," said Captain Drake, "though you are overseem with wine."

Captain Wynter swayed dangerously left to right as he stared at Captain Doughty. "You, sir, were supposed to be vice admiral, am I correct? I know I am correct. Vice Admiral, what happened to our exploration of Terra Austra . . . Austra—"

"Australis?" Captain Doughty said approvingly.

Captain Wynter nodded. "Yes. That's what I mean. I never gave my consent, gentlemen. I never gave my consent or allowance in any way to the taking of any ship or goods unlawfully on this secret mission."

Everyone stopped drinking. Captain Drake's smile vanished. Emmet felt as if all the air in the overheated cabin were being sucked away. Even the sleepy pages seemed to awaken. Diego's head lifted and he opened his eyes. Like the rest of the crew, none of the servants knew exactly where the ships were headed. Although the destination had been officially pronounced as North Africa, they were now sailing west away from the continent, toward the mid-Atlantic. The sudden change in direction had made everyone gossip and wonder and wager. Where were they headed? To the Caribbean?

"We needed supplies," Captain Drake growled. "Taking barrels of fish and four-hundred weight of biscuit from those ships was not contrary to our expectations."

"Surely the Spanish are our enemies. They are evil and loathsome and deserve to be killed as enemies of God. But leaving those poor, miserable Portuguese sailors marooned! Truly, sir, that was unchristian." Chaplain Fletcher took a breath, then added in a low voice, "We're no better than pirates."

"This is a ship, not a church, sir," Captain Drake replied. He took another quick sip of wine, and wiped his lips with his sleeve.

"A gentleman," Captain Doughty said, turning to his dining companions, "always uses a handkerchief."

Captain Drake frowned. "What mean you by such words?"

"Three Spanish fishing smacks off the coast of Cabo Cabo Agadir," Captain Wynter said, and giggled. "Three Portuguese caravels in Cabo Blaco Blaco. That makes seven, doesn't it?"

"You're moony, Wynter," Captain Drake said. He turned to Captain Doughty and repeated his question. "What mean you, sir?"

Captain Doughty winked and cocked his head to one side, as if this was a very private joke with the other preening noblemen and kinsmen of noblemen who had come to sea for the first time to seek their fortunes. "I mean to say that our general-corsair is a private man of mean quality."

Captain Thomas and Captain Chester held their hands to their mouths to stifle chuckles.

"I may not have your education, sir. Your sophistication. Your experience in matters of state," Captain Drake replied hotly. "But I am a fit man to serve against the Spaniards for my experience and practice in that trade."

Captain Wynter jabbed a shred of boiled beef with his knife. "In what trade, may I ask, sir?"

The vein in Captain Drake's neck began to bulge. His face turned a dangerous shade of red. "It is the very reason why the queen gave me this commission as captain-general and not you, Doughty. Girdling the globe is not the same as gossiping at court—the only thing you seem to know how to do."

"Tut, tut, sir. Let us be friends!" Captain Doughty exclaimed. He struggled to his feet. Emmet and the other servants rushed to refill their goblets. "To the queen!" Captain Doughty exclaimed, and lifted his wine. The others did the same.

No one said anything for several moments. Captain Drake drummed his thick fingers on the wine-stained table. From the lower deck came the sound of the gunner's recorder and the rhythmic stomping of dancing feet. Emmet wished he were there—far away from these ill-tempered officers and useless gentlemen.

"We should have some music," announced Captain Doughty.

He signaled to Emmet, who was not going to be allowed to enjoy being invisible any longer. "Since your lute is repaired, perhaps you can play and sing for us? Something soothing for wild hearts."

Emmet bowed and took the lute from the shelf. He tuned it quickly and began to strum. Softly he sang:

> *"Whither runneth my sweetheart?*
> *Stay and take me with thee,*
> *Merrily I'll play my part,*
> *Stay and thou shalt see me. . . ."*

When he glanced at Captain Drake, he could see that the music had had little effect. The captain-general stared darkly into his goblet of wine. He did not even seem to notice Captain Doughty and the others howling in unison at the chorus:

> *"Hey, ding a ding a ding!*
> *Hey, ding a ding a ding!*
> *This catching is a pretty thing!"*

Chapter Four

The five ships traveled west across the open Atlantic. With Diego's help Emmet had found his sea legs. He swung his body like a pendulum, knees bent, in a jerky, lurching trot that adjusted to the rise and fall of the deck whenever the ship punched through a wave. He felt delighted to be able to make his way across the deck on a clear, fine day in early February and not once stumble or lose his balance. He climbed upon a barrel and began sketching the vast blue sky and water.

Even though he was far away from all that was familiar, Emmet took comfort in looking out at the rolling gray-green ocean that reminded him of the boundless distance and infinity of horizon of Dartmoor when the wind rushed and winnowed through the gorse blooms. The play of light, cloud, color, and shadow of enormous sky over the Atlantic was the same as the play of light, cloud, color, and shadow over the moor.

Emmet sniffed. Far from land the Atlantic had no real smell. For a moment he tried to recall the aroma of the moor after a summer rain: pungent mud and rotting leaves mixed with fragrant bell heather and shiny marsh pennywort and dust.

"Odd job for a soger."

Emmet started with fear at the sound of Sky's voice.

"Seems like skylarking fit only for a lady," said Edwards in a high-pitched, mocking voice. He was a bald, big-boned sailor who had his initials tattooed above two knuckles.

"Aye," Moone snickered, "or the work of a Jemmy-Jessamy sort of fellow." Sky and Moone laughed.

Emmet smeared the page with his sweaty palms. He kept sketching waves, pretending not to hear.

"Don't draw no living gale," warned Moone, who poked his metal-colored finger at Emmet's sketch. "I heard of a Dutchman once who painted the wind, and out of nowhere a squall wrenched the mast clear away. Ship sank into the deep with all hands lost."

"Conjurer!" Sky spat.

"That's what they said," Moone agreed.

With shaking hands, Emmet rolled up the parchment, determined never again to draw in full view of the crew. *Too dangerous.* As he corked the bottle of ink, a familiar voice called to him.

"You there, page! Let me see what you've done."

Emmet froze with dread.

"'You there, page!'" Edwards softly mimicked Captain Doughty's singsong words.

"Fantod!" Sky said under his breath. He and his companions jostled each other with their elbows.

"To your duties, men!" Captain Doughty announced. Unlike Captain Drake, Captain Doughty's voice had little command to it. Sky and his companions seemed to sense his uncertainty the way a fox sniffs a lame rabbit.

"Yes, Captain," Sky replied in a sullen voice.

While Emmet and the others took off their caps and bowed,

Sky only lifted one finger to his brim. For some reason Captain Doughty acted as if he had not seen Sky's obvious breach of conduct, but Emmet noticed. He had heard the men complain that Doughty was the kind of gentleman who fiddled about protocol but had no practical shipboard experience. To Emmet this seemed an unfair judgement of Captain Doughty's character. A sweet orator, Doughty impressed Emmet as an excellent philosopher who had admirable knowledge of Greek and Latin, art and music. The problem, Emmet was beginning to realize, was that fine graces that meant so much among civilized people ashore had no value here at sea.

With relief Emmet watched Sky and his companions saunter away, chuckling. He handed Captain Doughty the drawing.

"There is something pitiless about the ocean, isn't there?" Captain Doughty said. "A subject difficult to capture in art."

"Yes, sir," Emmet replied. "Reminds me of Dartmoor, with its boggy places and deep mires where a man or pony can be sucked down whole."

"That is where you grew up?"

"Yes, sir." Emmet hoped he wouldn't ask about his home, his family, or the reason he had to leave.

Captain Doughty cleared his throat. "I've heard a person might be lost in the moor on a foggy, snowy day the same way a ship might be lost at sea."

"You have to know how to jump tussock to tussock in good boots to keep from sinking," Emmet said. He remembered countless moor crossings in foul weather, as he scanned the wind-swept sea. "Of course, in the wideness of the ocean there's no refuge for a land creature who can't swim."

"Calenture."

"What, sir?"

"The mistaken notion someone has when they believe the sea is land and leap from a ship to try to walk as if across a moor."

"A person who's ravished in his mind?"

Captain Doughty laughed with a slight bitterness. "Or someone desperate to escape shipboard life."

Encouraged by their frank exchange, Emmet took a deep breath. "Do you know, sir . . . Can you tell where—"

"Where we're headed? No, I am officially forbidden to disclose that information. It is a secret."

"Forgive me, sir." Emmet felt embarrassed to have asked such an impertinent question, a question that seemed to betray the bounds of hierarchy. Father Parfoothe had always encouraged questioning. He claimed that questioning was the only way a human being could understand phenomena. Aboard ship, Emmet realized, everything was different. One followed orders. One never asked why.

"Young man, are you worried about returning home?" Captain Doughty asked in a kindly voice.

Emmet sighed. He knew his old life was gone. How could someone like Captain Doughty, who had been brought up in luxury, understand Emmet's former existence? There was no way to explain what it had been like to live in a one-room cottage with a hard-packed dirt floor, gathering firewood, milking a cow, or chasing crows. There was no way someone like Captain Doughty would understand someone as complicated and contradictory as Father Parfoothe. "No, sir, I'm not homesick," Emmet lied. "I am quite happy aboard the *Pelican*."

"Excellent," Captain Doughty replied, and smiled. "*'Carpe diem, quam minimum credula postero!'*"

"Yes, sir. I'll try, sir," Emmet murmured. Nervously he glanced about the deck to make sure that no one else from the crew had heard Captain Doughty quoting Horace to him in Latin.

Seven hundred miles south of Cape Verde, the trade winds died out. Sails flapped listlessly in the humid, hot air. Diego and the other sailors called this the doldrums or the Devil's Sea. It was a dreaded, torrid zone of blinding tropical sun, glassy blue ocean, and cloudless sky.

One morning the sky darkened, lightning flashed, and rain fell. Exuberantly Emmet and the other servants rushed to scatter buckets and hang canvas tarps from the rigging to collect fresh water for drinking. The crew whooped as the sails filled. But as soon as the fleet had been carried only a few leagues, the wind and rain shower mysteriously vanished.

Clouds parted and the sun shone with even crueler ferocity. The rain, which had been greeted as a blessing, quickly became a curse. The humidity grew unbearable. Every other day the same torturous pattern of brief wind and showers followed by dead calm and scalding sun repeated itself. Sailors' clothes or blankets accidentally left on deck rotted with mildew. The whole ship stank with wet, moldering bedding. Soon fresh water and food supplies ran short. So did tempers.

One afternoon Captain Drake called Emmet to his cabin. He sat at the table in his shirtsleeves, gazing at the enormous, colorful navigator's chart decorated with spouting sea monsters and crisscrossed lines of red and green. Emmet lingered in the doorway, waiting patiently to be recognized and admitted. He removed his sour-smelling wool cap and picked away the writhing, biting nits that had plagued the crew since Cape Verde. As inconspicuously as possible he scratched the back of his left leg using his right foot. Flies buzzed around the open hatchway near the ceiling. The air was close, fetid.

Since he'd come aboard as the captain's page, he had learned how to wash, dry, and iron his captain's laundry; sweep his cabin; light a fire in the small brazier when necessary; and heat spiced rum the way the captain liked. He helped the captain compose letters in Latin with a proper pious tone, and he assisted him in keeping the log of compass readings, daily ship speed, and progress in neat script. He and Diego shared the job of turning the ship's sandglasses every half hour to keep track of time.

Emmet had not once been required by the captain to read from *The Key of Solomon* or to perform any charms using the crystal or Mosaical Wand. Nervously he glanced around the room and wondered where the captain had hidden these things that had rightfully belonged to Father Parfoothe. Perhaps in his locked chest? Deep down Emmet prayed that the captain was too busy directing the fleet to bother himself with such dangerous, powerful objects and rituals that Emmet had absolutely no idea how to evoke or control. If it were up to Emmet, he'd wipe from the captain's memory everything that had happened on that fateful day he'd come to Tavistock. Why, he'd—

"Your art supplies, you have them, do you?" Captain Drake said without even looking up at Emmet. "Why not put these doldrum hours to profit by sketching?"

Emmet was amazed and relieved by this suggestion. He was

supposed to be cleaning pots in the galley, but he eagerly retrieved his satchel with his pens and ink and parchment from the wooden box he shared with Diego. When he returned to the captain's cabin, he discovered Drake poring over the mysterious maps using the two-pronged dividers to plot a course. Sweat beaded his forehead.

"Draw," the captain commanded as he worked, without pausing.

Nervously Emmet took a seat on a low bench and arranged his parchment in his lap. He began to sketch the first thing he could think of. The day before he'd seen a great school of flying fish flash across the water during a brief, light breeze. For many moments he had watched them dance and sail over the water, more like birds than fish. Their strange, long fins on either side spread out like fanlike wings that carried them as far as an arrow shot from a crossbow.

Captain Drake mopped his brow with a piece of linen tucked in his sleeve, and glanced at Emmet. "What is that?"

"A flying fish, sir," Emmet replied. "Sometimes they lift themselves out of the sea and land on deck with a thud. I have had the opportunity to examine carefully one that was nearly two feet in length. A strange, marvelous species."

Captain Drake grunted. "I would think it might be more interesting to sketch their clever enemies—the dorado, albacore, and bonito. No sooner do the flying fish fall into the water than their able predators seize and eat them. A very amusing spectacle."

"Yes, sir," Emmet said. He was about to mention the beauty of the flying fish's eyes and the iridescent splendor of their fins in sunlight when he was interrupted by a sharp rap at the door.

"Enter," Captain Drake bellowed.

Sky crept into the cabin as stealthily as a rat into the ship's bread room. He removed his cap and gave Emmet a sneering once-over.

"What cheer?" Captain Drake said quietly to his brother. He motioned slightly with his head in Emmet's direction, as if in warning.

"Not . . . not much news to report, sir," Sky stammered. He looked smaller, thinner, and less powerful standing next to his older brother—the only individual on board he seemed to fear.

"Thought I told you to keep your weather eye lifting," Captain growled.

"I am, sir," Sky whined. "I tried, sir."

When the two men retreated to the far end of the cabin, Emmet acted as if he were concentrating on the flying fish. Try as he might, he couldn't understand a thing the two men whispered.

" . . . He won't blow the gaff," Sky hissed.

"When he's by the wind . . . damn his eyes . . . Lord Burghley," Captain Drake replied in a low voice. " . . . A ship of knaves . . . tell Doughty to come here directly."

"Yes, sir," Sky replied. He bowed very low before the captain, but as he left the cabin he gave Emmet another threatening look.

"I'll try that," Captain Drake said, and took a seat in his cushioned chair. He picked up the parchment that Emmet had been drawing on and dipped a quill into his fancy inkwell made of cow horn.

Emmet was so startled by the captain's sudden interest in

drawing, he did not know what to say. Obligingly he took out another piece of parchment and began to work on a dolphin's smiling snout. *Scritch-scratch-scritch.* He and the captain bent their heads and worked together in what Emmet sensed to be a shared, companionable silence. *Smack-smack-smack.* The way the captain restlessly tapped his foot made Emmet wonder if he'd rather be up and about on the poop deck. His crude, predatory bird with sharp claws and outstretched wings hovered at the top of the page.

Although Drake clearly had no talent as an artist, Emmet spoke up in a bold voice, "Sir, I admire your industry. The principle of drawing, my teacher always said, is the truth of the line—"

"Bah!" Captain Drake interrupted. "There's not a bit of truth in drawing. It's all pretending. Nothing more real than drawing love knots or mazes or loops and flourishes of ciphers, rebuses, and secret codes. This bird can't bite, can't claw no more than your fish can fly." His eyebrows furrowed and he glared at Emmet with disdain. "Not all of us is schooled by popish scabshinds. When I was a yonker, I grew up hard. No gingerbread quarters for me. My posy is: 'Win gold and wear it.'" Captain Drake smiled broadly. The fierce grin took Emmet aback.

"Yes, sir," Emmet said. Somehow he never knew what might set off one of the captain's moods. To keep from looking into his blazing eyes, Emmet studied the fine red hairs on the back of the captain's powerful hands.

"Good morrow, Captain-General!"

Captain Drake looked up and seemed surprised to see Captain Doughty standing in the doorway, even though he'd expressly asked Sky to bring him to his cabin. "You come upon us painting, sir."

"Beg your pardon for the interruption," Captain Doughty replied, and bowed. "I heard you sent for me. I came directly on the *Swan* to do your bidding."

Captain Drake kept sketching with great gusto. Emmet did not speak, although he tried to smile and bob his head in Captain Doughty's direction. The visiting captain remained at attention. Captain Drake did not invite him inside to sit down or speak.

"A true gentleman," Captain Drake said finally, "knows the value of the arts, the truth of the line, does he not?" He looked up at his visitor with disdain.

"I did not know you were trained in rendering such lifelike marine animals," Captain Doughty said, obviously impressed. "A fine flying fish."

Captain Drake smiled. "Yes, I am something of an accomplished artist," he said, admiring the drawing that Emmet had made as if it were his own. "There are perhaps many things you do not know about me."

Emmet felt his face flush. He would have liked very much to have Captain Doughty know the truth. But he could not contradict the captain without showing disrespect and risking punishment.

"You may go, page," Captain Drake announced to Emmet. "Shut the door behind you."

Emmet stood, bowed, and hurried belowdecks with his rolled parchment under his arm.

As soon as he opened the chest in the corner that he shared with Diego to store his few personal belongings, he felt the presence of a figure lurking behind him. He turned in alarm. "Who—"

"Didn't mean to scare you," Flea said.

"How dare you creep about like that?" Emmet demanded angrily. Ever since Flea's beating and remarkable recovery, the carpenter's mate had assumed the irritating habit of shadowing Emmet as if he were his only friend in the world. This was an embarrassment to Emmet, who would rather have nothing to do in public with unlucky Flea.

Flea shrugged. "Beg pardon. Just that I wanted to ask you if you seen a sea charm about."

"Why," Emmet asked in a cautious voice, "do you think I would know anything about a sea charm?"

"Just that," Flea said softly lowering his voice, "I'm hoping it'll turn up. Didn't take it. I told Edwards over and over I didn't steal his sea charm. So I'm hoping it might appear. You know, maybe the fellow who took it'll leave it someplace. You have sharp eyes. If I tell a few folks with sharp eyes, maybe the charm might turn up and I can return it and . . ." His voice drifted off.

"What does Edwards say it looks like?" Emmet said. He'd had plenty of experience observing his teacher interrogating people about lost shoes, spoons, and darning needles to know that it was important from the start to discover the object's correct description. There were so many different kinds of charms. Some were written on special unborn parchment—skins of animals cut from their mothers' wombs. These were often folded and tucked into black silk bags attached to strings and worn close to the body. Other written charms were hidden inside tin boxes or glass bottles. They were concealed under pillows or tucked above windows and doors. None were meant to ever be opened or read by the charm's owner.

Flea glanced nervously over his shoulder. "Edwards says he bought the charm for twenty shillings."

Outrageous! Emmet thought. His teacher never charged even so much as a farthing.

"Says it's a protective lease for sailors to keep him safe from rocks and stands and storms and tempests," Flea continued. "Just a piece of paper folded up tight inside a wooden pipe corked at both ends. That's a lot of money, twenty shillings."

Emmet couldn't see Flea's face in the darkness, but he could tell from his quavering voice that he was desperate. "I'll watch for the sea charm," Emmet promised in the same soothing voice he remembered Father Parfoothe had used when he tried to console a shepherd who'd lost a lamb he'd probably never see again. "I'm sure it'll appear. Don't fret, Flea."

As soon as Flea shuffled away, Emmet carefully closed the lid of the sea chest and sighed. Father Parfoothe had tried to teach him how to detect a thief's identity by staring into a crystal or a basin of water. Most of the time Emmet failed miserably. And yet the image Emmet had spied in the bucket belowdecks that first day aboard haunted him. Was Sky the thief who stole the charm? *What if I'm wrong?* There was no way he could accuse the captain's brother of theft without endangering his own life. *Best just to forget about it.*

Chapter Five

In the middle of February a steady wind picked up as the fleet approached the equator. Gunshots boomed. Word spread quickly on the lower deck that preparations would begin soon for "crossing the line."

"What does that mean, Diego?" Emmet asked nervously.

Diego winked. *"El bautismo."*

"A baptism? For whom?" Emmet suddenly felt sick.

"You, *amigo,* and others never crossed the line. I cross a hundred times." Diego puffed out his chest, but Emmet knew Diego well enough now to tell when he was lying. Diego had a habit of pertly heating up the truth until it sizzled.

A festive atmosphere took over the ship the afternoon that Captain Drake agreed to the ceremony. Beer rations were doubled. Men shot pistols into the air. With no work to do, the men enjoyed themselves with feats of daring, which provided plenty of opportunities for wagers. Athletic Diego, always willing to oblige any gambling crowd, balanced on the palm of his outstretched hand a harquebus, a heavy matchlock gun ordinarily supported on a forked rest during firing.

"Two minutes!"

"I say five!"

"Place your bets!"

The crowd roared with approval when Diego held his arm out for nearly six minutes—a new record.

"Now show your jump!"

Right away everyone had something to throw into the circle as a wager: a pair of bone dice, a pewter thimble ring, a pocket sundial made of wood, a carved birch whistle, a deck of worn playing cards.

"I say he makes the leap four times."

"Three. That's my bet."

"An even half dozen."

Diego set up two barrels side by side. He stood in one and grinned. When the gunner's mate shot a pistol into the air, Diego made a standing jump from inside one barrel to the other and back again. With great agility he tucked his long legs up against his chest as he lifted himself into the air and threw his arms over his head. He managed to jump seven times without even stopping for breath.

The crowd went wild. No one else in all the crew could perform such a remarkable feat. "Well done!" Moone said, and slapped Diego hard on the back.

Diego took a great swig of rum. "*¡Gracias!*" he said, and made a little bow. Fame did not seem to go to his head.

Emmet could not help but feel impressed. He was scrawny and stubby-legged and had none of Diego's strength and endurance. Secretly he wished he were larger, stronger, bolder. He wished he had skin that did not turn lobster red in the sun and peel like paint from a wooden church steeple. He wished his reddish hair did not stand out like boar's bristles. Most of all, he wished he were well liked, the way Diego was. But he knew he wasn't.

"Tail on here, bullies!" shouted Sky, who wore a dripping beard of seaweed and a comical crown fashioned by the copper from broken barrel staves. He stood beside a flimsy-looking stick that had been attached to a long rope that hung from the yardarm, the horizontal timber used to spread a sail. Trumpets sounded. Drums rolled. Sky waved a long pole in the air. "Gather round Old Neptune, you freshwater sailors."

Emmet noticed immediately that Captain Drake was nowhere in sight. This realization made Emmet more nervous than ever. On this topsy-turvy day, Sky and his friends had taken over the ship and were allowed free reign to do whatever they wished.

Emmet wondered where Captain Drake might possibly be hiding. Before Emmet could escape to find out, several drunken crew members grabbed him and the other dozen unbaptized sailors and shoved them into the middle of a circle of brawny sailors.

"Any lubber who refuses the dunking must pay in rum," Sky declared, and leered at his victims. He took a great swig from a bottle.

Like the others, Emmet had no money to pay the bribe to avoid the dunking. The first to be baptized was the gunner's mate. The sallow-faced boy of seventeen straddled the stick as a second line was tied around his waist. He made a little salute, then gripped for dear life the rope attached to the yardarm.

The yardarm was swung out over the water. A musket boomed. The crew gave a cheer and released the rope. The gunner's mate was plunged into the sea, yanked up, and unceremoniously dumped, coughing and retching, onto the deck. Someone clamped him hard on the back and gave him a swig of beer from a tankard and pronounced him properly baptized by Old Neptune.

Emmet had moved nearly to the back of the line in order to cautiously observe the ceremony. As usual, Flea cowered nearby. "Now, now," Flea murmured to Nipcheese, the half-bald orange ship's cat he held far too tightly in his arms. The fierce ratter had bitten or clawed every third crew member. For some reason, only Flea escaped Nipcheese's famous fury. "I don't know," Flea wailed, turning to Emmet. "I don't know this looks safe."

Emmet pretended he couldn't hear.

"What if we drown?" Flea demanded. "What if we break our necks?"

"We won't drown," Emmet replied quietly. "Hold on to the rope and be sure to land feetfirst."

When it was Flea's turn, Sky motioned with his scepter pole and commanded the terrified carpenter's mate to come closer. "Tail on here, Butter Box!"

Flea refused to budge. Nipcheese yowled.

"Don't have a choice, Butter Box. You need a bath. Get rid of some of that vermin."

Everyone laughed.

"Be a man!" one of the older sailors said, and gave Flea a good pounding on his shoulder.

This advice did nothing to change Flea's mind. He appeared as allergic to seawater as Nipcheese. The more Flea stalled, the more the others made fun of him.

"Dunk the cat, too!"

"Cat's worth more than a worthless carpenter's mate!"

"Hop up, man!"

Flea snuffled loud enough for everyone to hear. Emmet stepped as far away from him as he could, determined more than ever not to reveal his own terror and shame.

Edwards finally wrenched Nipcheese from Flea's arms. The battered-looking creature sunk its teeth into Edwards's hand and drew blood before streaking down into the hold.

"Look lively!" Edwards shouted angrily, and gave Flea a hard shove toward the yardarm. The tipsy crew roared with laughter at the cat's fierceness and speed.

Flea would not be as lucky as the escaping cat. Two seamen grabbed him by each arm and hoisted him onto the stick in spite of his oaths and kicking and screaming.

"Dowse that now!"

"Mama can't hear you squall."

"Only a few sharks down there."

"Dunk him three times," ordered Sky, "just to make sure he's baptized proper!"

The yardarm swung out with dangling, whimpering Flea. "Can't swim!" he screamed. The three tipsy crew members handling the yardarm dropped the rope. Flea hurtled downward with a great splash.

Everyone cheered on deck except Emmet. *I'm next,* he thought miserably. He wished he'd paid more attention to Father Parfoothe's charms for preventing drownings. Such a charm would come in handy, but of course he could not think of even a phrase, a word that might help him. Seconds crawled by. He took a great breath and counted. Weren't they going to pull Flea up? Were they really going to drown him the way they'd threatened?

Finally the sailors yanked the rope. Flea appeared, sputtering and soaked.

"Lower away!" someone on deck shouted.

"Let fly!"

Flea splashed again into the deep. Another round of cheers went up. He was hoisted up with a great jerk.

"Again!"

Flea was soaked once more. By the time he was finally hauled onto deck after the third dunking, his lips were blue and he was puking. Someone handed him a sloshing tankard, but he simply collapsed in a pathetic heap on the deck.

Secretly Emmet felt sorry for Flea. At the same time he felt a rising sense of revulsion. Emmet did not wish to stand too close to Flea for fear of contamination. What if Flea's cowardice might somehow infect him and make him just as weak and pathetic?

When it was Emmet's turn, he knew what to do. Quickly he straddled the stick. No one had to drag him forcibly to take his place. He waved grandly to the crowd and kept his jaw set so that there was no tremor of fear anywhere on his face. He tried his best to smile, to appear as if he had not a care in the world. The rope bit his fingers, he gripped it so tightly.

In a split second the ground underneath his bare feet vanished. He lurched skyward. In one dizzying motion he swung up and out over the water. The ocean below seemed miles and miles away. He scanned the surface for an evil fin or a set of vicious teeth—signs of the sharks that Diego always described with such delight.

Emmet shut his eyes. Before he could remember to take a deep breath, a roar went up from the crew on the deck of the ship.

He fell for what seemed several moments. His breeches ballooned, his shirtsleeves flew upward. He saw Father Parfoothe saying something in Greek. Emmet could not understand. Lukewarm water smacked hard against Emmet's legs and slapped his back. Darkness swallowed him. His eyes opened. Something scaly brushed against his face. The glance of a paper-thin fin, the scrape of sharp tail. Emmet's mouth snapped open. He screamed. Bubbles streamed past his cheeks, his chin. Instinctively he sucked in briny water. *No!* his brain shouted.

It was too late. His nose and throat burned with briny water. His chest felt as if it might explode. His eyes bulged. Desperately he clawed at the rope. *Pull me up!* What was taking so long?

And then, as if by a great miracle, the line jerked upward. He was yanked out of the watery darkness to the surface. He held on to the line for dear life. Bent forward, clinging to the rope, he coughed. Salt water poured from his mouth and nose.

Without warning he felt his body thump against something hard. The deck. He was on solid ground again. He coughed some more and retched until he thought his stomach might come up his throat. Nauseated, half-blind, half-deaf, he could barely make out the legs or the knees of people standing around him. Diego's arm, black and strong, reached down and shoved a tankard in his face.

"Swallow this, *amigo*. Not ocean!" His voice sounded faraway.

In spite of Emmet's aching gut and burning throat, and the salt water that filled his ears, his eyes, and his nose, he struggled to sit up. He would not lie here like a coward the way Flea had.

Emmet took the tankard in his hands and drank the beer as if what had happened meant nothing. Signified nothing. His lips trembled. His teeth chattered. Yet he forced himself to grin. A stupid grin. He wiped his mouth with the back of his trembling hand and handed the beer back to Diego.

"You baptized, *amigo*," Diego crowed. "You deepwater *marinero* now!"

Emmet watched the crew move on to their next victim, glad that the attention had shifted to someone else. Glad that he did not have to bear the crew's scrutiny for another moment. Now he understood the supreme unspoken rule aboard ship. If he wished to survive, he must always be afraid to seem afraid.

Chapter Six

As the fleet headed south and southwest along the treacherous coast of South America, rumors flew among crew members on the lower deck about exactly where they were headed. Some sailors said they were going to the Strait of Anian, which led to a northwest passage across North America. Others insisted the fleet was destined for the rich Spice Islands. A few crew members claimed they'd heard officers whispering about some place called Terra Australis, an undiscovered southern continent.

Whatever their destination, one thing was clear: They were going to shoot the Strait of Magellan on the far southern extremity of South America.

"Might as well say good morrow to Davy Jones," grumbled a sailor belowdecks one evening.

"Aye, we're all going to be dead men soon enough," another agreed.

Emmet listened with dread. When he cleaned the captain's cabin, he had managed to secretly read bits of Captain Drake's book about the Spanish-backed voyage of Portuguese navigator Ferdinand Magellan. Not until this moment did Emmet realize why the captain may have brought along this particular volume on the voyage.

Magellan was the only mariner in more than half a century who had successfully threaded the narrow, treacherous, 320-mile passageway now known as the Strait of Magellan. His success had come at a high price: 245 of the 280 sailors who embarked with him on the round-the-world voyage never made it home. Before entering the strait, Magellan faced mutiny and murder attempts from his crew. After managing to cross the perilous South Sea, or Pacific, he was hacked to pieces by natives.

Almost every sailor in Drake's fleet knew that once a ship entered the Strait of Magellan, there was no turning back. Contrary trade winds and terrible weather made the return journey even more impossible and dangerous than the outbound trip. And yet Captain Drake seemed to have cast their fate. Like the other sailors, Emmet had a hunch that in spite of the odds, the fleet was going to shoot the dreaded strait.

"The strait's the edge of the world," Moone said in a low voice. "Man-eating giants. Sea monsters. Whirlpools with human faces pull ships into icy, dark caverns. Sirens call men to their doom."

"I heard," said Edwards, rubbing the top of his bald head, "there's storms so powerful they suck clean the decks of ships, splinter vessels in half, and feed every last sailor to sharp-toothed fish and gulping whales."

"What do you think, Emmet?" Flea asked fearfully. "What's going to happen to us?"

Emmet shrugged. He tried to appear as if he didn't care. Deep down, he was terrified.

The debate on the lower deck continued, and seemed to have

spread to the officers on the poop deck, as well. On a particularly miserable hot afternoon, when the wind blew in unpredictable breezes that appeared and disappeared, Emmet and several crew members had been assigned to scrub the main deck with sand and sea water. They had done this twice already this week, and the heat and the lack of fresh drinking water or a bit of beer made the job especially miserable. Kneeling on the deck, Emmet and the others scoured the splintery wooden surface with rough pumice stones nicknamed "prayer books" by the sailors. Back and forth they scraped.

Above them on the poop deck several officers in velvet mandilion jerkins with hanging sleeves and scarlet-and-yellow trunk hose were playing cards. Every so often the sailors could hear them arguing about the strait and authority and something about being cast ashore on islands of demons. The officers sat under an awning and drank claret. Every so often they pointed and laughed uproariously at the crew members on their hands and knees, cleaning the deck.

"Will you listen to those peacocks!" muttered Sky. He stopped working and sat on his heels. "Worthless gentlemen don't labor or climb aloft. Don't know the first thing about a ship."

"We take the risks and do the work," grumbled Moone. "They get all the profit. You can be sure they'll be safe in their cabin while we risk life and limb shooting the strait."

"Six days shalt thou labor, and do all thou art able," Diego sang under his breath. "And on the seventh, *por favor*, holystone the decks and scrape the cable!"

"You there!" one of the peevish young gentlemen called down. "Get back to work."

Sky put his finger to his cap and forced a smile. "Quarter-deckers fall foul of each other!" he murmured.

"Careful," Emmet said under his breath.

"Mind your own business, Scowbank!" Sky warned. "And take care what gentleman's boots you lick."

Emmet knew he was talking about Captain Doughty. Flush-faced, Emmet went back to scrubbing. Sweat poured from his forehead so that he could not see. He paused and raised one hand to wipe his eyes. As he did he accidentally bumped Sky in the arm. Sky turned to Emmet and grabbed him firmly under the chin with a twisted handful of his shirt. "Dare knock me?" he demanded.

"Didn't . . . didn't mean to," Emmet stammered. He could feel the shirt tightening around his throat so that he could barely breathe.

In an instant the cleaning crew jumped up and began making wagers. There was nothing like a fight to end the boredom of meaningless chores.

"I should pound some sense in you about fantods," Sky snapped, dragging Emmet to his feet. He held Emmet close to his face so that Emmet could smell his onion breath, stare directly into his bloodshot blue eyes, and feel the spit fly from the corner of Sky's mouth. Before Emmet could protest, Sky kneed him in the stomach. Emmet flew against the railing.

Emmet managed to keep on his feet and turned just in time to see Sky flying straight for him, headfirst. Sky's big greasy head, like his big hard boots, was famously used in fights as a battering ram. Head down, Sky hurled toward Emmet. Emmet did the only thing he could think of. He jumped out of the way.

The able seaman crashed into the railing, which only made him more furious. He lunged back and tackled Emmet, grabbed him in a headlock, and squeezed.

"Stop! Stop, sir!" Emmet squeaked. Small white specks flew before his eyes. He blinked and gasped for breath. With all his remaining strength, he tried to pry himself free, but he was trapped in Sky's viselike grip.

Just when he thought he could stand the pain no longer, Sky let him go. Emmet staggered backward and rubbed his jaw. Several teeth felt as if they'd come loose.

"You there, page!" a voice boomed. Emmet looked up. He was collared by the bosun. "No fighting. Come with me."

Before Emmet could even really understand what had happened, he was dragged down into the hold. The lowest, darkest, most foul-smelling part of the ship, the hold had little air, no light, and smelled of putrid bilgewater. Deep in the bowels of the *Pelican* were stored timber and iron for repairs, kegs of gunpowder well sealed with pitch, gunshot, barrels of salted meat, spare weapons, and kegs of drinking water.

Rats scrambled past as Emmet was clamped in leg irons beside Sky, the other prisoner.

Emmet was certain he would soon be dead. Every crew member knew that Sky never went anywhere without his sharp dagger. He used the knife to carve, whittle, eat his food, and clean his fingernails. Sky liked to brag how he'd slit a highwayman's throat when he tried to steal Sky's horse on a trip to London.

As Emmet's eyes grew accustomed to the dim light shining from the carpenter's lantern at the other end of the hold, he noticed the profile of Sky, who leaned against the slimy wall. Was he asleep or awake? Where was his dagger? *Be afraid to show you are afraid.* "Sir," Emmet said, desperate to avoid any more attacks, "I beg your pardon for my clumsiness. I—"

"Dowse that now!" Sky barked. He did not speak again until after they were hauled up onto the deck before the entire crew.

For fighting, Sky received a round dozen—thirteen—lashes. The bosun flogged Sky's shirtless back using the vicious cat-o'-nine-tails, a whip with nine lengths of knotted cord fixed to its wooden handle. Sky did not cry out.

Emmet, however, was so terrified he felt as if he might faint. He knew that the punishment was unfair, since he had not provoked the fight. Yet he had no choice but to take the round dozen as best he could. The first smack against his bare back shocked him so much, he winced and screamed. Tears came to his eyes. Over and over he felt something as sharp as fire burn against his back. It was a searing pain worse than anything he'd known.

When it was over, no one helped him. No one offered him water. No one said anything.

Emmet crept onto his pallet and tried not to move. Every muscle ached. The last time he had felt so miserable was when he was knocked over by the sow and nearly trampled to death. Father Parfoothe had made him a poultice of something foul-smelling. Mustard, was it? Then he'd said the charm to stop the bleeding. By trying to think of the charm, Emmet kept his mind off the awful aching. He felt too bleary with pain to concentrate. He must have dozed off, because he heard someone's voice and awoke with a start.

"Drink this," Diego whispered. He pushed a tankard of beer in his direction.

Emmet groaned and sat up. He took a sip. Even his lips felt sore. Something inside his mouth seemed very peculiar. When he held up his hand and spat, a tooth flew out of his mouth. He stared at the tooth and thought of Flea. Never before had he understood how helpless it felt to be beaten by a larger, stronger opponent.

"A poor fighter you are, *amigo*," Diego said. "Sky will beat you again. Suffering he enjoys."

Emmet winced and tossed the tooth into the darkness. "You came here to tell me this?"

"A few lessons to be fighter might help."

"And then I land back in the hold again? No, *gracias*."

Diego smiled. "I can give you some good—*¿Cómo se dice en Ingles—consejo?* So next time, you kick his tooths."

"Teeth," Emmet corrected and flinched.

"Teeth," said Diego, grinning broadly. No one had ever knocked out Diego's teeth. They looked perfect. Maybe Diego could help him after all. "How is your back?"

"Back?" Emmet wasn't sure what he meant.

"From the cat. How is your back?"

"You mean the cat-o'-nine-tails." Emmet turned his head as far to the left as he could and tried to look over his shoulder.

"Let me see, *por favor*," said Diego, who inspected the places where he'd been hit. "Bleeding stopped." He looked surprised.

Quickly Emmet pulled down his shirt to cover his back. He'd never expected success with Father Parfoothe's words. "I don't think he was hitting me as hard as is his custom." Emmet hoped he concealed his amazed expression by taking another gulp of beer.

"*¡Buena suerte!*" Diego said, and stood up. "Now your fortune will improve. When we go ashore, our lessons begin."

"*Gracias*," Emmet said. He tried to feel hopeful.

The next day the fleet cruised close enough to the green coast of Brazil for Emmet and the others to experience the tantalizing tang of land: sweet flowers and blossoming trees, hot earth and baked grasses. It had been nearly four months since Emmet had walked on solid ground. He stood at the rail and looked with longing at the passing shoreline.

"Page!" the bosun shouted. "To the captain's cabin."

Startled from his daydream, Emmet hurried across the deck. *Now what trouble awaits me?* Anxiously he spat on his palm and tried to flatten down his unruly hair to make himself presentable. He hoped that the captain would not berate him for fighting.

As Emmet lifted his hand to knock, the cabin door swung open. Da Silva, his face dark with anger, stormed past Emmet. "You break your promise! *¡Fraude!*"

"Come in, page," the captain beckoned from the table. His cool eyes narrowed. "And shut the door behind you."

Nervously Emmet removed his cap and bowed.

"Disregard that pilot's disrespectful behavior," the captain continued. "He is upset that he must stay on with us. He is too valuable a navigator to be returned to his home in Brazil. And if he cannot adjust to his new life, there are ways to convince him of duty and discipline, are there not?"

"Yes, sir," Emmet said in a quavering voice. "I wish to apologize for fighting on deck, sir. It won't happen again, sir."

The captain removed a small silver-handled dagger from his belt and began to sharpen it with a whetstone. "Some men learn more slowly than others," he said. The knife made a harsh scraping sound as he moved it back and forth, back and forth. "I am a patient man, am I not?"

"Yes, sir."

"And a God-fearing man, am I not?"

"Yes, sir." Emmet felt sweat drip down his forehead.

The captain plucked a hair from his head and tested the sharpness of the knife blade. "When I give orders I expect them to be obeyed."

"Yes, sir." Emmet shuddered, recalling the dampness, the smell of the hold, the cold, heavy chains around his legs, the biting pain of the flogging against his back.

"I am glad we understand each other." He looked at Emmet and smiled. He put his dagger back inside its scabbard. "I have an important job you must do for me. It involves finding the truth regarding recent reports of infamous thefts."

"Thefts, sir?"

"It appears that someone has stolen from my stores taken from the Portuguese merchant vessel the *Santa Maria*, certain sundry items of value. I want to know the name of the thief." The captain stood and crossed the room, fumbling with the keys around his belt. He unlocked his great sea chest and rummaged about inside. "I believe you know exactly what to do." The captain handed him the crystal.

The glassy surface felt cool against Emmet's sweaty palm. "Sir, I doubt I can do much good."

The captain shut the chest and locked it. "You are not as dull as you look. Do I need to repeat my order? Or would two dozen lashes help you remember your skills as a scryer?"

"No, sir," Emmet said. He wet his lips carefully. "It is only that . . . it is only that spirits cannot be raised at the spur of the moment. Such gazing requires preparation. Nine days' fasting, attending Holy Communion—"

"I am in a hurry," the captain interrupted. "I need to know the name of the thief and I need to know it right now."

With shaking hands, Emmet placed the polished stone on the table. The crystal required special concentration, a calm heart, an open mind, his teacher always said. All he had to do was use the powers already at work in the universe.

"Heave, away, boy!" Captain Drake barked. "Get to work."

Emmet wished he could shrink into the floor and vanish. "Sir," he pleaded. "I need to know a few things first. What exactly was stolen? When was it stolen? Where was it stolen? I need to have some time in private. I need to make a sketch of what I see. I—"

"Fine, fine. Whatever you need. Just hurry." Captain Drake paced back and forth across the cabin. "Item: one gold ring with a ruby and dragon shape. Item: a pair of silver bracelets. Item: a pearl earring. All brought to my attention by the knave Captain Doughty, who falsely accuses my brother in the past week of committing this crime."

Emmet took a deep breath. "Sky, sir?"

"That is correct." The captain glared at Emmet. "What have you heard among the men on the lower deck?"

"Nothing, sir," Emmet replied in a miserable voice.

"Then get to work. I'll be on the poop deck, awaiting your answer."

As soon as the captain left, Emmet took out a piece of paper and a pen. He sat on a chair. He tried to calm his wildly thumping heart. His hands sweat so badly, he could hardly grip the quill. Desperately he tried to recall the procedure. Was it two Aves, a Pater Noster, a Credo? He closed his eyes. His mind was a blank. Something about three angels from the right-hand direction, wasn't it? "Who shall tell or show us," he mumbled, "the truth about these things which we shall ask?" After what seemed a very long time, he finally opened his eyes and stared into the crystal.

A young man's face quivered on the surface. Whose? He couldn't tell. He copied the features he could. A weak mouth, sparse beard, and bad-tempered, far-spaced eyes. Too much yellow bile, perhaps. A choleric individual whose humors were badly out of balance.

"So!" the captain said as he burst into the cabin. "What have you?" He grabbed the sketch from Emmet before he could finish. For several moments, Captain Drake stared at the drawing in silence.

"As I said, sir, it may not be an exact likeness. My teacher often found my work lacking—"

"God's eyes!" Captain Drake swore loudly. He crushed the drawing, then raised his fist.

Emmet cowered, shielding his face with his arms. To his surprise he felt no blow.

The captain tossed the portrait of Sky into the brazier. "That'll do, then," he said gruffly. "If you tell a soul what you saw, I will make a fray with you that will make you wish you had never been born."

"Yes, sir," Emmet said, his knees shaking.

Captain Drake picked up the crystal, shifted it once, twice

from one hand to the other, as if he were considering its weight. Then he tucked the crystal at the back of the shelf built into the wall. "You are dismissed."

"Yes, sir." Emmet stood, bowed, and rushed out the door.

That very day the missing jewelry from the *Santa Maria* miraculously reappeared on the captain's table. And the stolen charm belonging to Edwards was found hanging from the handle of his sea chest.

"Wonderful news!" Flea confided to Emmet. "No one can accuse me anymore of being a thief."

Emmet did not reply. The measure of Flea's happiness was as extreme as his own dread. How long, he wondered, before Sky discovered who had pointed the finger of guilt?

Chapter Seven

Contrary winds, fog, and storms dogged the fleet from mid-March onward for the next two months as the ships sailed south. Sudden tempests churned steep, closely spaced waves. The troughs between breakers buried the ships' bows. As the crew struggled to survive, there was no time for Sky or anyone else to suspect or torment Emmet. Keeping the ships afloat and staying alive were all that mattered.

Gales scattered the *Pelican* and the other leaking ships far apart. When storms temporarily ended, days were spent searching for lost vessels. The disabled *Christopher* was burned. The *Swan*, commanded now by Captain Doughty, vanished three times. Each rescue attempt revealed growing tensions between the inexperienced gentlemen and the overworked mariners.

As food supplies dwindled, Emmet and the others felt lucky to eat one hot meal—a small bowl of thin lentil soup—a day. The crew's supply of salt pork, too rotten to be salvaged, had been thrown overboard. With salt beef barely edible and the last of the cheese long gone, the crew survived on rations of stale ship biscuit. The sailors smacked the hard crackers against the edge of a table to knock away as many wriggling weevils as possible. Meanwhile, the officers and gentlemen dined on private stores of Portuguese ham, Spanish wine, and English marmalade.

By the time the fleet finally managed to reassemble in mid-May at Port Desire, a sheltered, rocky harbor only several hundred miles from the opening to the strait, conflict erupted on the deck of the *Pelican*.

"You, sir!" Captain Doughty called angrily to Captain Drake on the poop deck. "I wish a word with you. What gave you the right to strip my ship of provisions and everything usable? Do you know your men have purposefully set the *Swan* afire?"

Emmet, who had been helping four other crew members butcher the fresh meat of a sea lion, looked up from the bloody carcass at his feet. Everyone stopped working.

"Do not try my patience, sir. We have much work at hand," Captain Drake announced. He motioned to the shore where sailors collected drinking water in casks and hunted seals and seabirds. "Your ship slows the fleet. I am reducing our number. Now, if you will excuse me—"

"Sir, I will not be humiliated in this manner," Captain Doughty said. His velvet cape blew about him in the wind. "When we come back to England you will need me more than you will need any reward from this voyage."

"Peacock!" muttered a sailor, who wiped a bloody blade on a rag. "I seen him write in queer conjure language."

"And what about those books he reads?" another whispered. "Not a word of English!"

"Careful, man. T'ain't safe to hector a witch—no way."

Emmet gulped nervously but said nothing. He kept his eyes

on the two shouting commanders on the poop deck.

"I have seen how you flatter and beguile my men." Captain Drake prodded Captain Doughty's chest with one finger. "We will see to it, Thomas Doughty, that you can meddle no more." He turned and called to two nearby sailors. "Fetch a rope and tie this gentleman to the main mast. You will see what it is like to be an object of scorn and ridicule."

Captain Doughty struggled as he was lashed to the mast. "Miserable scoundrel!" he shouted and cursed. "Foul treacherer!"

Captain Drake simply smiled. "Two days you will remain here, sir. Please enjoy our humble accommodations," he said, and bowed.

"Why should I believe you?" Captain Doughty demanded. "Free me at once. Your word is worthless!"

At first many members of the crew jeered openly when they saw how a fine gentleman might be so easily abused. Sky and his friends seemed to take special pleasure as they mocked helpless Captain Doughty during the next two days.

Most of the sailors, however, kept their distance. Like Emmet, they awkwardly averted their eyes and removed their caps whenever they passed the humiliated officer tied to the main mast. Long-standing rules of conduct that measured everyone's lives seemed to have been brutally turned upside down. If a man like Captain Doughty—gentle born with status and education and power—could be humiliated in this unnatural fashion, no certainty existed anymore for the lowliest mariner among them.

For Emmet life aboard ship suddenly seemed more dangerous than ever.

* * *

With every passing day the air became colder. With every passing mile the fleet came closer to the heart of an unforgiving winter in the Southern Hemisphere. Shooting the strait would be delayed until August or September, Captain Drake announced, when the weather would be more favorable. In the meantime, the fleet would anchor in a safe harbor where the men could repair the ships and restock fresh food, fuel, and water.

On 20 June 1578, the ships passed desolate gray cliffs and entered Port St. Julian, the place that would serve as their anchorage.

No one seemed pleased. Word had spread quickly on the lower deck that this was the exact spot where, sixty years earlier, Magellan had crushed a mutiny. Somewhere on the beach Spanish officers had been hung from a gibbet. Ghosts of several other marooned mutineers were said to haunt the harbor.

"Here live giants," said Diego, pointing to the bleak shoreline and the dark forest beyond. He stood beside Emmet as the *Pelican*'s anchor was lowered.

"Perhaps," replied Emmet. He had read in Captain Drake's book about the seven-foot-tall men who were said to inhabit this barren place. Anxiously he gazed up and down the narrow strip of sandy beach for a sign of any movement.

After the ships anchored, Emmet and Diego were delighted to be among the small group of men sent ashore in the longboat. They were under the command of Captain Doughty, who seemed unusually subdued as they rowed toward the beach. Emmet and Diego were to guard the boat while Captain Doughty scouted for fresh water. Surgeon Winterhey, Master Gunner Oliver, and a half-dozen others were to hunt game with longbow and harquebus.

Secretly Emmet had brought along a small sketchbook, pens, and ink. As long as Sky and his companions did not go ashore, he felt he might be safe recording what he saw. Stepping on solid land for the first time in several months shocked him. Somehow his legs refused to work properly. His body expected the ground to buck and shift like a boat at sea. The very steadiness made him strangely dizzy, and he staggered like a drunken fool.

"Look at you!" shouted Diego, who seemed to have little trouble adjusting to solid land. He handed Emmet a cutlass and shield as soon as the hunting and watering parties disappeared. Emmet and Diego marched up and down the beach as if to show they took seriously their jobs as guards.

After a half hour of marching they lost interest. Low threatening clouds hung overhead. The desolate beach showed no sign of life except for an occasional seabird. From the woods came an invisible bird's harsh warning call. Emmet took a seat on the sandy ground and sketched what he could see of the sinister shoreline and the ships anchored off a nearby sandy island.

"You think Old Man can see us?" Diego said, pointing to the distant *Pelican.*

"In spite of what the captain would like us to think, he does not have godlike powers." Emmet put the finishing touches on his sketch of the ship.

"*¡Palabra!* Old Man just like anyone. One time I saw him use the head at the bow of the ship," Diego said and laughed. He made a little demonstration, wiggling his rear end as if he were shimmying out to the ship's pair of outdoor toilets—simple planks with holes cut in them that hung over the front of the ship. "'*Tengo dolor de estómago,*'" Diego mimicked Captain Drake's distressed voice as he held his stomach. *"Y tengo diarrea."*

Emmet laughed.

"What say you to fight?" Diego suggested.

"I need practice." Emmet rolled up his drawing and tucked it into the boat with the sword and shield. "Giant, beware!" he shouted, and ran at Diego, hoping to catch him off guard.

Diego hooked Emmet under his neck with his arm. Grasping him from behind, he swung him around hard, then slammed him onto the ground.

Emmet curled, rolled, and sputtered sand. "Cheat!"

Diego held up his fists, allowing Emmet time to scramble to his feet. Emmet swung, and missed. He swung again, missed again.

"¡Mucho ojo! Eyes open!" Diego shouted. He hopped and skipped backward, forward, sideways. "What I do next?"

Emmet panted. He swung again, but always too late.

"Move! *¡De prisa!"* Diego barked. He smacked Emmet on the side of the head. Blood spurted from his nose.

Undeterred, Emmet rushed forward, head down, and butted Diego in the stomach. Diego stumbled backward in surprise. He grabbed Emmet by the arms and flung him into the sand again.

"Gracias, Diego, but I will never fight as well as you," Emmet said, out of breath. He wiped his bloody nose with his shirt.

"Keep trying, *amigo."* Diego offered Emmet his hand and pulled him to his feet.

Emmet waded into the water up to his ankles and splashed his arms and face. Learning to fight seemed completely hopeless. He watched Diego wander down the beach.

"*¡Socorro!*" Diego shouted, pointing at something that looked like a mound of sand.

"Now what?" Emmet said. He rinsed the blood from his shirt. Diego was jumping up and down frantically. "Hurry!" he called and waved his arms. "*¡En Español!* See?" He dug with his hands around a large piece of wood partially covered by drifting sand.

Emmet hurried closer. Suddenly he froze. His face went pale.

"*¡Santa Maria!*" Diego shouted, and made the sign of the cross. Beside the piece of wood, staring up at them half-buried in the sand, were two hollow eyes inside a bleached skull. "*¿Quién es?*" Diego asked with a trembling voice.

"Mutineer," Emmet said softly.

"And this?" Diego said, pointing to the wooden post and fallen timbers.

"The gibbet," Emmet replied. He could imagine the scaffold where Magellan had drawn, quartered, and then hung his victim. He felt sick. "We must tell the others."

In the distance they spotted Captain Doughty rounding the point, approaching with his servant. Every so often he paused and picked up something from the sand as if to examine it.

"Sir!" Emmet cried. "Over here, sir!"

Captain Doughty hurried closer. "What's the matter?"

"We found something, your lordship," Emmet said, out of breath. "Bones, I think. Human bones. One of Magellan's men."

Captain Doughty calmly poked the skeleton with the tip of his sword. With the curiosity of a scholar he examined the carving on the post. "I can barely make out the writing. Perhaps this states the year. I believe you are correct. If we were to dig carefully we might find the remains of all three of Magellan's men," he said, then turned to Emmet and smiled. "This climate does make mutiny flower, does it not?"

Emmet glanced at Captain Doughty in horror. Digging up skeletons was the last thing he wanted to do. His only desire right now was to run as far away from this place as he could.

"What is he talking about?" Emmet whispered to Diego.

Diego jabbed him hard in the ribs. "For an artist, you see poorly," he whispered.

Emmet scowled. He was about to protest when he noticed a startling sight lurking at the edge of the forest.

"Giants!" Diego cried.

Between the trees two boys appeared as silent as ghosts. Neither were especially tall, though they both appeared very strong, with thick muscular arms. Their faces were painted with red circles. Yellow circles were painted around their eyes. Their hair was cut short and their scalps were daubed white. They wore furs wrapped around their shoulders and legs. They carried thick bows and quivers of arrows tipped black and white.

"*Por favor, señor.* Should I kill *los canibals*?" Diego asked eagerly, even though neither he nor Emmet had their swords. Emmet glanced at the boat farther down the beach, where their weapons were hidden.

"Steady!" Captain Doughty said. "I don't believe they mean us any harm. Stay where you are."

Diego and Emmet did as they were told. The wary native boys trudged closer, until Emmet could see that they stood perhaps three inches taller than Diego. On the boys' feet were enormous fur boots.

Emmet longed to speak to them and have them understand.

He had never before been so close to boys his own age from such a distant place. Somehow he felt oddly disappointed that they weren't stranger and fiercer than he'd imagined. "In the book Magellan said his men came only to the giants' waists," Emmet said to Captain Doughty in a quiet voice so that he would not scare away the natives by accident. "Do you think, sir, there are other, older ones in the forest much larger than these?"

"I do not know," Captain Doughty replied cautiously. He smiled and opened his hands wide to show their visitors that he had no gun, no knife concealed. "As I recall, it was not a particularly happy visit with Magellan. That giant did not wish to be kidnapped and taken back to Spain. I cannot blame him."

Emmet tried to keep breathing as the native boys circled them slowly, inspecting their clothing. Suddenly from across the bay, Emmet noticed the swift pinnace from the *Pelican*. Standing in the back of the boat was Captain Drake, scowling. Meanwhile across the beach marched the hunting party with longbow and harquebus. The native boys' eyes darted in both directions. Even though they were armed they did not prepare to shoot their arrows. Instead they stood perfectly still.

Once ashore Captain Drake rushed across the sand, followed by two sailors carrying fowling pieces. "What do you think you're doing? Where are your weapons?" he shouted at Captain Doughty. "Get back to the ships at once! You are fostering an unsafe situation."

"What need we of weapons," Captain Doughty replied in a haughty voice, "if we come in peace among peaceful people?"

"Are you talking sedition? Get back into the longboat and return to the ship," Captain Drake barked. "Immediately."

Diego, clearly chagrined by his beloved captain's reprimand, retreated toward the longboat. Emmet trailed behind him, followed by Captain Doughty, who could be heard grumbling to himself. "An unsafe situation," he mumbled.

Emmet felt disappointed to not have been able to spend more time ashore. He might have drawn the boys' picture. He, too, felt resentful to be sent back to the ship. Using all their strength, he and Diego tugged the longboat into the shallow water and set the oars to begin rowing Captain Doughty back across the bay.

Just as they shoved the longboat into the water, Emmet spotted the two boys vanishing into the trees. To his surprise, two older, taller men carrying bows strode out of the forest. "There are your giants, Diego," he said.

Emmet, Diego, Captain Doughty, and the others watched from the rocking boat as the native men appeared to be engaging Captain Drake and his men in a friendly arrow-shooting demonstration.

"*¡Atención!*" Diego said, as if certain of Winterhey's farther shot. When the surgeon placed an arrow in his longbow, something went terribly wrong. The bowstring broke. At that moment, the native man slipped an arrow into his own bow. In rapid succession he shot two arrows into the surgeon's arm and leg. The other native bowman shot the gunner through the chest.

"Go back! *¡De prisa!*" Diego shouted. He splashed the oars into the water to return to shore.

Emmet could not look away. He could not move.

"Well, I don't . . . don't—" Captain Doughty stammered, his face pale as he clutched his fine leather gloves to his chest. "Perhaps we should—"

"We must help them!" Diego said, pulling on the oars.

"Shields!" Captain Drake bellowed to his men on the beach. He grabbed a cutlass and herded the mariners toward the pinnace. "To the boat!" he ordered. The captain retrieved Oliver's harquebus and primed it. A native plucked an arrow from the quiver, set it in his bow, and was about to shoot when Captain Drake pulled the trigger. A loud blast echoed across the beach. Blood splattered in every direction as the native plunged facefirst into the water.

Immediately the other native man fled into the woods.

The remaining crew members had only time to limp with wounded Winterhey to the pinnace, leaving Oliver's body behind. Before they'd shoved the boat out into the shallow water, a dozen warriors charged out from the trees and tugged off Oliver's shoes and hat.

"To the ship!" Captain Drake shouted to Emmet and Diego. Captain Doughty seemed too terrified to speak. He gripped the sides of the longboat as Diego and Emmet pulled hard on the oars. Emmet felt terrified that another group of bowmen might have been hiding in the trees, ready to attack.

Back on board the crew members were eager to fire at the shore with cannons and set the forest aflame. These giants, the men said, were nothing but animals to have skulked and killed their comrades. Captain Drake forbade acts of revenge. In the morning, he said, someone would go ashore to retrieve the body for a proper burial.

"We still need food and water," Captain Drake announced to the assembled crew. "There is no reason to go to war with the natives over what might have been a misunderstanding."

Captain Drake's speech did nothing to dispel Diego's anger. "¡Pronto! I go ashore, kill everyone!" he declared.

Emmet did not reply. In the longboat he had felt a terrible kind of numbing fear. He had no will to go back into the danger of flying poisoned arrows. His only thought was to flee. Such thoughts filled him with shame. Secretly he wondered if Diego had sensed how cowardly he'd behaved.

Later that evening in the captain's cabin Emmet was about to remove the basin of water that Captain Drake was using to soak the hand he'd injured with the cutlass. "Boy!" he shouted.

"Yes, sir." Emmet said, certain he would be beaten for his cowardice.

"I have eyes everywhere. Stay away from Doughty. Do you hear?"

"Yes, sir," Emmet said. Terrified, he picked up the basin of bloody water and retreated out the door.

Chapter Eight

Soon after the fight on the beach, Winterhey died from his injuries. A few crew members crept back to shore and recovered Oliver's body. The natives had left their own warning. The body had been stripped of its clothes and an English arrow protruded from the man's left eye. Winterhey and Oliver were buried in a grave on the sandy island off the main shore. The sailors made quick work with their shovels. They cursed the dead men for their bad luck. They cursed them for their incompetence.

"Winterhey never was a decent archer."

"Yaw-sighted Oliver warn't much better."

"Come on, now, boys, stand off. Who shall have this?" One by one the bosun held up the belongings of the dead men. With his back turned so that he could not see the pitiful objects—a wooden comb, a whistle, a rosary, a deck of cards—Edwards called off the name of a member of the crew. It didn't take long for both men's sea chests to be emptied.

Emmet found the ritual strange and hard-hearted. The gunner and surgeon were the first fatalities of the voyage. Who among them might be next?

The following day was bleak and windy. The crew went

through the motions of routine maintenance of the ships: caulking the seams with fresh oakum and tar, repairing sails, splicing rope. No one worked with a will. Everyone seemed to keep a wary eye on the desolate shore.

Without warning, a trumpet sounded. Emmet, who had been mopping the floor of the captain's cabin, looked up in surprise. "Tumble up!" the bosun shouted. When Emmet assembled with the others on the deck, he discovered that everyone from the fleet was being ordered to assemble at attention on the small island.

"What's this about?" Emmet asked Diego as they rowed to the sandy shore, where a table and chairs had been set up.

"Court martial," Diego whispered.

Was this another one of Diego's exaggerations? "Whose court martial?" Emmet demanded.

"Doughty."

Emmet stared in horror as Captain Doughty was led in manacles to one of the chairs that had been set up on the windy beach. His face was pale and drawn. He seemed to meet no one's gaze directly. Captain Drake strode to the table, where he deposited papers.

"Thomas Doughty," Captain Drake boomed loud enough for everyone to hear him, "you have here sought by diverse means, in as much as you may, to discredit me to the great hindrance and overthrow of this voyage." He sternly surveyed the nervous crowd of sailors standing at attention. "If found guilty in this trial, Thomas Doughty will deserve death."

"Sir!" Captain Doughty protested. "It shall never be proved that I merited any villainy toward you."

Captain Drake shook his head. "By whom," he said, turning to Captain Doughty, "will you be tried?"

"Why, good General," Captain Doughty said in an earnest voice, "let me live to come into my country and I will there be tried by Her Majesty's laws."

"Nay, Thomas Doughty, I will here impanel a jury on you to inquire further of these matters that I have to charge you with all." Captain Drake paced in front of the chair where Captain Doughty sat. He signaled from the crowd the forty sailors and officers he had already selected to serve as jurors. They stepped forward. Each of them, Emmet knew, was loyal to Captain Drake. They were quickly sworn in and told to listen to Captain Wynter, their foreman. John Cooke, one of the captains who could read and write, sat at the table with pen and paper to officially record the trial.

Captain Doughty crossed his arms in front of himself and cocked his head to one side. "Why, General, I hope you will see your commission be good."

"I warrant you my commission is good enough!" Captain Drake snapped.

"I pray you let us then see the paper stating you have been put in charge of the fleet by the Crown," Captain Doughty said, half smiling.

To see the queen's signature! The crowd rumbled in anticipation.

Captain Drake faltered for a moment, his face flushed. "Well, you shall not see it." He turned and faced the crew. "My masters, this fellow is full of prating!"

Captain Doughty leaped from his chair and tried to grab Captain Drake by the throat. Sky and his henchmen quickly forced him to sit down again.

"Bind me his arms," Captain Drake cried, "for I will be safe of my life! My masters, you that be my good friends—Thomas Hood, Gregory, you there—my masters, bind him!"

As Captain Doughty was tied to the chair, Captain Drake accused him of poisoning the Earl of Essex.

"The Earl of Essex, you say? In September 1576 it was you, not I, who did that bloody deed," Captain Doughty said in a calm voice. "Without my connections, my patrons, sir, you know you would be nothing."

"My friends, do you see how he threatens me?" Captain Drake announced to the crowd. "How he would kill me with poison too, if he could?"

The crowd murmured. Nervously Emmet watched the recorder scribble a few more lines.

Captain Drake called for witnesses. The first was Carpenter Ned Bright, a small, jittery man with a balding head. Bright stood with his cap in his hand and told how back in England he had heard Captain Doughty say that he wanted to break away from Captain Drake and take the ships' plunder to give to the queen to bribe her into giving him amnesty for his actions.

"Liar!" Captain Doughty declared. "I only told you that if we brought home gold we should be the better welcome, but yet even that is more than I remember."

Captain Drake accused Captain Doughty of revealing the secret mission to Lord Burghley, against the queen's orders. "Lo, my masters," he cried. "What this fellow hath done! God will have his treacheries all known."

When Captain Doughty's friend Leonard Vicary, a lawyer, declared that the entire trial was illegal, Captain Drake told him to sit down and be quiet. "I have not to do with you crafty lawyers," he said, "neither care I for the law, but I know what I will do." Captain Drake, with a dramatic flourish, looked through the pile of parchment and letters. "God's will!" he said, then admitted he'd left the queen's official letter of commission in his cabin. He signaled to Emmet to go back to his cabin on the *Pelican* to bring the paper to the trial.

Emmet did as he was told. Frantically he searched through the papers strewn about the cabin table. He could find nothing that appeared to be a fancy order from the queen. When he tugged on the lock of the captain's great sea chest, nothing happened. If there were no official letters from the queen, did that mean that Captain Drake had no right to try Captain Doughty?

As Emmet rummaged through the papers one last time, he realized the truth. He and the others had been deceived. Captain Drake had sent him on a wild goose chase just to make it appear as if such a document existed. When Emmet rushed empty-handed back to the beach, he arrived in time to hear the end of Captain Drake's speech.

"—And now, my masters, consider what a great voyage we are like to make," Captain Drake bellowed triumphantly. "The worst in this fleet shall become a gentleman."

The crowd cheered with excitement as if they'd completely forgotten about the queen's document. Clearly the queen's signature no longer mattered. Captain Doughty slouched forward in his chair.

"And if this voyage go not forward," Captain Drake continued, "which I cannot see how possible it should if Thomas Doughty lives, what a reproach it will be, not only unto our country but especially unto us. Therefore, my masters, they that think this man worthy to die, let them with me hold up their hands."

Emmet watched as every single person in the jury raised his hand. The crowd cheered again.

"The worst in this fleet shall become a gentleman—you heard him," Edwards murmured happily.

"A gentleman," Diego said, and smiled.

"How do you wish to meet your end?" Captain Drake demanded of Captain Doughty.

Ashen-faced Captain Doughty replied, "As a gentleman. Under the ax." He was led away to spend the next day locked in the hold of the ship.

Emmet rushed to Chaplain Fletcher. "Please, sir," he begged, "isn't there some way you can convince the captain to spare Captain Doughty's life?"

With a shaking hand Fletcher placed the orange peel he always carried to his nose. He shook his head, then scanned the crowd to make sure that no one had heard Emmet's question. "It's God's will," he said, and walked away.

When Emmet tried to visit Captain Doughty in the hold of the *Pelican*, he was barred by guards. What could he do? He was only a lowly page. The rest of the fine gentlemen had disappeared aboard the cabin on the *Elizabeth*, the ship anchored farthest from the vessel of vengeful Captain Drake. It seemed to Emmet that the entire world had abandoned Captain Doughty. He had been betrayed and now he was condemned to die.

That evening the air rang with the chilling sound of digging as crew members prepared Captain Doughty's grave. The next morning Emmet and the rest of the company met on shore to watch the execution. Emmet felt sick to his stomach. Like every other crew member, he was not allowed to look away. To close one's eyes, Captain Drake had warned, would mean severe punishment.

Captain Doughty, dressed in black, knelt on the ground. In a surprisingly strong voice he prayed aloud for the queen and for the success of the voyage. Then he stood and asked forgiveness for himself and his friends. When he knelt again, he removed his long velvet cape and revealed a bright red scarf wrapped around his doublet. "Strike clean and with care, for I have a short neck," he politely asked the brawny sailor with the ax. Then Captain Doughty turned to the assembled sailors and declared, "*'Crudelius est quam mori semper timere mortem.'*" Calmly Captain Doughty placed his neck on the wooden block.

The ax fell.

No one cheered. No one spoke.

Stunned, Emmet watched as Captain Drake stepped forward, grabbed the fallen head by the hair, and held it in the air. "Lo," he shouted, "this is an end to traitors."

Emmet stared numbly at the lifeless body of Captain Doughty, the only honorable officer in the fleet. The only man among them who would quote Seneca in Latin as a warning: "More cruel to always fear death than to die."

"Told you," Moone whispered.

Edwards nodded. "Aye. Them words Doughty used was conjure words."

Doughty's bright red scarf flapped in the wind. Blood pooled in a dark spot on the sand. Emmet looked away. No matter how hard he tried, he could not banish from his ears Captain Drake's rallying cry: "The worst in this fleet shall become a gentleman."

Now Emmet knew for certain. He was on a pirate ship.

And there was no escape.

Chapter Nine

25 June 1578

I will tell my thoughts here in Latin. The only words
with which I may be safe to bare my heart.

Emmet hid what he'd written on a piece of drawing paper
folded and tucked inside a satchel, buried beneath his only
extra shirt in the bottom of his sea chest. If anyone discovered
his words scribbled in tiny letters, he might be found guilty of
mutiny or, even worse, of conjuring. And yet he knew he must
write in order to make sense of what was happening to him.

Since Doughty's execution, fear haunted the powerless and
powerful alike aboard ship. On the lower deck no one sang,
played the tabor, or threw dice. No one hunted rats for sport or
laid wagers on cockroach races. The mariners were silent and
sullen as they mended sails or repaired rigging.

Officers, too, seemed unusually quiet and nervous. Small arms
that once stood on racks against one wall of the lower deck had
been locked in the hold with kegs of gunshot and gunpowder
well sealed with pitch. Twice in one day Emmet had seen Captain
Wynter go below on the *Pelican* to check that the guns and ammunition were secure. Captain Thomas gave orders with a tentative
quality to his voice, betraying an uncertainty he never had before.
The officers appeared to spend as little time as possible among
the men on the lower deck. They moved quickly and warily

through the forecastle, past the sullen sailors and dark shadows.

One afternoon as the ship lay at anchor off the sandy island near Port Julian, Emmet went to Captain Drake's cabin to empty the jordan. Cleaning the pewter chamber pot, a wide jug with handles, was one of his least favorite duties. Emmet was startled to see Sky slouched against the wall outside the cabin, with a pistol tucked inside his belt. His arms were folded and he appeared to be sleeping.

Sky opened one eye. "What you want, boy?"

Emmet's heart raced. He didn't like the way Sky looked at him, as if he were trying to come up with a reason to give him a good beating. "J-j-jordan," Emmet stammered in spite of his attempt to appear brave. "Captain's orders."

"All right, then. Look lively." Sky stood away from the door and waved Emmet through with surly pride.

Emmet hurried inside. At the table Captain Drake fumbled with something and looked up. His face was blotched with red. "What do you want? Can't you knock?" he exploded. "I should thrash you."

"Sorry, sir." Emmet took off his cap and bowed. He wasn't certain, but he thought he'd caught a glimpse of something glimmering in Captain Drake's hands. For a moment Emmet dared not even breathe. *The crystal!*

"Be about your duties, then," Captain Drake said brusquely.

Emmet retrieved the sloshing jordan. As the door shut behind him, he took off at such an anxious trot, he did not notice Sky's outstretched foot. Emmet sprawled on the floor. The jordan overturned, then clanged against the wall.

"Going somewhere, your grace?" Sky snarled in a low voice.

Flushed and furious, Emmet picked himself up. The contents of the jordan had spilled all over his tunic, the floor, and the wall. Now he'd have to clean up the mess.

Sky laughed as though he thought his humiliating joke were very funny. "Don't want to make Captain upset, now, do we?" he said, and began to carefully wipe the barrel of the pistol with a dirty rag.

The three remaining ships—the *Pelican*, commanded by Captain Drake and piloted by da Silva; the *Marigold*, commanded by Captain Thomas; and the *Elizabeth*, with Captain Wynter in charge—set sail from Port Julian on 17 August under a cold, angry sky and a north wind. No one regretted leaving Blood Island, the name the crew had given the melancholy place where the gunner, the surgeon, and Captain Doughty lay buried.

Out in the open sea again, the ships hustled south and west toward the Strait of Magellan. Everyone knew they had only a month of good weather left to make the passage. On 21 August the ships entered the deep bay that led to the strait. It had been described in great detail in the book about Magellan. Emmet and the others stared out at the bare, flat land on either shore. In the distance floated smoke from what seemed to be campfires.

"*Los canibals,*" Diego whispered.

August late

After several days sailing through narrow channel, we take shelter in the lee of island we call Cape Contrary because the northerly wind will not let us pass. For two weeks we wait until the wind turns to south and we proceed. Fires on both sides of Strait. Water so deep, no bottom touched.

The ships came to anchor near three small islands that Captain Drake named Elizabeth, St. George, and St. Bartholomew. The islands teemed with black-and-white birds that seemed to have fur, not feathers. Emmet and several other sailors were sent ashore to hunt the waddling birds, which one of the Welsh mariners called *pen gwyns,* meaning "white heads."

"Come on!" Diego shouted to Emmet. *"¡Pronto!"*

The melancholy birds, about the size of mallard ducks, did not even try to fly away as the hunters waded ashore. The fearless, stupid birds simply stood, innocently squawking with rumbling voices.

Sky picked up a stick and cudgeled a bird's skull. He quickly did the same to another, and then another. With each thwack a bird fell to the ground. Killing the birds was so easy that soon everyone who'd come ashore began crushing skulls left and right until the ground was littered with heaps of dead black-and-white bodies. *Whack-thud-whump.* It seemed like a child's game, it was so easy. A kind of relieved frenzy swept over the men. Shooting the strait was not dangerous or impossible after all. No whirlpools, no monsters, no demons. Only stupid birds. *Whack-thud-whump.*

"Over here!" Diego called in an exultant voice. *"¡De prisa!"* Signaling the other sailors, he rushed with glee at a new group of birds that did not seem to have the sense to flee. He clubbed them until his shirt was black with sweat.

Emmet watched Diego and the others slaughtering the flightless birds. He heard the thud of clubs and saw the birds resist—always too late. The sickening scent of blood and wet feathers filled his nostrils. He wanted to raise his voice against the killing. But somehow Emmet could not speak. All he could think of was Doughty's black doublet, the white collar, the red scarf. Doughty's willingness to lean forward, head down upon the block. The way his eyes looked, beseeching, but not protesting. The growing pool of blood.

Before Emmet could stop himself, he was puking.

That day the rest of the crew went on to kill more than three thousand birds.

During the next two weeks the ships maneuvered among strong, treacherous currents through winding channels. At one point the passage shrank in width to only six hundred feet, making it difficult for the ships to pass without using cables and anchors. Rising on either side of the channel were high, snow-covered mountains and pockmarked glaciers of a surprising blue color. The glaciers stood like walls two hundred feet or more in height. Icy, moaning wind rocked the ships and made Emmet and the others shiver. The water in the strait was so cold that anyone unlucky enough to fall in would be able to live only a few moments.

6 September

The men call the Captain's luck remarkable. We see no
Monsters. No Whirlpools. We pass along without any real
hindrance of weather. High land on both sides covered
with snow yet the Strait is free of ice, fair, and clear.
Stunted trees on hills. Being out of the Strait on the other

side we cheer and praise God for our Deliverance.

Now we hold our course for Northwest into South Sea.

The fleet had accomplished in just sixteen days what had been a thirty-six-day ordeal for Magellan. The fabled South Sea stretched and glittered to the horizon.

"What say you to the name *Golden Hind*? The symbol of my honored friend and patron, Sir Christopher Hatton," Captain Drake announced that evening. He and Chaplain Fletcher and a few other officers sat together at a triumphant meal in the captain's cabin. Captain Drake had been drinking heavily. His face was splotched with crimson patches and his speech was slurred.

Emmet, who stood motionless against the wall, watched as the ship's chaplain picked at his stringy helping of boiled penguin. Like other dinner guests, Chaplain Fletcher seemed to suffer from lack of appetite. "My revered and honored captain-general, is not the pelican the emblem of our sovereign lady and esteemed queen? Sir, could a change of name bring us bad luck?"

"I am Captain-General! I can name my ship whatever I wish." Captain Drake thumped the table so hard that the frightened chaplain nearly jumped from his bench. "As good luck would have it, a new name signifies a new beginning, does it not?"

In an instant the door flung open and Sky leaped inside. "What service, sir?" he asked, pistol in hand.

"Caps off, fool!" Captain Drake declared. "I didn't call for you. Out of here!" His brother tugged off his hat, bowed, and backed out the door.

Captain Drake raised his goblet. "To the *Golden Hind*."

With obvious reluctance Chaplain Fletcher and da Silva did the same.

Before the crew had much time to boast of how they had easily surpassed Magellan, whom they called a "Spanish dog," the wind shifted. Heavy swells, growing larger by the moment, struck the bows of the fleet's ships like boulders. Wind forced the *Pelican*, now renamed the *Golden Hind*, up over the crests of enormous, granite-colored waves. Lifted in a sickening, nearly forty-five-degree tilt, the ship dropped with a thud into deep troughs between the waves. The ship was lifted, tilted, dropped. And each time, the movement was steeper, harder.

Inside the captain's cabin, plates skittered across the table and crashed onto the floor. Goblets of wine sloshed and tumbled. Hissing waves sucked overboard anything on deck that was not securely tied down. On the lower deck thousand-pound bronze guns strained and creaked in hemp harnesses. Barrels rolled. The cooking fire sputtered out. Nipcheese hid deep in the ship's hold.

"All hands!" the bosun cried.

Emmet and the others hurried up from below. Sailors scrambled up into the rigging to clew up and haul down, reef and furl. On the horizon, shifting gray-green slabs of waves broke, splintered, then reformed larger than ever beneath dazzling whitecaps. And then the brief glimpse of distance snapped shut. Rock-hard rain, sleet, snow, and wind pelted the ships. Even the toughest sailor turned his back to the penetrating gale that was forcing the fleet south, in the opposite direction than they intended. A loud cracking noise rose from the rigging and spars of the *Golden Hind*.

The ship's masts bent and thrummed as if they might snap. The whole ship seemed ready to break apart.

"Clew up the fore and main topgallant sails!"

"Damn you, scowbank! Show a leg there!"

"We going under?" Emmet shouted desperately to Moone.

Moone grinned. "Get a handspike and hold it down hard in the water scuppers!"

Emmet couldn't tell if he was joking.

For the next three weeks storms slammed the ships. On the last day of September the *Marigold* vanished from sight. Some said late one night they heard the sound of cries for help from the *Marigold*'s twenty-nine-member crew. Others were certain they'd spied a wave as big as a church crush the tiny ship. In early October the *Elizabeth* disappeared. For days the sailors on the *Golden Hind* searched the raging sea for the sign of a light or sound of a gun that might indicate that either ship might still be afloat. To Emmet the vast sea seemed lonelier and more threatening than ever, knowing that the *Golden Hind* might be the sole survivor of the fleet.

Short-handed because so many of the crew were sick from scurvy, Emmet's normal duties as the captain's page were suspended as he helped the crew wherever he could. He hauled ropes, furled sails, and pumped water with four other men who slipped and slid in the hold in fetid, icy bilgewater up to their knees. Back and forth they pressed levers to desperately pump out the ocean that was pouring in through gaps in the hull planks and holes bored by sea worms. Emmet would rather have been above deck, where he could see what was happening. In the darkness and cold of the hold, every jolt, thud, and crash seemed to signify that the ship was going down.

For two days straight, Emmet had no sleep. He was constantly wet, constantly cold and hungry. He wondered if Diego was still alive. He wondered how many men had gone overboard. *How many of us are left?* Water dripped down from the beams and ceiling and slid along the walls.

"Ice ahead!" he heard someone shout above.

"Hard up the helm!" his companion, a Welshman, murmured. "Keep her off a little. Ever seen a iceberg, boy?"

Emmet shook his head as he pressed against the pump.

"A terrible beauty. Creviced and brittle. Tall as a mountain and twice as sharp. Floats and bobs like a giant animal big as an island. When I was a young fry I joined a whaler. Saw enough ice to last me the rest of my life."

There was nothing they could do but keep pumping. But with every jolt Emmet half expected to see a great piece of ice piercing through the fragile hull like a cutlass.

As the ship was buffeted farther south, ice cloaked the rigging. What sails were set stiffened like iron. Men who went aloft hauled in the canvas bare-handed while balancing on slippery, ice-coated rigging. One false move and they'd land in the sea or against the hard deck. The remaining longboat and pinnace had been hoisted on deck and could not be used for rescues. Any man overboard was as good as dead.

For days they had been unable to glimpse the sun, moon, or stars and depended on dead reckoning, guessing their position by log and compass. Da Silva desperately stood on the lurching deck so that whenever the storm cleared enough he could hold the backstaff to his eye to try to measure the angle between the horizon and the slight blur that might be the sun. This was their only reading that might tell them their latitude. Although his attempts were usually in vain, everyone sensed they were headed south instead of north. And everyone knew what lay to the far south—deadly icebergs.

One morning the wind shifted and sent the ship east. To take advantage of the change in wind direction, Captain Drake ordered the crew to unfurl the sails. Before the work could be finished, another storm struck with piercing wind, snow, and sleet. The mainsail, partially unfurled, flapped and thundered in the gale. The rigging quickly caked with ice. Diego and two other sailors were ordered aloft to secure the sail before the cloth was ripped to shreds.

Emmet stood on deck and helped coil rope. For a moment he paused, shielded his eyes from the snow, and watched his friend clamber high into the rigging. Diego and two other mariners made their way along treacherous lurching footholds in ratlines—pieces of rope dipped in tar and fixed to the rigging—as the ship bucked and plunged. For better grip they inched their way without shoes or gloves. Leaning over the yard, they grabbed the stiff sail and struggled to secure it with a rope. Every so often, Emmet saw Diego stop and move his arms. What was wrong? Maybe he was beating his frozen hands against the sail to revive his circulation.

"What's taking them so long?" Captain Drake shouted.

"Look lively up there!" the bosun called, even though his voice was lost in the wind.

The impatient captain turned away.

For a split second, the ship lurched violently.

Emmet saw his friend fall, saw his body splash into the frigid water off the starboard side. It was as if Diego had been floating, falling slowly as a feather through the air and dropping soundlessly, invisibly into the raging waves. Emmet's mouth opened to yell, but nothing came out for what seemed many minutes. Finally the frozen sensation that gripped his mouth, his arms, and his legs melted away, and he heard himself screaming, felt himself running, not even realizing that he still gripped the coil of rope in his hands.

"Man overboard!"

In one great arc Emmet flung the rope over the side to the place where his friend had vanished, even as the ship was racing away, slicing through the waves, abandoning Diego forever. And then, like a buoyant chunk of iceberg—not brittle but breathing—Diego surfaced. Alive! Arms flung upward, black hair plastered over his eyes, mouth gasping, somehow he reached out and caught the rope.

Everything that happened next occurred so quickly that Emmet did not know for certain if he truly saw it. Other sailors crowded at the rail. Together they hauled Diego through the water, up over the side, and onto the deck.

"What's this all about?" Captain Drake demanded.

Emmet and the huddle of sailors crowded around shivering Diego. One had draped him with a blanket. Another had given him a swig of precious rum. In spite of the height of his fall, he had not broken any bones. Diego managed a weak smile when he saw Emmet.

"A miracle," Flea said. "If you hadn't seen him go down, Emmet, he'd be dead."

"Take him below," the captain growled. "Back to work!"

No fires could be lit below. No warm food could be prepared. The best anyone could offer Diego was a collection of half-damp blankets to revive him.

Emmet felt as if what he'd done had been accomplished by someone else, someone outside himself. He didn't feel particularly heroic—only relieved that somehow he had been able to help his friend, who had nearly slipped out of sight forever.

At night Chaplain Fletcher made prayers in a voice barely audible above the raging storm. Emmet, who stood nearby, overheard the terrified pastor mumble to no one in particular, "God has pronounced a judgment, till he has buried our bodies and our ships also in the bottomless depths of the raging sea."

Days passed without a hint of sunlight. Night blurred into day, day into night. And still the wind howled, shaking the shrouds and whistling through the rigging.

Emmet and the others fell onto their pallets in soggy clothing. Some who had stood up on deck on watch were too stiff to bend their knees. They gulped beer, ate biscuits and small chunks of cold salt beef, and fell asleep until the next shrill bosun's call woke them. The sailors did not joke or sing or whistle. No one dared.

For a short time during one of the storm's lulls, Nipcheese reappeared on the lower deck. As soon as the cat saw Flea sitting down in a rare dry spot on a sea chest, he turned once, twice, in Flea's lap and curled into a ball. Flea stroked the mangy cat. "Do you think if we get home—" he began in a sorrowful voice. He stopped when the others looked at him as if they might slit his throat.

No one mentioned home at all anymore. The men who had

scurvy lay on their pallets, too weak to rise. With every passing day the amount of supplies grew smaller. Rations were cut, even though the men were working harder than ever. When the beer rations were halved, the men began to grumble about taking the ship back to England.

"A jinx, that's what it was. To kill Doughty."

"Storm's a conjurer's curse. You heard what words he used before the ax. Sure enough, he hexed us."

Emmet was too cold, too wet, and too tired to care. Between watches or turns at the pumps, he fell onto his pallet in his wet clothes, covered himself with a sodden blanket, and fell, dreamless, asleep. Even Diego, who had recovered with remarkable resilience, seemed quieter after his icy plunge.

Just when Emmet thought he could stand it no longer—when he thought he'd go mad to hear the howling of the wind, the shaking of the ship another day, another night—a shout rang out from deck.

"Land, ho!"

Every man who could rushed to deck to spy in the distance through patches of fog a bare, broken island girt with rocks and ice and stunted vegetation. Everyone agreed it was the most beautiful place they had ever beheld.

Chapter Ten

October 1578

At fifty-four degree we anchor behind an Island. Captain
sends ashore a pinnace with eight men to look for fresh
game—perhaps ducks, penguins, or more seal meat. Peter
Carder of Cornwall and seven men and boys—among
them Artyur the Dutch trumpeter and Richard Joyner,
servant to Scoble. The last we see of any of them. They
had neither compass nor food. The Captain has stopped
looking for the open boat. Our anchor cable broke in
violent winds and we were driven farther south. At last
we find harbor off a more promising island. I shall miss
Carder's songs of Devon. God save them all. We have lost
the rest of the fleet and more than half the crew. Only
the *Pelican*, renamed *Golden Hind*, remains with less than
five dozen aboard, nearly three-quarters weak and
afflicted with scurvy. Swollen legs and gums, loose
Teeth, unhealed wounds.

Emmet and Diego rowed ashore to gather scurvy grass while
six other sailors were assigned to cut wood for fuel, shoot
ducks and seabirds, and fill barrels with fresh water. Emmet
felt tremendous relief as he stepped ashore on the small, rocky
island. He tried to convince himself that the terrible storms
were at last behind them. "Over here!" he called to Diego.

Together in the sandy, stony soil along a small rivulet of fresh
water they searched for scurvy grass—what Father Parfoothe had

always called spoonwort. An odd name Emmet had never understood. Nothing about the plant looked like a spoon.

"This?" Diego asked, pulling up a great weed by its roots.

"No," Emmet replied. "Look for a small, low-growing plant with long stems and white flowers."

"This?"

"No. Fleshy, heart-shaped leaves are what we're looking for." Emmet plunged into a brushy area, and after several moments came out with a small green plant. "Here!" he called joyfully. "Smell it."

"Phew! *¡Qué barbaridad!*" Diego said, holding his nose. "Why Old Man want this?"

Emmet explained how they'd crush the leaves with a pestle. Then they'd use the pungent oil to make a drink with boiled water that would help cure scurvy. Diego nibbled a leaf and made a face. "*¿Vasa tomar vino?*"

Emmet laughed. "*Sí. ¡Mucho vino!* Wine will make it taste much better." He enjoyed his Spanish lessons with Diego, a patient teacher. The language seemed easier and more melodic to Emmet than Latin or Greek.

Diego pulled up a clump of scurvy grass and stuffed it inside the bag. "I should tell you this," he said, not looking up. "*Gracias.*"

"*¿Por qué?*" Emmet asked. He wondered if this was part of the language lesson.

"For my life."

Emmet brusquely sorted through the plants, pulling leaves, discarding roots. "You would have done the same for me."

"Would I? How are you so sure? *¡Mucho ojo!*" Diego laughed.

Emmet laughed too. On board ship everyone joked about the

cheapness of life. What else could they do? With so many dead or disappeared, they had to somehow keep their sense of humor, however dark.

When they finished gathering scurvy grass they rested on a large, flat rock at the southernmost part of the island. Every so often sunlight pierced the gloom, providing at least the appearance of warmth. Breakers pounded the windy shoreline. To the east loomed another dark, hulking shape—another rocky island. Beyond that to the south, open ocean stretched to the horizon. According to the biggest map in Captain Drake's cabin, this was where Terra Incognita—the mysterious Southern Continent that the captain seemed to study with such enthusiasm—was supposed to lie

"What you will do with your gold?" Diego asked. He picked up a rock and hurled it. The rock bounced against a boulder.

"What gold?" Emmet asked. He stared at the vast space and tried to imagine what kind of Southern Continent he would draw if he were an artist of maps. It would certainly be a bountiful place. Not anything so barren as this rocky island, inhabited mostly by seabirds and seals.

"Your share of *el tesor* after we attack Spanish galleons," Diego said with enthusiasm. "Surely you have thought of treasure, have you not?"

Emmet scratched his head. Up until recently he had not been certain he would live long enough to find a safe harbor, much less enough food to fill his stomach. "We have not seen one Spanish ship since the strait. Any sensible captain would avoid this ocean altogether."

"When we go north, you shall see," Diego said with confidence.

There are great ships filled with gold. Old Man knows. We all become rich."

"You like the idea of being a pirate?"

"*¡Si!*" Diego declared. "One day I buy grand carriage with six horses. I take my *madre* for rides up and down the mountains. Eat on fine plates, like Old Man. Plenty of sugar and marmalade and raisins, *la mantequilla* and *el queso* every meal. And you?"

Emmet stared at his filthy feet. He had never admitted to anyone before how much his conscience troubled him. Piracy meant theft, murder—everything he had been taught by Father Parfoothe never to commit. And yet to confess his reluctance, his anxiety, and his dread would only make Diego laugh. Diego the pirate. If any of the other crew members discovered Emmet's true feelings, he'd be tormented. Perhaps even thrown overboard.

"My family will welcome me with a great celebration," Emmet declared. "My father the mayor will make a feast, and invite everyone in the village. They will be glad to see me because I will bring gifts. Gold spoons, gold combs—"

"*¡Bueno!* And do not forget gold shoes! And the harness for your horse, the one you race every Sunday. Gold too?"

Emmet nodded. He hoped his grin looked believable. "A gold harness. And a gold saddle."

"Why you leave such a wonderful family?"

Emmet felt sweat trickle down his arms. There was no one left at home who meant anything to him anymore. He could never go back. "I told you before. I left home to seek my fortune," he said quickly. "My father and my mother anxiously await my return."

Diego gestured with enthusiasm. "My father was the chief, and my mother, she was escaped slave. They tell Old Man, 'Take our son, but bring him back *opulento*.'" Emmet had heard Diego's exaggerated story a hundred times. How he had joined Captain Drake at Nombre de Dios when he was only eight years old. How as a young boy he had single-handedly saved the captain from attack by alerting him of approaching Spanish horsemen.

Emmet sighed. Sometimes it was a lonely feeling not to be able to speak the truth about his past. Even though Diego was his closest friend, he wouldn't understand. To confide the true story, Emmet knew, would be his own death sentence. Aboard ship there could be no secrets. Someone was always watching. Someone was always listening.

Suddenly a gun boomed from the ship. *"¡De prisa!"* Emmet said. He and Diego hurried to their feet, grabbed the sack, and rushed back to the beach where the ship lay at anchor.

1 November

Captain demands I sketch his picture. Seeking out the southernmost part of the Island, he casts himself down, groveling, upon the Island's outermost point, and so reaches out his body over it. He says to me, "I shall tell all who ask that I have been on the Southernmost known Land in the World, and more farther to the Southwards upon it, than any of them, yea, or any man as yet known." He looks a fool sprawled there, but I do as he commands. Diego stifles his laughter, which would have cost him his life.

No sign of *Marigold* or *Elizabeth*. We fear they are lost from us for good. In completely calm sea, trumpeter Brewer standing on the poop sounding his trumpet, is knocked into icy cold water by a rope that seems to flail out of its own volition. Line cast to him, and he is pulled to safety. Brewer is one of the men who put Doughty to his death. Is his falling overboard and rescue some sign of forgiveness?

In late October the ship weighed anchor and sailed north, tacking northwest then northeast in search of the coast. After nearly three weeks what little meat they had was eaten. When another cruel storm hit, some of the men belowdecks grumbled that perhaps they had become lost. What if they had somehow fumbled their way east to the Atlantic again?

On the morning of 25 November the weather cleared. From high in the mainmast a lookout shouted, "Land, ho!"

Emmet and Diego ran to the rail and looked out at the low smudge on the horizon. Mocha Island—their first landfall in nearly a month. This was the gateway to one of the largest gold-mining cities in South America, a place where Spanish *encomendaros* commanded thousands of Indian slave laborers to dig for gold. The men hoped that here they could find fresh food, firewood, and drinking water.

As a precaution, however, Captain Drake ordered all British flags—and any indication of their identity—stowed out of sight. Trespassing in Spanish waters, the *Golden Hind* was alone, outmanned, and outgunned. The ship leaked. The rigging and sails needed mending. The hull, riddled by sea worms, required careening and repairs. The men were still weak from hunger, thirst, and scurvy. Neither the ship nor the crew were in any shape to attack a well-armed Spanish vessel with a well-fed crew.

The idea that the *Golden Hind* might try to strike a heavily laden Spanish gold ship seemed foolhardy.

Exactly something Captain Drake might try.

When the *Golden Hind* came closer to Mocha, the crew did not spy any signs of Spanish merchant vessels. Indians crowded the shore. The air smelled of smoke from campfires on the beach. Canoes crisscrossed the harbor.

Emmet watched nervously as two canoes filled with Indians paddled past. The Indians did not pause or hail the *Golden Hind* in a friendly manner. One paddler shouted harsh words in their direction.

"What's he saying?" Emmet asked Diego.

Diego shrugged. *"No se."*

On the first day of their arrival, eleven gunners and bowmen were sent ashore to trade for food. What little they brought back included shellfish and two bony sheep. The following day another party was sent ashore for water. This time Captain Drake accompanied the group, which included Emmet, who was assigned as a rower. Eager Diego volunteered to serve with the group.

As the *Golden Hind*'s longboat made its way to shore, Emmet saw women and children scurry like phantoms between the trees. Palm leaves rattled in the wind.

"Anchor here," Captain Drake ordered. As the heavily loaded longboat bobbed in shallow water, Brewer and Flood rolled water barrels down the beach.

Suddenly a shot rang out. "Look lively!" the captain shouted, and waded toward shore, weapon drawn. Diego was right behind him, brandishing a pistol. All seven of the remaining harquebusiers and bowmen were ordered ashore. Only Emmet was told to remain behind to guard the boat.

Helplessly Emmet watched as the mariners charged straight into an ambush. Before Diego or the others could reload, two dozen Indians leaped from the reeds and surrounded them. *Zing! Zing!* Arrows sliced through the air and riddled the sailors' backs, arms, and necks. More warriors poured from between the trees. They pelted rocks and shot more arrows. Emmet watched in horror as the beach filled with confusion—the screams of men and the stench of gunpowder. Somewhere in the chaos Diego had vanished.

"Back to the boat!" the captain shouted, trying to rally a retreat. Men with pistols backed toward the water, fumbling to reload. A few managed to get off second shots but were pinned on the shore by a fresh assault of arrows.

"To the boat!" Captain Drake shouted at the water's edge. He hacked two Indians with his cutlass. Blood seeped into the water, staining it pink.

Emmet pulled on the oars. With all his strength he tried to maneuver the boat so that the wounded sailors could be dropped inside. A cloud of arrows whizzed past.

"Weigh anchor!" Captain Drake waved his sword in the air. Nearby a longbowmen hurtled facedown into the water. Another crew member tried to drag the bowman toward the longboat. His back and shoulders bristled with arrows. The water swirled dark red.

Emmet pulled a dagger from his belt and tried to slice the rope that moored the longboat to the anchor. Closer, closer, crept an Indian with his knife raised. The rope seemed too tough for the dull blade. Emmet sawed faster, faster. A shot rang out. Blood splattered Emmet's face, his arms. The Indian pitched forward into the water.

"Hurry, you scabshin!" Captain Drake bellowed. The pistol in his hand smoked. The shaft of an arrow protruded from his face, just below his eye. Bright red smeared his face.

"Diego!" Emmet shouted. Desperately he scanned the beach littered with bodies. "Where is he?"

"We'll all be killed if we wait. Heave to!" Captain Drake commanded. With one hand he cradled his bloody arrow-wound.

"But he's still in there—" Emmet glanced again toward the trees. Any moment, any moment he expected Diego to emerge. He had to be all right.

"I said, heave to!" Captain Drake shouted. He pulled a dagger from his belt. "Pull those oars or I'll kill you."

"He's still—"

"Pull!"

Emmet gripped the oars and pulled. The longboat rocked dangerously against a wave. As long as he could, he kept his eyes on the shore.

When they finally managed to return to the *Golden Hind*, the injured from the longboat were hauled up with ropes onto the deck. The heavy, limp body of Great Neil, the Danish gunner, was pulled to safety.

"He's dead," someone mumbled.

Emmet turned and heard shouting from shore, the sound of exultant celebration.

"They've got Brewer and Flood. Diego, too," someone shouted, peering through the glass.

Emmet could not believe it. Could not believe that his friend was still there, being butchered with the rest. He didn't want to look. He didn't want to hear.

The groaning wounded were laid out on the deck. Flea and a few others rushed about with strips of rag and buckets of what precious water had been salvaged, trying their best to remove arrowheads and bandage wounds.

"Leave me alone!" Captain Drake bellowed. He pulled the arrow from his face himself. The fistful of rag he held beneath his eye quickly soaked with blood.

"Sir, let me help you," Chaplain Fletcher begged the captain. The pale chaplain looked as if he might faint. Even da Silva, who ordinarily seemed calm in emergencies, appeared distraught as he offered swigs of rum to the wounded.

Onshore the mob was singing and dancing around an enormous bonfire. "They've got a head on a pole, sir," said Edwards, staring through the glass. His voice was almost hushed. "Can't see whose, sir."

"Load the guns, Captain?" Sky demanded eagerly. "Blast them to pieces?"

"And waste good shot?" Captain Drake replied. "No. They think we're the Spanish, their enemies. We'll weigh anchor and find a place to bury what dead we have aboard."

"Sir?" Emmet asked, stunned. How could the captain so callously abandon Diego and the others who had risked and sacrificed their lives for him? Indefatigable Diego, who would have gone anywhere, done anything for Old Man—no matter how impossible, how dangerous. "What about the ones left behind?"

"Are you disobeying my orders, boy?" Captain Drake demanded. "That's an act of mutiny."

"No, sir," Emmet replied, cowering.

"Raise anchor! Look lively!" Captain Drake barked. The bosun whistled.

Emmet and the six men who were fit enough turned the capstan, heaving with all their might. Every time Emmet trudged forward, pushing against the capstan bar, he glanced toward the rising smoke on shore. No one spoke of gold. No one spoke of attacking a Spanish ship.

"Ever think how we might be marooned here?" Moone murmured.

Edwards nodded. "Aye, with no certainty of return."

Emmet scarcely listened. He was too stunned, too overwhelmed to care. Diego of the buoyant heart, the only one who knew how to help him when he was fearful or crazy. Diego, gentle and strong. Diego his brother, his comrade in arms. Diego, his friend, was gone.

Chapter Eleven

November

Little sorrow among the crew. All goes on as usual. I
walk and eat and talk and act as if nothing happened,
pretending that Death is not the King of Terrors to me,
one of the survivors, the one who mourns. Can I shut my
eyes and let nothing touch me? Diego was here once,
now he's gone. I can still see him entertaining the crew
with jumping tricks. I should have died, not him.

The ship set sail on the afternoon of the ambush, and did
not come to anchor until a week later at the Bay of Quintero,
350 miles to the north.

Something aboard had changed. Emmet and the other crew
members had crossed a line. More than eighty men and boys
from the fleet had vanished since the strait—some from perilous
seas, some from disease. The surviving crew members of the
Golden Hind had seen their friends wounded. They had seen their
friends die and their bodies left abandoned, to be mutilated by
the enemy. Emmet and the other mariners were in the midst of a
strange kind of war with rules that did not seem to make sense.
Their foe—faceless, formless—might appear between the
shadows of trees or cruise on well-equipped ships, then vanish as
quickly as fog. Between moments of surprise attack and terror
stretched long hours where nothing happened.

Only waiting.

One night as the ship sailed north, the sea cascaded with

specks of fire—phosphoric gleams that snapped and danced as the water bucked. Overhead so many stars studded the sky that Emmet felt dizzy when he gazed upward. Below and above he was surrounded by terrible beauty made even more profound by the knowledge that at any moment he too might suffer the fate of Diego, Great Neil, Brewster, Carder, or any member of the crews of the *Elizabeth* or the *Marigold*.

On 5 December they approached the port of Valparaíso along the coast of New Spain. A captured fisherman who was brought aboard for questioning claimed that a great ship lay at anchor in the harbor. Speaking in Spanish, he told da Silva that the *Los Reyes*, known locally as *La Capitana*, was filled with gold.

Captain Drake, with a bandage over his right eye, assembled the crew on deck to describe how they'd attack *La Capitana*. "Listen close!" he shouted. "For if you disobey my orders you will find yourselves flogged and thrown overboard. We will haul up the Spanish flag. Eighteen men, heavily armed, will go to meet her in a pinnace. Your arms will remain hidden, and only Spanish shall be spoken when you board her. Take all pilots, crew, and passengers prisoner. No one touches anything aboard without my orders."

Emmet was surprised to discover that he was among the men selected to board the ship. It was because of his ability to speak Spanish, Captain Drake said. He depended on Emmet to call out in the correct tongue where they were from and where they were headed in order to trick *La Capitana*'s pilot.

"You're a lucky one!" Flea whispered as the crew prepared their weapons.

Emmet did not feel the least bit fortunate. Nervously he

watched the horizon as they sailed closer to Valparaíso. At nightfall they approached the harbor. Emmet was relieved to see only one ship anchored there: *La Capitana*. He had overheard da Silva tell the captain that the ship had served nearly eleven years earlier as the flagship for Pedro Sarmiento de Gamboa, a famous navigator. De Gamboa's expedition from Peru to the Solomon Islands and back had covered nearly eighteen thousand miles in twenty-two months. This was a ship that had traveled even farther than the *Golden Hind.*

Over and over in his mind Emmet rehearsed his greeting. Closer, closer they approached *La Capitana* until he could see the faces of the men on board. Captain Drake gave him the signal.

"*¡Buenas noches!*" Emmet shouted in a friendly manner.

Across the bay came the sound of a drum. "*¡Bienvenido!*" the Spanish sailors shouted a message of welcome.

"What are they saying?" Captain Drake hissed in Emmet's ear.

"They want us to visit. They say they have wine," Emmet replied.

"Good!" Captain Drake signaled to the men, who lowered the pinnace. Quickly and silently Emmet and the other men clambered down into the pinnace and began rowing toward the unsuspecting ship. Their weapons lay concealed beneath a canvas tarp.

Emmet sat in the bow near Sky. "Keep your mouths shut!" Sky growled. "Nobody speaks till we're safe aboard." He peered through the spyglass. "They're waving to us," he whispered. "Five, six, seven Spanish dogs. That's what I'm counting. Can't see too well."

"May be more below," Moone cautioned.

Emmet wondered if they were completely outnumbered.

It seemed to take forever for the pinnace to make its way across to the ship. A line was thrown down to tie up the pinnace. Emmet took a deep breath. His voice had to sound friendly, convincing. He could not betray how terrified he felt as he shouted in Spanish that they were coming aboard.

"*¡Bienvenido!*" the sailors howled.

Emmet crawled up first, according to Captain Drake's orders. Up close now he could see that the ship needed paint. Above him patched sails flapped. *La Capitana* was apparently being used as a coastal trader carrying ordinary cargo—nothing like its dramatic cross-Pacific exploits of a decade earlier.

"Be careful," Flea had warned when Emmet left. "She may still have some fight left."

As Emmet recalled those words, he froze halfway up the rope ladder. Sky, climbing up behind him, jabbed him hard with the barrel of his pistol. Emmet took a deep breath. *How Diego would have liked to be here at this moment!* Emmet could imagine him, teeth flashing, as he climbed aboard the Spanish ship. *I can do that,* Emmet told himself. He reached up to put his hand on the rail of the ship and felt a sudden surge of energy. "*¡Hola!*" he called in a loud voice that surprised himself.

Before he could make the brief speech that he had rehearsed, Sky pushed over the ledge past him, quickly followed by Moone. "*¡Abajo, perro!*" Moone shouted, and slugged the pilot with the butt of his harquebus. The man fell to the ground.

This was not part of the plan. No one was supposed to shout "Get below, you dog!" Emmet wasn't sure what to do next.

"*¡Piratas!*" the Spanish sailors cried in confusion.

In an instant the shouting crew of a half-dozen men aboard *La Capitana* dove for cover and knocked over the wine cask. Before they could scramble to grab weapons, poles, anything to beat back the intruders, the armed men from the *Golden Hind* quickly surrounded them. The *Capitana* crew and three slaves silently raised their hands in the air.

Sky poked one of the men with a gun and glanced at Emmet. "Tell them to go below. We'll lock them down there."

Emmet gave them the order, which they quickly obeyed. He felt delighted to exercise this new power. After so many failures, they finally accomplished what they'd set out to do without any injuries or deaths. Triumphantly Sky whistled to Captain Drake to signal their success.

Splash!

"What's that?" Moone demanded.

Emmet ran to the side and heard what sounded like someone swimming toward shore. "A sailor got away!"

"God's eyes!" Moone swore an oath. "Now the whole town'll know we're here."

"If you hadn't ruined everything with your dramatic entrance, this wouldn't have happened," Sky told Moone.

"You shouldn't be one to talk—"

"Quit your jawing-tackle," Captain Drake barked. Everyone, including Sky, quickly removed their caps and bowed as the captain climbed aboard. "We must move swiftly."

The trembling Spanish crew was brought up on deck and tied together so that they could not escape. Captain Drake went below to inspect the cargo: two huge chests that were filled with gold pesos. In the hold were casks of wine and stacks of sawed lumber.

"Who is pilot here?" Captain Drake demanded, using Emmet as translator.

Juan Griego, a small, dark man with a goatee, stepped forward and bowed. He handed over his detailed set of charts and sailing instructions for all the ports on the coast. "Better than gold!" the captain declared. "Here is something the queen will want to see. You are going with me, Juan the Greek, to be my pilot."

Frowning, Griego bowed. He was obviously not pleased to be kidnapped and renamed by an English pirate.

Without waiting for daylight Captain Drake ordered the men into the pinnace and *La Capitana*'s longboat. "While some of you stand guard, the rest will come ashore with me. This time there will be no mistakes," Captain Drake announced severely.

Emmet was among those selected to row into the town in case any translation was necessary. They were going into the heart of danger, he knew. Anything or anyone might be waiting for them in the town. They could be ambushed and wiped out by the Spanish viceroy's soldiers. They could be massacred by hiding villagers. Except for the yapping of a dog, the village appeared silent. No light shone.

Emmet sat in the boat and gripped the oar until his hands ached. He stared into the darkness, desperate to see something—anything. He leaned forward and listened, but all he heard was the wind, the lapping water around the boat, the dripping from the oars. The oppressive silence from the village howled in his ears. Every sound, every thud, every movement of wave or palm leaf reminded him of the beach at Mocha where Diego had been killed.

The boat rocked. Emmet's heart raced. He wasn't waiting in Valparaíso anymore. He was back in Mocha again, waiting for the ambush—the gunshots, the whiz of arrows, the sound of men screaming in pain and terror. *Now! Now!* Emmet wanted to shout. He wanted to leap from the boat, wade through the water, and charge toward the shore, as if this time he might save Diego, he might bring him back alive.

"Steady now, my bullies," Captain Drake murmured. "Pull her in and go to work. You know what to do to Spanish infidels."

The boat thudded softly against the beach. Emmet barely heard Captain Drake divide the men into two groups, with instructions to return to the boat when they heard the trumpeter. Emmet and his companions, under the leadership of Sky, grabbed loaded snaphance pistols, cutlasses, and short hunting swords. They pulled the boat high onto the beach, then scuttled toward the black outlines of a cluster of buildings.

Anyone might be hiding in the shadows with arrows or rocks. Emmet didn't care. Fearlessly he charged toward the village. He did not think about being killed. He did not think about dying. He did not care about living. Only one thought consumed him, carried him, propelled him forward: white-hot revenge.

Sky slammed against the door of a hut with the butt of his harquebus. Nothing happened. He kicked the wooden door, and it finally flew open. "Light torches," he said, pointing to a fire in the hearth.

When Emmet held a burning torch aloft, he paid no attention to the rough-hewn table, stool, and pallet covered with a ragged blanket. He was too busy searching for any enemy who might be hiding.

"Miserable Spanish must have just escaped," Moone said with disappointment. The blanket had been thrown back in a hurry and lay crumpled against the grimy wall, as if someone had just jumped from the bed. On the table a spoon gouged half-eaten beans in a wooden bowl.

Sky overturned the pallet, revealing, wedged among the slats of the bed frame, a faceless doll made from a corn husk. The sight of that mocking doll enraged Emmet. He picked up the stool and hurled it against the wall with all his might. The wood splintered. At that moment right spilled into wrong, order blended into chaos. He did not know why he was there, what he was doing. It was as if he'd left his own body and could no longer control his actions as he tore a crude crucifix from the wall and tossed it into the fireplace.

"Well done," Sky said, grinning. "No gold or silver here. Burn everything." He touched the pallet with the torch. In an instant, fire crackled and leaped.

Emmet stampeded with the others to the next house. And the next. There was nothing of value in any of the ramshackle places—just a bit of food and a few sticks of furniture. Nothing worth stealing. They set more fires. Flames raged and danced. The men seemed to gain courage from the flickering light. Now that it appeared that no one would stop them, their voices became louder, brasher. They whooped and hollered as they rampaged through the village, destroying houses, clothing, belongings.

Emmet, too, felt a strange kind of elation. He didn't know why. The more he destroyed the better he felt. For the first time the hurt and pain of Diego's death didn't touch him. Memories of Doughty's death and betrayal by Captain Drake vanished. As he moved through the houses, knocking over furniture and setting walls on fire, he became consumed by reckless power. No one could stop him. No one could touch him. He was as powerful as a vengeful god.

"Good work!" Sky shouted. The others cheered as another house went up in flames.

It was so easy, so pleasurable. Emmet crashed through a wooden fence and kicked open a small shed. A terrified, bony pig raced out and nearly knocked him over in its mad dash to escape. Emmet was too quick. He tackled the animal, stabbed it repeatedly with the cutlass until his arms were covered with blood. Emmet did not hear the pig's piteous squeals. "This one's for you, Diego," he said in a hoarse voice.

Emmet stood, unaware of the way the felled pig's legs jerked and jolted as if it were still running away. He wiped his cutlass on his sleeve and hurried to the next building, where he heard shouting.

Moone had found the warehouse. The door stood wide open. In the corner were casks of wine and sacks of grain and rice.

"Take everything," Sky ordered. "Load what you can carry into the longboat." Emmet and Flea hauled sacks of corn from the warehouse.

"So easy!" Flea announced in a merry voice as he carried a bag on his shoulder. "Now the girls have hold of the tow rope, and can't haul the slack in fast enough!"

There wasn't much in the warehouse, perhaps because the villagers had had time to hide what they could. In a small struggling village, Emmet knew that every bit of food was probably precious. Yet he felt no guilt as he rolled a cask of wine out of the warehouse. He was hungry and thirsty too, wasn't he? What was he supposed to eat and drink?

Nearby they could hear the loud voices of Sky and Moone. They had obviously broken into the casks of wine and were enjoying themselves as they set afire a small barn with a thatched roof. Lowing cows with great rolling eyes fled in the firelight. Moone laughed and shot one of the animals.

Piles of looted food grew in heaps along the water's edge. More men from the boats had come ashore to help carry the cargo and enjoy the pleasures of a village where they could do whatever they wanted. A crew member stumbled out of a house wearing a woman's shawl. Another appeared carrying a broom, a pot. There were few items of value in such a poor place, but the men seemed determined to uncover hidden chests of gold or silver plate.

"Over here!" Moone called. He and a group of drunken crew members had entered the little church. In a matter of moments they had broken through the wooden door and found the chalice, some cruets, a shabby priest's vestment made of damask, and a missal.

"Present those popish presents to Fletcher!" bellowed Captain Drake, who had joined the looters on shore.

It seemed to Emmet as if the days of humiliation and suffering, the days of privation, the days of witnessing wounded and dying friends had all been swept away. Nobody could stop them from enjoying the present moment. They drank free-flowing wine and staggered through the empty town in stupefied, gleeful abandon. Like the others, Emmet felt invincible. And throughout the loud carousing, there was Captain Drake—encouraging the loudest, most destructive behavior of all.

Emmet laughed when he saw Flea prancing in a woman's dress.

Eager to outdo Flea, Emmet stumbled through a hedgerow into the little cemetery beside the church. With a will he went to work on the headstones, knocking them over, tugging them flat. Sky and the others shouted approval when they saw Emmet's cleverness. Soon three or four sailors joined Emmet, tossing sad bouquets into the air and urinating on the graves.

Emmet staggered onto a soft mound, surprised when his feet gave way slightly beneath him. *Fresh grave.* He jumped off. Breathless, heart throbbing, he felt a tremendous burning in his gut. Only a few feet below him he knew there was a Spanish corpse—perhaps only a few days old. And yet even the presence of someone newly dead beneath him didn't stop him. Why should it? The corpse was an enemy's, wasn't it? In a frenzy he bent and cracked the wooden grave marker between his fists. He felt no slivers, no pain, no remorse. These defilements meant nothing to him. Nothing. He was past feeling anything for himself, let alone anything for the families of the dead.

Crash! Something shattered. Men shouted with delight. Emmet rushed into the church, eager to find some new amusement.

"Don't," Flea said, and tried to grab his arm.

Emmet pushed past Flea and cursed him. "Get out of my way."

Half a dozen men were already pulling down the large crucifix on the wall, knocking over benches, overturning the altar. They had just broken all the glass from the church's sole window. One of the men was wearing the priest's vestment and pretending to bless his drunken friends.

Emmet picked his way carelessly over the broken glass. A ladder leaned against a wall. Overhead was a small opening in the ceiling that probably led to the bell tower. Curious, he tucked his cutlass inside his belt so that he could use both hands to scurry up into the church loft.

In the darkness he crossed the beams that led to a dusty tower shaft. Small slits at the top opened on all four sides of the shaft. Outside in the square below he heard the sound of the crew's laughter and shouts of delight as they danced around a bonfire.

Beyond the firelight stretched the darkness of the woods. Some of the villagers might be hiding there at this very moment, watching them in horror. Even if they spied Emmet high in the church bell tower, they couldn't stop him. They couldn't reach him. Not even an archer hiding in the trees could pick him off. No one could kill him. He was too powerful.

Emmet looked up into the dark circle that he knew was the gaping mouth of the church bell. He reached out with one hand and felt something against the wall—another ladder. Now he had another splendid idea. Perhaps this bell might be worth something. A rope hung down from the enormous clapper. Emmet gave the rope a hard yank. The bell echoed with a sonorous *DONG* that nearly deafened him. Inspired, he shimmied up the second ladder to the very top of the tower. Using his cutlass he began to saw away at the stout rope from which the bell hung. The cold metal bell was so heavy it did not even budge as he worked.

He sawed and sawed. Little by little the frayed rope tore and shredded. With a surprising silence and swiftness the bell whooshed and tumbled. It crashed down through the wooden beams of the tower and with a series of satisfying crashes and hollow metal thunks disappeared into the dark abyss below Emmet.

Emmet was not aware how he managed to make his way so quickly to the ground. He expected to be greeted as a kind of hero by the others, who cheered when they heard the bell fall. By the time he reached the fallen bell, someone had already torn away the cracked plaster wall to uncover their prize—the only thing of real monetary value they'd found in this miserable village.

The other crew members peered into the opening with torches. The bell was so heavy, four of the brawniest crew members had to use all their strength to tip it so it might be rolled down to the beach to be loaded aboard the ship. They had only managed to budge the great metal bell when they stopped. Everything stopped. The shouting. The shooting. The talking. The laughter.

"What the devil—" Flea whispered.

Wedged beneath the hard edge of the bell's lip were two small, pale bare legs. The feet were curled together, toes touching, the way a child sleeps—careless and comfortable.

"Move it!"

"Heave the thing!"

Someone held a torch higher. The men lifted the great bell, which had crushed and cut in half a boy no older than nine or ten years of age. He must have been hiding in the secret alcove inside the church when the bell fell. His thick hair was very black. His dark eyes were as flat and lifeless as those of a trapped fish. The boy's full lips curled half open, grinning.

Emmet stared, certain that the boy was smiling at him. He gulped. "He's dead?"

"Couldn't be deader," someone joked.

Another sailor laughed. "Stupid bastard. Why didn't he run away with the rest?"

"Maybe he was guarding the church."

"Stupid bastard."

Emmet did not hear anything. He kept staring at the boy's

mouth. He looked as if he might speak, as he if he might say something.

"Let's get out of here," Moone said.

"Nothing more we can do."

The crew, now snapped out of its madness, silently rolled the bell down toward the beach. The metal *thonked* and thudded against the rocks, the ruts. Only Flea and Emmet remained.

"Come on," Flea said quietly. "It was an accident."

Emmet shrugged away Flea's tugging hand. Emmet couldn't stop looking at the dead boy. Finally when Emmet glanced down at the front of his own tunic, he noticed that it had been stained with blood. *Where did this come from?* He couldn't remember anything. He couldn't remember the pig or the fires or climbing up into the tower. He felt nothing. Not even shame.

A trumpet sounded from the beach. "We've got to get out of here before the Spanish soldiers come," Flea said. In the firelight Emmet did not notice how months of sleepless nights, days of meager food, the constant strain of storms, and the bullying from other crew members had aged Flea. The boy's sad, tired eyes were as dull as an old man's. "Let's go," Flea insisted. He took Emmet firmly by the arm and led him to the shore.

Chapter Twelve

7 December

Fourth hidden strongbox of treasure discovered on *La Capitana*, four hundred pounds of the finest Valdavian gold. Worth more than twenty-four thousand pesos. I saw the captain plunge his hands in the gold, then lift and inspect it. When Edwards tried to do the same, the Captain ordered everyone on deck to watch Bosun chop off two of Edwards's fingers. No one looked away. We take the ship *La Capitana* and replace the crew with twenty-five of our men and sail north. *Elizabeth* and *Marigold* gone for good. I am sick of the voyage, sick of what it is doing to us, sick of myself and what I am becoming. God help me.

Because firewood and fresh water were once again in short supply, the two ships hugged the coast in search of a stream where the men might refill the water casks and search for wood. At the Bay of La Herradura, Captain Drake ordered the ships to anchor, and sent ashore a dozen men in a pinnace. Emmet and Flea stayed aboard the *Golden Hind* to help build another pinnace with lumber from *La Capitana* that had been stowed in the hold. The swift second pinnace would be used in future raids.

Expertly Flea moved the plane back and forth to form neat white curls of wood. He did not seem to mind that Nipcheese slept in the wood chips. "Something vexes you?" he asked

Emmet. He did not look up as he sawed a board in half. "Since Valparaíso—"

"I am fine," Emmet interrupted in a sharp voice.

"You shout when you sleep."

"You are mistaken." In one savage movement Emmet gathered up the unused ends of wood and hurled them into a pile. He wasn't going to talk about nightmares, visions of that boy's face staring at him. Not here. Not on deck, where anyone might be listening. Why couldn't Flea mind his own business?

"Next week's Christmas," Flea said, as if anxious to change the subject.

Emmet only grunted.

"We been gone little over a year."

That long? Emmet stared out at the green trees, the white beach, the azure water. Christmas and home seemed like distant, half-forgotten visions. He felt as if he'd been gone for more years than he could count.

"Just thought you might like to know, that's all," Flea mumbled. He sat in the shade for a moment, his back leaning against an empty keg. His knees were bent and he slumped forward, staring hollow-eyed at some place in space.

Emmet, too, took the moment of peace to crouch in a shadow. He ached with exhaustion. For a second his eyes must have shut. When a shout rang out from the lookout, he was on his feet, dazed but instantly awake. Like everyone else aboard ship, he searched the shore for a sign of the watering party.

A cloud rose in the distance. Along the ridge above the beach galloped what appeared to be a huge body of armored Spanish horsemen. Their helmets gleamed in the sunlight. "Two hundred

Indians running alongside!" the lookout shouted.

Captain Drake ordered the signal gun shot off as a warning to the men on shore.

"There they are!" Emmet called out. He could see the watering party wading out to a large rock where the pinnace had been anchored. The men stumbled and splashed. The horsemen came closer and closer.

Emmet and the others on board called out and waved, as if by doing so they might somehow save their comrades. "Should we go ashore, Captain?" Moone asked eagerly.

Captain Drake shook his head. "Prepare to fire."

They were too far away to do much damage with nine-pound balls shot from the long-range demiculverin. From this distance they would barely be able to blast the edge of the sandy beach. But it might be enough to scare off the Spaniards.

Eager to do something—anything—the crew in charge of the slim, deadly artillery went to work. They loaded swivel-mounted falconets with shot. Before they could begin sweeping the shore, another shout went up from the lookout.

"Captain! They're in the pinnace now. They're coming this way."

"All of them?" Captain Drake bellowed.

"No, sir."

"Who's missing?"

"Minnivy, sir. He's—he's . . . I can't believe what he's doing, sir."

Captain Drake grabbed the glass from his mate and held it to his eye. "Good God."

All eyes turned toward the beach where the horsemen galloped at full speed. A hundred yards, ninety yards, eighty yards separated them from the naked bellowing figure who waded out into the water. Minnivy had stripped away his clothing, his hat, his armor, and stood raving with only a harquebus loaded with one shot—one shot against two dozen Spanish horsemen and two hundred Indians shooting arrows. His wild, long hair stood out in all directions. He howled in defiance, shot the harquebus, managed to kill one rider, and then at the last moment raised the gun itself as if it were a weapon. He was surrounded by horses and arrows and vanished from view.

For what seemed like forever, no one on board spoke. Minnivy's stand was so improbable, so fantastic. It was madness. "Berserk," Flea mumbled. "He's gone berserk."

"Fire!" Captain Drake bellowed to the men below loading one of the bronze cannons. "Damn your eyes, fire!"

The cannon belched smoke and the shot arced and fell short, plummeting into the water several hundred yards south of the fleeing pinnace. The men in the pinnace rowed furiously toward the ship even as arrows hurtled over their heads.

"¡El Draque!" the crowd of horsemen and Indians on the beach shouted. They held aloft a pike. And even from this distance aboard ship Emmet and the others could see that it was Minnivy's severed head spiked on the end. They waved the head and taunted, "¡El Draque!"

Hours later, after the horsemen and Indians had disappeared, Captain Drake sent ashore two sailors to retrieve what they could of Minnivy so that he could be given a proper burial. One shoe was the only belonging of Minnivy's that they were able to find along the beach. His beheaded body was so riddled with arrows and cut to pieces that it was unrecognizable. The sight of what had been done to Minnivy filled Emmet with something hard, cold—merciless. He turned away during Minnivy's burial. He did not pay any attention to Chaplain Fletcher's swift prayer.

"A real hero," someone said after the burial had ended.

"Aye, did you hear how he shouted?"

That night Emmet dreamed again of the boy in the bell tower. He awoke drenched in sweat, his heart beating fast. In his dream he had become wild-eyed Minnivy, lighting fires. Berserk.

Shaken and wide awake, he crawled up on deck for air. Stars crowded the sky. A slight wind rocked the ship. The rigging creaked. Overhead he searched for the constellations Father Parfoothe had taught him. The stars seemed lost and scattered in unfamiliar regions of the sky. Emmet would have given anything to be able to speak to Father Parfoothe, if only for a moment. Just to ask him what to do to be forgiven.

"Help me," Emmet whispered. He heard no voice, no answer. Never in his life had he felt so forsaken, so alone.

During the next month the *Golden Hind* and the hijacked *La Capitana* moved slowly north along the coast in search of food, water, and Spanish ships to loot. The ships skirted the great Atacama Desert, which Juan the Greek, the *Capitana* pilot, said stretched nearly five hundred miles along the coast of New Spain. There was little hope of finding fresh drinking water. Most of the rivers were pitifully small, and disappeared into the ground before they reached the sea. With each passing mile, the men became more restless and anxious for fresh water, decent food, and plunder.

Finally the ships reached a good harbor called Bahia Salada, where Captain Drake ordered the men to finish caulking the pinnace and make ready the sails. He took Juan the Greek and a crew of fifteen and sailed the pinnace south to scout for water. When the expedition returned empty-handed, Captain Drake decided the crew should careen the *Golden Hind* on the beach and repair the leaking hull.

This was hot, dirty, backbreaking work, with little beer and no fresh water to drink. First the ship had to be emptied of all cargo. Valuable treasure was stored in *La Capitana* for safekeeping. Everything left on board the *Golden Hind* was lashed down. At high tide the ship was brought as close to the shore as possible. She lay like a giant beached whale while the carpenter, Flea, Emmet, and others went to work hammering makeshift wooden posts and ramps into the sand. A system of ropes and pulleys attached to the mastheads were connected to stakes farther up the beach. Slowly the tide went out. Teams of men chanted and pulled so that the ship listed far to one side. With every tug of the line, they sang out in a kind of yell: "Yeo heave-ho!"

As soon as the ship was secured, scraping began. Stripped to their waists, Emmet and the others chipped away sharp-shelled, limpetlike creatures that clung ferociously to every square inch of the ship below the water line. Shipworms had honeycombed some parts of the hull. Emmet's hands and fingers bled as he scoured the wood. Whenever he came upon a gash or shipworm holes, he called out to the carpentry crew, who repaired damaged areas with patches of melted lead that were later painted with hot tar.

The air filled with the smell of wood smoke and heated tar,

and the sound of hammering and sawing. Inside the hold, crew members hauled out filthy rock ballast while struggling to keep their balance atop slimy boards. Rats darted past their legs as they emptied stinking green bilgewater with buckets.

When it was Emmet's turn to work inside the ship, several of his companions found a way to make sport of the job.

"Get him!" they shouted. One of the men with fair aim struck a rat with a marlin spike.

Everything had to be done in a hurry. As long as the *Golden Hind* was unballasted and careened, she was easy prey for any passing Spanish ship. When the crew finished with the starboard side, they tipped the ship in the opposite direction and began work on the larboard.

Everyone was on shore, working late into the night by firelight in a desperate attempt to finish by sundown the next day. On board *La Capitana*, Emmet was required to serve Captain Drake and da Silva their dinner, in addition to his other duties. After Captain Drake returned to the shore to oversee the careening, Emmet stacked the plates. His stomach growled as he worked. When he was sure no one was looking, he scooped up remaining crumbs of moldy cheese—what little was left from the captain's meal.

Da Silva unrolled an enormous map and placed it on the table.

It was unusual for Emmet to have the chance to speak with da Silva without Captain Drake present. The Portuguese pilot, who spoke three languages—his native tongue, English, and Spanish—seemed an intensely private man. Nevertheless, Emmet decided to use what Spanish he had acquired to ask da Silva about his home. *"Perdone, por favor, señor. ¿De donde está usted?"* He cleared his throat and glanced curiously at the map decorated at its edges with dragons and fanciful fish.

"*Allí*" said da Silva, pointing to Portugal. "*En el oeste.*" He leaned closer and ran his finger along a small rugged coastline, then stopped at a point. He gazed at the spot with a kind of longing.

"Your home?" Emmet asked.

Da Silva nodded. "*Sí.* On a hill there is a rose garden and a terrace where vegetables grow. And a swing from a tree where my children play. *Tengo una hija, un hijo.*"

Emmet tried to imagine da Silva's daughter and son running up the hill. He tried to imagine their laughter.

"They were but five and seven years old the last time I saw them," said da Silva, who seemed unusually talkative. He described his daughter's love of music and his son's fear of thunder.

Portugal and everyone da Silva loved seemed so very far away. "*Está lejos,*" Emmet said.

Da Silva smiled with a bittersweet expression. "*Sí.* Too far to run."

Emmet nodded. "We are both prisoners."

"*Sí,*" da Silva agreed. "*Por las buenas o por las malas.*"

There were things for good or for ill that Emmet wanted to tell da Silva. He wanted to speak of Doughty and Diego, of Dartmoor and his teacher. Yet he knew he couldn't. These subjects were too dangerous even for fellow prisoners. The walls might have ears. "How is it, *señor,*" Emmet whispered, "that you have managed to survive so far from home for so long?"

Da Silva paused. "*Quién porfía mata venado,*" he said quietly.

"*Por favor, señor,*" Emmet said. "Can you explain?"

"It might not be a pleasure exactly to survive," da Silva confided. "But it's one's solemn duty to live another day if only to spite the enemy."

"*¿Cómo?*"

"Part of you may live alone inside, like a stone at the bottom of a well. The other part must never give up."

Emmet looked down at his scabby arms, his bleeding fingers. He searched the older man's face. "Not giving up sounds much easier than it is."

Da Silva sighed. "To sing sad songs or lie awake at night, looking at the rafters, is sweet but dangerous, *amigo*. It is better to look at your face in the reflection of the rain barrel. Watch out for lice and for spring nights. Eat every last piece of bread. And don't forget to laugh heartily."

Emmet sucked his lower lip. He could not remember the last time he had laughed. "*Señor*, what of your children? What of your wife? What if she stops waiting for you because she thinks you're dead?"

Da Silva rubbed his eyebrow with the tip of his ink-stained finger. "*Ya lo creo.* That would be terrible. Like the snapping of a green branch inside me," he said. For several moments he was silent. He looked quickly at Emmet, as if with a renewed urgency. "Do not think of small, confined places—like gardens of orchids. Concentrate on the vastness of the sea, the vastness of the mountains. Read and sketch and write without rest. I advise weaving. Making mirrors. Making maps."

Emmet could not help himself. He chuckled. *What nonsense!*

Da Silva placed his hand on Emmet's shoulder with a fierce grip. He stared hard into his eyes. "You can pass any length of time—ten years, twenty, maybe more—in this prison. As long as the jewel on the left side of your chest keeps shining. *Cada día.*" He thumped Emmet hard over his heart with his knuckle.

Every day? Emmet gulped. *Truly easier said than done.*

The door swung open. In stepped Captain Drake. "Didn't you hear me calling?" he bellowed at Emmet. "What kind of worthless servant are you?"

Emmet stared at the jagged half-healed wound beneath the captain's right eye. He had never noticed before how much it reminded him of the coast of Portugal. "Yes, sir. Sorry, sir." Emmet bowed, and bowed again. As he followed the captain out the door, da Silva's advice lingered in his ears. *Live one more day to spite the enemy.* How could he live to spite the enemy, he wondered, when he already felt dead?

Chapter Thirteen

19 January 1579

Our ship becomes a floating artillery battery. Eighteen artillery pieces—thirteen bronze cannon, and the rest of cast iron. Cannons spike through seven portholes on each side of the ship. The rest mounted above, two large cast iron decks on the poop, two smaller guns in the bow. We sail north again with *La Capitana* and stop at Morro de Jorje, where we find water and steal dried fish packed in bundles. Not enough to fill our stomachs. I am hungry nearly every waking hour.

A gunner ought to be sober, wakeful, lusty, hardy, patient, prudent, and quick spirited," shouted Captain Drake as he paced the deck before the assembled sailors. It was another ferociously hot day—too hot to again practice the loading and firing of guns. This didn't stop the captain, who seemed determined to whip the ship's undisciplined gun crews into shape. Emmet glanced around at the sun-blackened men, who appeared anything but sober, wakeful, and prudent. There were fewer than fifty sailors fit for fighting service—barely enough to man the guns. Scarred, pockmarked, bowlegged, and mostly toothless, the ragged crew stood hatless under the scorching sun. For the past five hundred miles at sea they had been underfed, overworked, and beaten into submission.

"Ahead lies plunder the likes of which you waisters have never seen before," declared the captain. "I will make you into a disciplined fighting machine, or I will kill you all trying."

"I'll weather him out, even if he was the devil himself," a low voice grumbled behind Emmet.

"Who speaks?" Captain Drake shouted.

No one moved. The crew knew enough about Drake's rage to keep still. Sometimes if a fellow prayed hard enough, they said, the captain's violence passed like a harmless waterspout.

But not always.

"You, Edwards!" Captain Drake bellowed. "Step forward. Bosun's mate, show this man the proper way to stand at attention."

The bosun's mate made a secret apologetic grimace to Edwards. Then he punched Edwards so hard in the gut that he doubled over. "Stand!" the mate growled.

Edwards gripped his stomach and struggled to keep upright. He glared at the bosun's mate with the sharp hardness of the ballock knife everyone knew he kept hidden in his sea chest. From now on it would be best for the mate to sleep with his eyes open.

"That's better," Captain Drake said, and smiled. "Somewhere ahead, I have been informed, sails the Silver Ship. She's on her way from loading silver from the mines at Potosí on the eastern slopes of the Andes. She is King Philip's richest ship in the South Sea."

The men murmured in eager anticipation. Suddenly they seemed revived. Now *here* was some real Spanish plunder! Emmet, however, wondered if they should believe the captain. He had lied to them before. After weeks at sea all they had encountered along the coast had been pitiful fishing smacks. Onshore they'd robbed a caravan or two or llamas carrying bars of silver. Nothing extraordinary. Nothing like the riches Captain Drake had promised when they'd left Mocha.

"You dogs, hear me!" the captain shouted. "Soon we come upon Spanish galleons equipped with guns. We will surprise our enemies, make a fray with them, and seize their ships. I will ride every man down like the maintack who cannot follow orders to my satisfaction. Bear a hand!"

Flea shot Emmet a look of worry as they hurried below to the lower deck. They were assigned to the same gun crew, which consisted of four men who had to hunch forward to keep from bumping their heads on the low ceiling.

A breeze blew through the lower deck, where the wooden lids of seven portholes on each side of the ship had been flung open. Emmet and Flea took their positions beside a heavy bronze muzzle-loader on the starboard side. The gun, with a ten-foot-long barrel decorated with lion's heads and mermen, had been rolled into position on a kind of wooden carriage with four solid wooden wheels.

"The Silver Ship!" Flea whispered. "Now there's a ship I'd like to meet."

"I'm sure she'd like to meet you, too, Butter Box," growled Hawkins, a taciturn gunner from Bristol who was known for his quick temper and abiding affection for the three-thousand-pound ordnance he called Murderer. "No holding on to the slack this time, Butter Box. Ye hear?" he said to Flea. Hawkins picked up a nine-and-a-half pound cast iron ball. "This sweetness can tear through the hull of a ship at two hundred yards. Smash the frames and spars and pierce the planking. It's the flying slivers, Butter Box, that kills Spanish dogs."

"Yes, sir," Flea said nervously.

"Get the gunpowder, Horse Marine," Hawkins ordered Emmet.

Emmet hurried to the powder magazine in the hold, where kegs of gunpowder were well sealed with pitch. This heavily restricted area, which also contained gunshot, was guarded and patrolled twice daily. Any stray candle or spark near an open barrel of black powder could blow up the ship. A mariner handed Emmet a powder cartridge—a packet of gunpowder wrapped in paper.

"Make ready!" Hawkins shouted, and gave Murderer a pat.

Using a scoop, Emmet shoved the crinkly powder cartridge down into the gun's barrel. Next a cannonball was rammed inside, followed by a cloth wad to keep everything in place. Hawkins demonstrated how to seal the barrel with a wooden plug called a tampion. This went in last, he said, to keep any splashes through the porthole from wetting the powder.

Hawkins used a wire rod to clean out the touchhole at the back of Murderer. With a quick poke he pricked a hole in the powder cartridge. Then he poured a small amount of extra gunpowder from a powder horn into the touchhole. With all their strength, Emmet and the three other gun crew members rolled the heavy gun into place.

"Aim!" Captain shouted.

Hawkins deftly adjusted wooden wedges to line up the carriage.

"Fire!"

A light was rushed to Hawkins and each of the other gunners, who carefully gripped a linstock. This long stick had been carved at the end with the head of a dragon. The dragon's open mouth held the end of a length of rope, which had been wrapped around the linstock's handle. The tip of the slow-burning rope was carefully pressed against the touchhole. This was the most dangerous moment of the cannon firing. A stray spark could start the ship on fire and blow up the ship's store of ammunition.

Emmet's job was to have ready a leather bucket of water, just in case of an accident. He held his fingers to his ears as the slow match sizzled and sparked against the touchhole. The explosion of Murderer and the six other guns caused a deafening blast that rocked the ship. Shots sailed across the water and landed with a resounding splash.

Meanwhile the gun crew on the larboard side of the ship made ready their guns, aimed, and fired. The gun deck filled with thick black smoke that smelled of brimstone and rotten eggs. Emmet coughed and felt as if he could not breathe. The men cheered and congratulated each other.

"Faster this time, you lousy whip-jacks!" Captain Drake shouted above the din. "Aim for a Spanish galleon!"

Flea grinned at Emmet. His face, blackened by powder, was streaked with sweat. Even without saying a word, Emmet knew exactly what Flea was thinking. The Silver Ship!

The next day the pinnace was hauled out and the crew aboard was drilled on boarding procedures. Everything depended upon obedience, speed, and silence. "You are worthless knaves!" Captain Drake shouted. "But we cannot afford to lose even one of you waisters. No one fires unless ordered. Is that understood?"

For two days the crew was timed with a tipped hourglass. The pinnace was lowered and a dozen armed men stealthily clambered down the side of the *Golden Hind* and took position, hiding their guns, hunching forward, and rowing as fast as they could to the stern of *La Capitana.* The idea was that the pinnace would serve as a reconnaissance vessel, cruising the waters a mile or two from the *Golden Hind.* When a likely plunder target was sighted, mirrors would be flashed from the pinnace to the flagship. For now, *La Capitana* was serving as the mock Silver Ship.

After the pinnace crew went through the motions of disabling the rudder, they grabbed their weapons and scaled the side of the ship as swiftly as squirrels. Over and over again Captain Drake made them repeat the drill, until Emmet thought he might be able to climb aboard an enemy ship in his sleep.

Still Captain Drake was not satisfied. He cursed the men, bullied them, pushed them to the limit. "You're weak as a woman, Hawkins!" he screamed. "Your crew is a worthless band of sogers!" The captain's insults only made Emmet's gun crew work harder and faster. They held together like burrs. When one man was offended, one and all would revenge his quarrel.

"If there was no Silver Ship, do you think the crew would endure this?" Flea whispered to Emmet that evening as they ate yet another meal of boiled fish washed down with sour beer.

"Silver Ship. Silver Ship," said Emmet with irritation. "Can you not speak of anything else?"

Flea looked dumbfounded. "Why should I? As soon as we find the Silver Ship we'll all be rich. When I get home I shall buy a house with a chimney. I will eat pudding at every meal, and feed my dozen fine hounds mutton. What will you do with your fortune?"

Emmet shrugged.

"Surely you must have some kind of plan for your share."

Agitated, Emmet stood. "No, I don't," he said, then turned to take his plate back to the galley. Flea would never understand. Not only did Emmet refuse to believe he'd ever make it home alive, but he didn't care.

On 6 February they had their first chance to put their practice to use. When they sailed under a Spanish flag as a ruse into the harbor at Arica, they spied two barks and three fishing boats. The lookout scanned the decks of the larger ships and reported that they appeared to be deserted.

Captain Drake gave the signal, and the pinnace went to work. Just as they had practiced, the crew rowed in silent discipline. Might one of these be the Silver Ship? Emmet watched from the deck of the *Golden Hind* as the men scrambled up the side of the Spanish ship and quickly took over. Another group rowed swiftly to the other ship and did the same before the two slaves on board could warn anyone onshore.

Unfortunately both ships had been recently unloaded. "Too late!" Captain Drake murmured as he watched the crew through his glass. "Damn their eyes."

When a messenger returned to the *Golden Hind*, the crew discovered that the only valuable cargo left on the ships was thirty or forty bars of silver, a dozen women's hats and dresses from Spain, and a few barrels of wine. The wine was carried to the flagship, where it was quickly consumed by the crew. Drunken sailors blasted guns into the air. "Music!" Sky shouted, and gave Emmet a shove.

"Do you think . . . Do you think this is a good idea?" Emmet asked. Shouts drifted across the water from the village. By now the citizens must have discovered that the two Spanish ships had been looted.

"Play!" Sky insisted.

One sailor played the tabor, a second the pipes, and a third the fiddle, while Emmet strummed the lute and sang:

> *"As I lay musing in my bed,*
> *Full warm and well at ease,*
> *I thought upon the lodgings hard,*
> *Poor sailors had at sea.*
> *Our ship that was before so good,*
> *And eke so likewise trim,*
> *Is now with raging seas grown leakt,*
> *And water comes fast in."*

No one seemed to notice the ominous words of Emmet's song. They were too busy enjoying the wine. The men shouted, danced, and skylarked on deck. Meanwhile Captain Drake was nowhere to be seen. Only later, after one of the hijacked ships burst into flames because of a drunken guard, did anyone discover that the captain, in one of his dark moods, had stayed below on the *Golden Hind*.

When the flames from the captured ship shot into the night, two guards on board had just enough time to leap into a pinnace and row back to the *Golden Hind*. Early the next morning before Captain Drake had a chance to send to shore another party to ransack the harbor storehouse, sixty horsemen armed with spears, harquebuses, and longbows assembled on the beach.

"All hands, tumble up! Men, tumble up!" shouted the bosun. A shrill whistle pierced the ears of the hungover sailors. He gave the signal to weigh anchor. Captain Drake ordered his fleet of three ships—the *Golden Hind, La Capitana,* and the surviving stolen bark—out to open sea to find other, richer places.

It had been a disastrous performance, in spite of their disciplined drill. Emmet and the others sensed they were no better off than when they'd anchored at Arica. The Silver Ship remained as elusive as ever.

Chapter Fourteen

9 February

Fuller and Marks are so drunk they start the surviving captured ship on fire. Captain orders us to unload provisions of his choosing from *La Capitana*. We clap her helm fast on the lee and let her drive to seaward without any Creature in her. She is a phantom Ship now, and whoever finds her will Wonder about where she came from and why her crew is missing. Edwards says no sight so much disturbs a Seaman as coming upon a derelict Ship. Like meeting an old friend whose mind has strayed, he says. I tell not a soul what I believe: that it pleases the captain to cause Fear and Confusion with whatever he discards.

Early evening darkness cloaked the harbor of Callao as the *Golden Hind* prowled closer. Less than six miles inland lay Lima, *Los Reyes*, the City of Kings—said to be one of the biggest, richest cities in the New World. Callao served as the trading point for galleons with holds full of silver bullion and merchantmen carrying silks and spices. And somewhere among these unsuspecting ships might be the greatest catch of all: the *Nuestra Señora de la Concepcion*, the Silver Ship.

No one spoke as the crew reduced sail. The *Golden Hind* groped along a narrow channel that led to the point of land where Callao stood. They needed a minimum depth of thirteen feet, or at least two fathoms of water, to pass safely. Emmet stared into the inky black water and listened to the splash of lead weights as a leadsman on each side of the ship leaned over the bow and dropped a line to test the water's depth. "Four fathoms!"

"Three fathoms!"

The *Golden Hind*'s keel squealed. Emmet felt the terrible scraping of wood and shoal as the ship shuddered, then stopped. For a moment no one breathed. If the ship stayed grounded, they'd be trapped—nothing more than easy prey for Spanish soldiers. There would be no escape now that *La Capitana* was gone. In the darkness everyone could hear the captain curse. "Leadsman, the sounding?"

"Two fathoms."

The abrupt stillness seemed strange—almost dizzying. "Good as dead," someone whispered.

"May Drake burn in hell," another hissed.

Chaplain Fletcher murmured a desperate prayer. Without even thinking, Emmet pursed his lips and silently whistled. Later he would not even remember why he did this, or what possessed him to think such action might help.

"The sounding, leadsman, damn you!"

"Still two fathoms, sir."

Miraculously, wind flapped sail. Just enough breeze carried the *Golden Hind* over the shoal, and she drifted free. Emmet felt his entire body relax with relief. "God be praised!" Chaplain Fletcher said in a low, fervent voice.

"God's eyes!" Captain Drake growled. Emmet heard a soft thud as the captain punched their pilot, Juan the Greek, squarely in the gut. "I'll hang you by the neck from the nearest spar if that happens again."

Juan the Greek stammered incoherent apologies. Like the rest of the crew, he knew that the captain meant every word he said.

Splash! "Three fathoms."

Sweat trickled down Emmet's arms. Only Drake would be so crazy, so bold, as to try slipping past dangerous shoals at night into a harbor where the troops of the Viceroy of New Spain were said to be stationed. In the distance Emmet counted the dark silhouettes of ships rocking quietly at anchor. Twelve. Fifteen. Seventeen. What if the enemy had long-range demiculverins? What if they had bowmen?

"Belay it now, boys," the captain muttered. "Remember, no prey, no pay."

The dozen men armed with pistols and hangers waiting on deck, ready and alert, seemed a very different group from the cocky raiding party that Emmet remembered from the earlier days. No one joked or bragged or bet with one another. Instead the sailors crouched or leaned, waiting with a kind of nervous resignation, a barely restrained sense of fear. They had witnessed death and abandonment, beheading and mutilation. They knew such horrors could happen to them, too, if they were unlucky.

Alongside the *Golden Hind* the water parted with a hush as the black bow of a merchant ship slid past. "Hail her in Spanish," Captain Drake ordered da Silva, "and ask where she's from."

"¿Cuál es su nombre? ¿De dónde viene usted?"

When the merchant ship answered, da Silva told the captain that their vessel hailed from Panama, loaded with Castilian goods for Lima. "Sir, she wants to know who we are," da Silva said. "What shall I say?"

"Tell them we are Miguel Angel's ship from Chile," the captain replied, "and ask them if they've seen the Silver Ship."

Emmet listened carefully as da Silva did as he was told. But the translated response was not what the captain wanted to hear. The Silver Ship had not been loaded yet. The bullion was still in the warehouse under Viceroy guard.

Captain Drake cursed. "Too early!"

Emmet and the other men waited impatiently. What were they supposed to do now? Inside the harbor the *Golden Hind* was outnumbered. Yet Captain Drake did not seem daunted. He stood, turned, and then looked up at the flapping topgallant sail as if to check the direction of the wind. It was blowing out to sea.

"My sword and sharpest ballock knife," Captain Drake said to Emmet. Emmet handed him his elegant, basket-hilted sword, and his dagger in its leather sheath. The captain's request could only mean one thing. They were going to attempt to take a prize—in spite of the terrible odds.

The bosun ordered the lowering of the anchor and the preparation of the pinnace. "You're coming too," the captain told Emmet. "Do as I say or you'll be hanging alongside Juan the Greek."

Just as they had practiced again and again, Emmet and the rest of the raiding party slipped barefoot down the rope ladder into the pinnace with their weapons. Quickly they muffled the squeaking oarlocks with pieces of rag. "Steady now," the captain murmured as the oars dipped silently into the water and they headed toward the nearest ship.

The galleon loomed overhead like a great black wall. The pinnace pulled close to the anchor cable, which descended from the bow into the water. Captain Drake ordered Emmet, the smallest among them, to shimmy up the anchor rope with the knife in his teeth and cut the anchor free. As soon as he'd sliced the anchor rope, he was instructed to drop back into the pinnace.

"Don't make a bloody noise," whispered the captain. "And don't drop my bloody knife."

"Aye, sir," Emmet said in a hoarse voice. The men around him yanked him toward the prow just as the cable bumped against the pinnace. The captain handed him his ballock knife. For a moment Emmet felt paralyzed with fear. What if he accidentally stabbed himself? What if he fell into the water? Somebody jabbed him hard in the back to get him moving. Everyone in the pinnace was watching and waiting. His hands shook uncontrollably, and he was certain any moment he might puke.

"Make your worthless father proud," Captain Drake growled.

Anger seared across Emmet's face. He stood with the sheathed knife clenched in his teeth, grabbed the cable with both hands, and pulled himself up. Slime coated the thick hemp anchor cable. He had to grip the rope as hard as he could to pull himself up hand over hand, the way he'd learned to move along the rigging of the *Golden Hind.* He tried not to look up toward the great ship's deck or down into the inky black water. Instead he concentrated on hauling himself up to the place where the cable attached to the rope. Fortunately this section of the anchor cable was not so slippery. Sharp fibers bit into his fingers and palms and the sides of his bare legs and feet.

Pulling the knife from the sheath, he reached beneath himself and began to saw away. He knew the knife was sharp. He had personally whetted the stone and sharpened it for the captain only two days ago. Why was it taking so long to sever the anchor cable?

Someone overhead shouted something in Spanish. Another man answered. Had they been detected? How many sailors were aboard this ship? How many were armed? Emmet worked faster. He barely had time to sheath the knife, clench it in his teeth again, and hold on with both hands as the rope finally split apart. He swung out over the dark water. Someone grabbed his legs and pulled him safely down into the pinnace. It was Sky who lowered him into the boat. For once he did not insult Emmet.

In an instant they paddled on to the next ship. And then the next. One after the another, Emmet climbed up the cable and cut away the anchor on half a dozen ships. The wind would send the ships drifting out to sea before the owners realized what had happened. Then all that the *Golden Hind* crew would have to do, the captain told them, was retrieve the ships and pillage their cargoes. After Emmet and the others had managed to cut free nearly a dozen ships, disaster struck.

The wind died.

The captain changed his orders. They were going aboard the remaining ships to cut down the masts. Emmet gulped. This was the most daredevil idea yet. Even so, the other crew members seemed eager to scale the sides and use their weapons if necessary to begin some looting. "Enough of rowing about and catching crab," one of them grumbled. "When do we carry a ship?"

Just as they approached the first ship to begin the dismantling of the mast, a shout went out from the harbor.

"Back to the ship," the captain ordered.

As soon as they clambered back on deck of the *Golden Hind,* they spied a small pinnace approaching with a torch.

"*¿Cuál es su nombre?*"

"Tell that blasted customs official your master's Miguel Angel from Chile," the captain whispered to Emmet.

Emmet called down to him. When the customs official answered, however, Emmet translated some bad news. "He says, sir, that Miguel Angel's *Nuestra Señora de Valle* has already arrived from Panama. He's coming aboard."

"God's eyes!" Captain Drake cursed. "Anyone who speaks dies."

The customs official's launch pulled close enough so that the fat man could haul himself breathlessly up the ship's ladder, over the gangway, and onto the deck. He had barely climbed over the rail and lifted his lantern when he found himself staring into a cannon's mouth. "*¡Los franceses!*" he screamed. "*¡Los franceses!*" Frantically he scrambled back into his waiting launch.

"See how they call my name in terror," Captain Drake said with pride.

"They think we are French pirates," da Silva said in a low voice to Emmet. "A prudent man would cut his losses and run."

Not Drake.

The wind had begun to blow softly again. One of the anchorless ships floated past. "Take the pinnace and board her," the captain ordered. "Give way now, you scum of the earth."

"Let us escape, sir, before we are hunted down," da Silva said, and bowed. "The alarm has gone up in town. Soon the soldiers will come and—"

"Belay it!" the captain said in a threatening voice. "The anchorless ship we just spied was the *San Cristobal*. We did not cut that ship's cable. The Spanish did. Which means that the crew's panicked and abandoned ship. Now do I need to repeat myself?"

Emmet stood on board the *Golden Hind* and watched through the gun port as the pinnace approached the *San Cristobal*. Like the other sailors left aboard the *Golden Hind*, he was ordered to man the guns.

"Surrender!" demanded one of the *Golden Hind* crew members in the pinnace. "Heave to and receive boarders!" The sailor's bold, careless command in English gave away their identity.

"*¡Piratas! ¡Inglés!*" the Spanish sailors shouted. The *San Cristobal* answered with a blaze of shot. In the pinnace a man crumpled. Three others managed to fire back.

Meanwhile the *Golden Hind* gun crew went into action. "Ready! Aim! Fire!"

Three bronze cannons on the starboard side lobbed shot. When the smoke cleared it was possible to see the gaping hole in the bow of the *San Cristobal*. Emmet and the other men cheered. It was their first successful strike.

"*¡El Draque! ¡El Draque!*" the remaining crew of the *San Cristobal* called as they leaped into the water and swam to shore.

Bells rang. The town would soon be completely awake. Already the harbor echoed with the sound of panicked, angry voices. How long before the Viceroy's soldiers arrived?

"What we need is some wind," Flea said to Emmet as they stood on the main deck and looked out toward the harbor town. Flea sighed. "We will never get out of here."

Shouts and gunshots echoed across the water. How soon before the townsfolk assembled to chase and capture "El Draque"?

"No sogering, page!" Captain Drake barked at Emmet. "Go to my cabin. I need a clean shirt. I cannot think in this shirt."

"Yes, sir," Emmet said miserably. By the time he returned with the captain's clean clothing, Drake had changed their plan again. After transporting the wounded and one dead man, the crew from the pinnace was ordered to board the *San Cristobal* and search for treasure.

Unfortunately the only treasure they managed to find was one small chest, barely two feet long and ten inches wide, of silver. When Drake inspected this trifling prize in his cabin, he became so enraged he broke a chair. "And in the warehouse in Lima are two hundred thousand pesos of silver!" he shouted.

Emmet tried to right the chair as best he could.

"Sir," da Silva said in a calm voice. "We must away. The wind is steady westward."

Emmet felt the ship begin to creak and roll. The wind was so light it barely filled the sails. And yet they did not have a moment to lose. From shore came the sound of gunfire.

Captain Drake composed himself and went back on deck, where he ordered the bosun to have all topgallant sails set. "Tell them to look lively!" the captain growled.

Sailors unfurled sail. Miraculously the wind increased. Sails billowed. And the ship had legs. With a surprising swiftness, the *Golden Hind* headed out to the open sea with one man dead, three wounded—all for a pitifully small box of silver.

Chapter Fifteen

20 February 1579

Bury Thomas at sea. One more sailor for fish meat.
The captain boasts that Juan the Greek will tell the
viceroy everything about us. Was it wise to leave him
behind in Callao? The further north we go, the closer we
come to danger, da Silva says. More people, more ships,
more guns. Already the Spanish may be pursuing us.
They call us El Draque—despised English rovers—and
know our ship by sight. If we cannot seize the Silver Ship
before she reaches Gulf of Panama, we will have to let her
go. We bend all sail our ship can carry to hurry north
after the captain's obsession: the Silver Ship. The Spanish
call her *Cacafuego*, or Spitfire. Not only is she laden with
treasure, she is heavily armed, as well. God preserve us.

What news of *Cacafuego*?" Captain Drake demanded each
time they came upon unsuspecting frigates, barks, fishing vessels, or anyone else who had the misfortune of appearing on
the *Golden Hind*'s horizon. Ships were boarded and searched,
and crews and officers were questioned. The news always
seemed to be the same about *Nuestra Señora de la Concepcion*.

"She's three days away."

"Gone. We don't know where."

The only plunder worth taking they'd found as they collected
information was sixty jars of wine, two boxes of wax, some
bread, a dozen chickens, and a pig.

In late February the *Golden Hind* rounded Parina Point and headed across the wide Gulf of Guayaquil. One afternoon all hands were called on deck. Captain Drake rocked back on his heels and clenched his hands behind his back. Dark circles rimmed his eyes. "You waisters and whip-jacks know our prey," he bellowed. "Remain vigilant. Whosoever should first spy the Silver Ship will have this." He took from his neck the heavy gold chain that hung nearly to his waist.

The men cheered. Emmet too waved his cap in the air. He knew how fine that chain was. He cleaned it every week for the captain. Drake did not go anywhere without it. For him to offer the gold chain as reward was remarkable. Nothing else proved how desperate he was to capture the Silver Ship.

"What I could do with that gold!" Flea said. He and Emmet sat on the deck and repaired sails, using long needles and heavy twine to mend the sails. As fellow gun crew members, they had become friends. "Each link of that chain's as genuine and solid as bullion," Flea said with confidence.

Emmet licked his lips and threaded the needle. How much would the captain's gold chain be worth back home? Up until this moment he had given up hope of ever seeing England again. The idea of riches and the opportunities they might provide him seemed to revive his spirits. He knew he could never go back to Tavistock, but perhaps there was somewhere else he could go. Someplace where no one would recognize him. Somewhere he could begin again. Just like the captain, he might live in a fine house and ride a fine horse. He, too, might wear velvet capes and fine leather gloves and eat grand feasts and—

"Sail, ho!"

"All hands on deck."

"Make all sail," Captain Drake ordered. "Brace the yards round."

"Aye, aye, sir," the bosun said. As soon as he left the poop deck he began shouting the new orders to the crew. "Time to do some sailors' work, if you can remember how!"

The crew jumped at his command, hauling halyards, trimming braces, letting go buntlines and clew lines.

"Might be the Silver Ship."

"Look lively, my bullies!"

Never before had Emmet seen so much enthusiasm among the crew as they set almost every inch of the available four thousand square feet of sail carried on the galleon's three masts. For the first time the *Golden Hind* almost seemed like a happy ship. Drake's promise of the gold chain had worked upon the crew like an elixir. Fear, dread, and stupor vanished. The men sang out walkaway shanties in unison: "Way, hay an' up she rises! Patent blocks o' different sizes . . ." For once even da Silva smiled. Perhaps he thought that if the Silver Ship were captured he too might find a way home.

The *Golden Hind*'s prey, a heavily laden merchantman, traveled northward with speed. The captain accompanied his crew in the pinnace, fully rigged with sail, to pursue her. Emmet came along to serve as translator. He was given a snaphance pistol and was instructed to keep safe the captain's fancy swept-hilted rapier. But after long hours of chasing the merchantman, they realized that she was not *Cacafuego* after all.

"God's eyes!" Captain Drake cursed.

"Watch out. Fur and blood for supper," mumbled one of the rowers behind Emmet.

Meanwhile the pinnace marksmen took aim and splintered a few of the Spanish ship's spars, which fell with a loud crack. The *Golden Hind* mariners hoisted the black flag, indicating that they were pirates. In terror, the Spanish crew signaled surrender. The men from the pinnace scrambled up and over the rail. A few more shots were fired. The last rebellious Spanish sailors were subdued and locked with the rest in the hold.

By the time the captain and Emmet boarded, the small group of wealthy gentlemen and friars in clerical robes huddled in terror on the poop deck. The ship's owner, Benito Diaz Bravo, begged Drake and his men not to kill them. Tears streamed down his face as he spoke in rapid Spanish.

"He says they have only some fishing tackle and provisions on board," Emmet translated.

"Liars!" the captain exclaimed. "Demand their money and valuables."

"*Perdone, por favor. ¿Tiene el dinero?*" Emmet asked, and waved the pistol in a menacing fashion.

The prisoners exchanged confused glances.

"Give us your silver, your gold," Captain Drake shouted. "Your *plata*, your *oro!*"

From their pockets and bags the prisoners came forward to offer a bag of silver coins, a jeweled pendant, and three gold crucifixes.

The captain unsheathed his rapier and made a vicious slashing motion near one of the friar's faces. "Where's the rest? This can't be everything."

"*¿Algo más?*" Emmet demanded impatiently.

The prisoners shook their heads. "*No hay mas.*"

"*¿Algo más?*" Emmet asked again. They were wasting precious time here while the Silver Ship was sailing north.

Diaz Bravo and the other prisoners opened their empty hands to show they had nothing more.

"Tell them," the captain shouted at Emmet, "in a few moments I shall have them all conveyed aboard my ship. Then my men will search this vessel from stem to stern. If they discover any hidden items they have not told me about, I will have each of them hung."

As soon as Emmet repeated the captain's threat, the prisoners scuttled below and returned with a heavy gold cross, a bag of emeralds each as big as a man's finger, a bag of coins, and a chest containing forty bars of silver and some gold.

"I'm taking the ship," the captain announced. "She's fast and fine. We'll have a great banquet to celebrate. Of course, our hosts will be pleased, won't you?"

Diaz Bravo made a desperate bow. As darkness fell the crew from the *Golden Hind* came aboard to enjoy a noisy feast of roast pig, gingerbread, and wine. Captain Drake sat at the head of the heavily spread table in Diaz Bravo's fine cabin. He insisted the gold-rimmed plates be used to serve the small group of prisoner-guests, who seemed too terrified to enjoy the candied aniseeds, olive pie, and bottles of sack from their own hold.

Captain Drake stuck a large knife into a boiled capon and held it in the air. Frightened Diaz Bravo at his right tried to smile. Meanwhile Emmet, dressed in the despised doublet, strummed upon the lute for the diners' entertainment. Only Captain Drake seemed to enjoy himself.

Why are we wasting time here? Emmet wondered as he strummed and sang. Above deck he could hear the crew drunkenly shouting and singing. It would take hours for the sailors to become sober enough to make ready and begin the chase again.

"To the Queen!" the captain bellowed and raised his glass. The prisoner-guests unwillingly did the same. Drake laughed uproariously at the sight. "May the Queen's Catholic enemies never make peace!"

The next morning Captain Drake's mood swung in a dark, dangerous direction. He announced he wasn't taking Diaz Bravo's ship after all. The foresail and foresail yard were ordered cut down. Some of the sails were wrapped like a shroud around the anchor, which was cut from its cable and heaved into the sea. In his fury, he had the ship disabled so badly it would be nearly impossible to control or bring into harbor.

"There's gold still hidden on board, I know it," the captain shouted. "You think me stupid, but I shall prove you wrong." Ropes were thrown over one of the spars, and nooses were slipped around the necks of Diaz Bravo and three other gentlemen officers. "Tell me the truth. Where is the gold?"

The Spanish prisoners shook their heads and frantically repeated over and over again that there was no more gold. They swore by all the saints that no silver was still hidden on board.

"I don't believe you," Drake replied, and gave a signal. Delighted sailors from the *Golden Hind* gave the prisoners a push. They were lifted off the deck, choking, red-faced. They kicked, breathless.

"Now will you talk?" the captain demanded. He made a sign for them to be lowered to deck again. "No? Very well, I will hang you one by one until the whereabouts of the hidden treasure is revealed. I have ways to prove that you are lying."

The gasping prisoners, whose hands were tied behind their backs, gazed in helpless horror as if their last moment had come.

A thin, slope-chested clerk, who looked only a few years older than Emmet, was singled out by the captain. With tears streaming down his pockmarked face, he was shoved to the ship's rail. A rope was thrown up over a spar so that it swung over the water. A noose was tied and secured around the clerk's neck.

"Give us the treasure!" Captain Drake shouted.

"Es imposible," the clerk wailed, and shook his head.

"Where is the treasure?" Captain Drake shouted louder this time.

"¡Es imposible!"

Captain Drake motioned with one hand toward Sky. Sky smiled and shoved the clerk out over the water. He hung for just a moment. As if rehearsed, Sky leaned over and cut the rope with his knife. The clerk fell with a loud splash. A few sailors from the *Golden Hind* roughly fished the clerk out of the water and hauled him, coughing and sputtering, onto the deck.

"Take this. You know what to do," the captain ordered under his breath to Emmet. He handed him a satchel containing the Mosaical Wand. Emmet turned pale. "But, sir—"

"You heard me."

Emmet made a small bow. His hand shook as he removed the forked hazel dowsing rod no longer than his arm from elbow to wrist. Members of the *Golden Hind* crew, who had been raucous when the Spanish clerk's hanging began, were now strangely silent. Emmet gulped. He had no idea what he was doing. And if he failed he'd be as good as dead. Captain Drake would see to that.

"This Mosaical Wand," declared Captain Drake, "will find where the treasure is hidden on board this ship."

Emmet moved around on deck gripping the wand in his fists. The end was pointed toward the ground. He felt like an aimless ghost pacing back and forth. Unable to concentrate, unable to breathe, he simply went through the motions in a desperate pantomime. All eyes were upon him. The men from the *Golden Hind* stood silent, mouths agape, waiting for a miracle Emmet knew he couldn't perform.

Without warning, one of the prisoners cried out, fell on his knees, clutched his hands against his forehead, and began to wail piteously. Another scurried into the hold, where he revealed a chest of silver bars and two plates of gold that had been hidden beneath the casks of wine.

Emmet took a deep breath. The wand was slippery with sweat. He looked with irritation upon the shivering group of Spaniards. They could have avoided a lot of trouble if they'd simply revealed where the treasure was in the first place.

"You see, my friends," Captain Drake boomed to the crowd, "how powerful my magic is?" He clamped Emmet on the shoulder with a viselike grip. Once, twice, he patted his shoulder with a congratulatory thump. "Well done," he whispered in Emmet's ear. "I'll see you'll have your share."

Emmet felt his ears burn. It was the first time the captain had ever praised him. *Well done.* He had been promised part of the plunder. He was more than a pirate. He had become Drake's henchman, Drake's treasure seeker, Drake's archconjurer. As Emmet made his way across the deck to the pinnace to be rowed back to the *Golden Hind,* the crowd of sailors shuffled backward to let him pass, keeping a careful distance from him, as if he had the plague.

"Could have told you," someone's voice whispered.

"Aye, always knew. Something odd about him."

Chapter Sixteen

That evening fog rolled in as the ship sailed north. Nearly every square inch of sail had been set since they'd abandoned Diaz Bravo. Too much sail, the crew grumbled, for such terrible visibility. Yet everyone knew that two Spanish ships and two hundred soldiers were following them. How far away? Maybe less than ten leagues. That was what one of Diaz Bravo's slaves had told Flea, who passed this reliable information along to everyone else. The Spanish authorities had vowed to hunt down "El Draque" and kill him and every one of his men.

"If you ask me, we wasted too much time torturing Diaz Bravo's crew," Moone complained. He ate his meal quickly. Emmet never took his eyes off him or Sky on the lower deck. Emmet sat apart from the others, always careful to keep the hatchway in view in case he needed to make an emergency exit.

"Aye," the carpenter said solemnly. "We're in a hurrah's nest all alone. Don't look to the Queen to save our bloody necks."

The bell sounded for the next watch. Early morning darkness and fog shrouded everything above deck. It was Emmet's turn to climb forty feet up into the crow's nest. No matter how high he scrambled, the view didn't change. Fog pressed against his body so completely he could barely see the mast six inches from his face.

Dib-dib-dib. He tried to ignore the way his knees drubbed in a twitchy rhythm against the mast. Any height more than thirty feet, he'd been told, would kill a falling man. *Just more time to ponder your life on the way down.* He pulled himself up hand over hand.

Once he was perched on the cramped platform of the crow's nest, he peered into the haze for some faint outline, some shape of anything familiar. No sun, no stars, no moon. Fog muffled sound as completely as if he were wrapped in a wool blanket. Only the nearby thrum of rigging and the snap of sail registered distinctly in his ears. Below him the sailors' grumbling voices sounded miles away. Emmet strained to hear breakers, the passing of another ship—anything.

On the moor on nights like this, when the fog shrouded everything, folks said pysgies led poor travelers astray. The wee folk might guide unsuspecting travelers through woods and waters, through bogs and quagmires and every kind of peril. Perhaps the ship was being pysgy led. Somewhere out there lay the treacherous coast of the Viceroyalty of Peru. One wrong bit of guesswork at the helm and the ship would be torn apart on the rocks.

Emmet leaned against the mast with his knees bent, his arms wrapped around his legs. He rubbed his eyes, determined not to think about the horror of the day before. The clerk dangling from the rope. The pleading voices. He shook his head. *Something pleasant. Think of something pleasant.* The gold chain. The satisfying heft in his hand. Glimmering gold links. He tried to recall each one. Fifteen, sixteen, seventeen—

"*River of Dart, oh, river of Dart—*"

Emmet sat bolt upright. Had he been sleeping? From somewhere in the fog came a faint voice. Or was it the call of an owl? They were too far out to sea for owls, weren't they? Emmet shivered and stood. He tucked each hand under an armpit for warmth. How long had he been up here?

"—*Every year thou claim'st a heart.*"

"Who's there?" Emmet demanded. He peered into the darkness. Must be Moone or some other sailor from Devon or Cornwall. Anybody from the West Country knew how a year never passed without the drowning of one person in the River Dart. "Can't frighten me, Moone!" Emmet called. He laughed, but somehow his derisive, manly chuckle sounded more like a nervous squawk.

To his surprise, no one answered.

Emmet shifted from one foot to the other. He rubbed his eyes with his open palms. The fog was making him crazy. Why else would he be hearing strange voices? He knew how bullbeggars could shoot up to unnatural heights. Was that whose ghastly voice he heard? Desperately he tried to recall the words to banish ghouls and apparitions. He remembered nothing.

"*River of Dart, oh, river of Dart, every year thou claim'st a heart.*"

Emmet froze. The voice, loud and clear this time, wafted from overhead. He was sure of it. Immediately Emmet's hands began to sweat. "Father Parfoothe?" he squeaked. His teacher's voice seemed to be coming from atop the flagstaff—higher than the topgallant, the highest and most precarious place on the ship. "What are you doing up there, sir?"

"*River of Dart, oh, river of Dart,*" the voice howled with grief. "*Every year thou claim'st a heart.*"

Emmet gulped hard once, twice. "I know what you're thinking, sir, about the way I abandoned your cottage." He tried his best to control the whining in his voice. "They were going to kill me. That Tavistock mob burned everything. All of your books, your work. I'm very sorry about that. As for the crystal, the wand, the book, Captain made me take them. Didn't have any choice." He shrugged sheepishly. "What harm was done? I only pretended I knew what I was doing—"

"River of Dart, oh, river of Dart!" the voice mocked in a singsong chant. "Every year thou claim'st a heart!"

Something red-hot surged through Emmet. How dare he accuse me of betrayal? Emmet gripped the rail of the crow's nest to keep himself from madly scrambling farther up the mast. "You don't know what it's been like, sir, aboard this ship. The things I've had to do. Wasn't my fault. Only following Captain's orders. And the others, too, they—"

"River of Dart, oh, river of Dart!" the voice scolded. "Every year thou claim'st a heart!"

Emmet clenched his teeth. Maybe Drake had been right. What great service had his master's powers and good works ever done him? Nothing. "What you taught me, sir, makes no difference here. Your civilized poetry. Your Plutarch. Your high ideals. 'Obey God, do right, be honorable in all things.' Doesn't mean anything." The bitter words stung his lips, but he couldn't stop. "I did what I had to do. That boy—that boy—how was I supposed to know he was hiding beneath the tower?"

A mournful breeze furled and unfurled the stolen Spanish flag that flew atop the topgallant. Snap-snap-snap.

"Leave me alone," Emmet muttered.

Snap-snap-snap.

"Watchman!" someone shouted angrily from the deck below. It was the bosun. "What are you saying up there? D'ye spy something? Answer!"

Emmet blanched. What if everyone could perceive Father Parfoothe perched above him? "Nothing to report, sir!" he called down. He took a deep breath and closed his eyes tight.

Then he tilted his head up and hissed softly, "Father Parfoothe?" The ship creaked. Wind moaned. No matter how hard he peered through the fog or cocked his head intently in the direction of the topgallant, he could not see or hear anything. The voice did not return. Father Parfoothe seemed to have vanished.

Good. Emmet relaxed his shoulders. He rubbed the back of his neck, which ached from staring for so long skyward. *Forget about it.* He'd concentrate instead on something pleasant. Something to take his mind off his shaking hands, his queasy stomach. *The gold chain.* Glimmering links. He tried to recall where he'd left off. Eighteen, nineteen, twenty . . .

Gradually the fog crept away. Slanted beams of early morning sunlight emerged from behind the clouds. Emmet squinted and stretched his arms over his head as if he'd just awakened from a terrible dream. Where the sky touched the blue-green water a bright white shape hove in the distance. Too big to be a whitecap. Was it a retreating wisp of fog? Perhaps his eyes were playing tricks on him again. He shielded his eyes with his hand. The more he stared, the more certain he became.

"Sail, ho!" he shouted as loud as he could.

"Where?" demanded the bosun.

"Slightly to leeward."

The captain, who never seemed to have left the poop deck, gazed with his glass in the direction Emmet had indicated. Emmet and everyone else working on deck waited in anxious anticipation. Captain Drake took the glass from his eye. No one breathed. He looked through the glass a second time. And then he smiled, nodded, and gave the signal to the bosun. The bosun blew the shrill whistle to alert the crew.

"Silver Ship!" the bosun shouted. "Twelve miles ahead slightly to leeward. All hands!"

The men cheered and threw their caps in the air. It was as if they'd already captured the Spanish merchantman, boarded her, and divided the spoils. They joked and jostled one another as Emmet slid down the mast from the crow's nest to receive his reward. Someone slapped him hard on the back. Another shook his hand as if he were a fine gentleman. Emmet basked in the warmth of their approval, delighted to be the center of so much attention and goodwill. He'd never felt so needed, so successful.

The captain waved ceremoniously from the poop deck. He beckoned Emmet to come closer. "Well done!" the captain said, beaming. Never before had Emmet seen him look so joyous. His ginger-colored beard bristled in the sunlight. He took the gold chain from his neck and held it high so that everyone could see. A trumpet blared. A drum rolled. The men cheered again.

Emmet made a little bow. With a dramatic flourish the captain presented Emmet with the gold chain. The gold felt cold on the back of Emmet's neck. When he stood he was surprised by the weight of the chain, which draped past his waist.

"Careful not to hang yourself," Captain Drake warned in a low voice.

Does he jest? "Yes, sir," Emmet replied. He glanced at the captain's face. His eyes appeared as cold and gleaming as gold.

The plans for the capture of the well-armed Silver Ship required different tactics from anything they'd attempted. There would be no racing after the Silver Ship or hunting her down with the pinnace. Instead, Captain Drake announced, they'd keep the pinnace, with furled sails, hidden alongside the Golden Hind. "Just as we can see Juan de Anton, he can see us," said the captain. "We must not alarm his suspicions."

The crew was ordered to fill empty wine jars with water and tie them to a long rope.

"What's this?" Flea demanded.

"You'll see," Sky said, and winked. "An old pirate ruse."

Under full sail, the line of jars was thrown off the stern to act as a drag. To any innocent bystander the *Golden Hind* appeared to be a well-laden merchantman capable of only slow headway even with every sail set. Meanwhile the cannons were run out, loaded, and primed. Weapons—harquebuses and longbows—were silently, secretly distributed from the armory. Men fastened leather tunics around themselves and donned helmets.

The captain remained alert on the poop deck throughout the afternoon. He seemed unable to take his eye away from the glass for even a few moments. And sure enough, like a rabbit too curious for its own good, the Silver Ship changed course. "She's coming closer!" the captain said, and flicked his tongue over one sharp, pointed tooth.

Emmet watched the captain's bristly red chin bob as he spoke, and couldn't help but think of the jaw of a fox. "Yes, sir," Emmet said, and nearly dropped the captain's elegant rapier as he presented it to him in preparation for the attack.

"Clumsy page!" the captain scolded. He brusquely fastened the buckle himself.

"Beg your pardon, sir." Emmet bowed, certain that the cumbersome gold chain knocking against his knees would make him trip and fall. *Everyone's watching.* Blushing, he stood upright with great care. The links pressed against his chest like a heavy hand.

The sun crawled across the sky during the endless afternoon. With equal, painful slowness the Silver Ship veered closer, closer. The *Golden Hind* seemed in no hurry to meet her. The English ship, flying the Spanish flag, cruised under full, creaking sails— yet always steering just out of reach. Clearly Captain Drake meant to delay their encounter until nightfall, when darkness might help ensure his ship's disguise as long as possible.

At eight o'clock, they could make out the Silver Ship's gun ports and count the cannon.

"Belay it, scowbanks," Captain Drake silenced the anxious crew. He ordered them all to pray with trembling Chaplain Fletcher, who asked for God's blessing, then retreated to safety belowdecks as fast as he could. "You know your duties," the captain said. "I'll scupper any one of you who ruins our little surprise for Señor Anton."

An hour passed. Closer, closer the Silver Ship sailed until it drew alongside the *Golden Hind*. Nervously Emmet scanned the Silver Ship from the poop deck, where he had been ordered by the captain to stand at attention in his doublet. Somehow the Silver Ship did not appear as enormous and legendary as he'd imagined. The three-masted Spanish galleon floated low on the water. Guns gleamed through its portholes. Spaniards smiled and waved in welcome. *"Buenas noches. ¿Cául es su nombre?"* one called.

Captain Drake secretly nudged da Silva with the tip of his rapier. "Tell them to strike sail or we'll send them to the bottom."

Da Silva relayed the message in Spanish to Juan de Anton, who burst into laughter and shouted a reply. "He says," da Silva translated slowly, "'What old tub is ordering me to surrender? Come and do it yourself.'"

Captain Drake's face flushed with anger. "Old tub? We shall see about that." He nodded to the *Golden Hind* trumpeter. The horn blasted.

Suddenly a line of archers with enormous war bows and gunners with harquebuses rose from their hiding places behind the *Golden Hind* deck rail. Porthole doors flapped open. Seven guns flashed and roared from the lower deck. Shot splintered the Silver Ship's mizzenmast. The mast plunged onto the stern, dragging a tangle of rigging. Before the Spanish crew could dodge for cover, *Golden Hind* archers and marksmen filled the air with deadly arrows and shot.

The Spaniards howled in pain. A few tried to jump over the port side but were stopped when a band of pirates swarmed up rigging from the pinnace, which had come around during the first surprise blast. The pinnace crew quickly herded the terrified Spaniards into the cabin on the Silver Ship's poop deck. Captain San Juan de Anton was locked up and placed under guard.

In less than a minute the attack ended. The Silver Ship surrendered. The *Golden Hind* crew roared with delight. Emmet slipped one finger under the chain where it seemed to bite the back of his neck. He felt relief and a kind of pride in their swift work.

To avoid any premature celebrating and to evade any ship that might be hunting them down, Captain Drake ordered half his crew to immediately man the Silver Ship. They crowded sail and made away from land, following the *Golden Hind* farther north-northwest to safer water. This time Drake seemed determined to avoid past mistakes.

The next morning Emmet laid out the best silver plate in the captain's cabin and served Captain Drake and Captain de Anton a hurried meal of rich cheeses, manchet, and roast goose looted from the Silver Ship.

Suspicious Captain de Anton, still nursing a wound on his face, spoke English with a heavy Spanish accent. He was a small, thin man with elegant, long fingers and a sorrowful expression. "*Señor*, what will you do with us?" he demanded.

"Don't distress yourself, for such are the fortunes of war," the captain exclaimed in a hearty voice. After regaling Captain de Anton with their exploits, real and imagined, and describing his special license from the queen to rob Spanish subjects, Drake rose from the table. He was clearly eager to count the Silver Ship plunder.

The Silver Ship treasure was more fantastic than Emmet or anyone else on board the *Golden Hind* had thought possible. There were 1,300 silver bars weighing twenty-six tons, and thirteen chests filled with silver coins, all amounting to nearly 362,000 pesos. The treasure also included eighty pounds of gold and bullion and jewels with an estimated value of 40,000 pesos. Stashed in the hold were plentiful stores of victuals, such as salt pork, sugar, and flour; and brand-new ship fittings, including tackle, sails, canvas, and cable. A crew from the *Golden Hind* rowed the pinnace back and forth to the Silver Ship to haul five full loads of treasure. After six days everything of value had been looted and transferred into the *Golden Hind* hold.

When Captain de Anton, his servants, crew, and passengers were finally released several days later, they were given insulting farewell gifts by the captain. To Captain de Anton Drake presented a German musket and a basin of gilded silver with the name Francis Drake written on the bottom. To a timid clerk from the Silver Ship he presented a steel shield and a sword so that he might appear to be a man-at-arms. Captain Drake laughed heartily as he gave away a pickax, a cask of tar, a gilt corselet, a few pesos, and a pruning knife to various terrified prisoners.

While the Silver Ship, now stripped of its most valuable cargo, headed for Panama, the heavily laden, leaking *Golden Hind* sailed north toward Isla de Caño. Caño was nearly a week's journey away. Emmet had heard the captain say that this was the nearest spot to find fresh water and perhaps safely careen the ship.

In the meantime, Sky and a few other thugs were assigned to watch the treasure in the hold all day and night. The captain was taking no chances that a sailor might try to pluck even one valuable item from the stash.

"Strict rules shall be followed for safekeeping of treasure until our return to England," the captain announced before the assembled crew. "No man shall take any pillage or make any spoil before proclamation made, upon pain of death."

This edict was taken seriously by the crew. They'd already witnessed what happened to Edwards. His missing fingers were a constant reminder of what could happen by touching Captain Drake's plunder.

In only a few days, however, the elation of the easy conquest of the Silver Ship began to fade. The reality of hauling so much treasure began to weigh heavily not only on the ship but on the men as well. The ship moved more slowly. When the sea was high, she labored, took on water, and became difficult to maneuver. The boisterous men, too, had become more difficult to control. Fights broke out belowdecks among men who wagered parts of their future shares of treasure in card games. Soon arguments erupted over every kind of belonging—a misplaced wooden comb, a borrowed set of shoes, or a stolen set of bone dominoes.

The *Golden Hind* was still thousands of miles from England. Now that the Spanish authorities had been thoroughly alerted, it would be foolhardy and dangerous to return the way they'd come. Who knew how many Spanish galleons might already be following them? The question that seemed to be in every sailor's mind was how they would make their retreat. East or west? Back through the strait? That seemed unlikely given the trade winds' direction and the storms. Would they push west to the Spice Islands?

No one on board the *Golden Hind* had ever circumnavigated the globe—not even experienced navigators like Drake or da Silva. The crew knew what had happened to the survivors of Magellan's round-the-world voyage after he "shot the globe." In the South Sea, Magellan's starving mariners had sailed out of sight of land for so long that they were forced to eat rats, sawdust, and shoe leather to stay alive.

"Don't trust no one," Flea whispered one evening when he saw

Emmet removing the gold chain from his neck. Emmet placed the chain deep inside his seaman's chest for safekeeping.

"What have you heard?"

"They say a man's life isn't worth a bosun's damn anymore. One less sailor only means a bigger treasure share for the rest."

Emmet gulped. Flea wasn't imaginative enough to lie.

That night Emmet slept uneasily, with the gold chain around his neck. As he lay in the darkness of the creaking ship, he thought he heard the treasure shift and clink in its chests. The cocky, greedy captain would never be satisfied—that much was certain. They were surrounded by rich Spanish merchant ships waiting to be taken, wasn't that what he'd said? It was only a matter of time, Emmet knew, before Captain Drake would order him to use *The Key of Solomon* to gain more wealth and power.

And then what would he do?

Chapter Seventeen

26 March 1579

Two days after we arrive on the island of Caño we search for beach to careen the leaky ship. Pinnace keeps watch for pursuers or prey, and spies merchant ship sailing south. Three shots fired and they surrender. Only a few silver bars—hardly worth effort. Sky stomps a prisoner's crucifix and throws it into sea. We take their ship and kidnap their pilot, named Colchero. He begs release, says his wife and children will starve. Up coast the stubborn man refuses to guide us to the port of Realejo, so that we may burn the town. Captain strings up Colchero with rope. Two times he hangs by neck; two times he is cut down. Still he refuses to pilot us. Captain locks him in iron Cage in the hold. I bring him food, water, but he will not speak to me in his own tongue. How will we cross South Sea if he will not cooperate? In anger I kick the slop bucket. He looks at me as if to say, *There is nothing you can do to me.* What am I becoming?

The *Golden Hind* and the small commandeered Spanish vessel sailed north past the port of Sonsonate on a beautiful, balmy dawn in early April. Emmet sat on deck with pen and paper and observed the changing colors of sky and water: vermillion, yellow, pale blue, and then something like purple but even darker. The color of the inside of an iris. If only he had paints to capture the scene! Suddenly rumbling echoed in the northeast. **As they sailed closer, black smoke wreathed a mountain range. Sparks of fiery orange shot skyward.**

"Devil's work," Flea said. He glanced over Emmet's shoulder at his sketch of the glimmering, fitful volcano in the distance. "Hot enough to broil a hen, I wager."

Emmet nodded absentmindedly. Drawing was the only thing that gave him pleasure anymore. Since the incident with the Mosaical Wand, no one from the crew bothered him when he sketched on deck. Was it out of respect or fear? Emmet did not know. Perhaps spying the Silver Ship and winning the captain's gold chain had also worked some kind of magic on the other mariners. Whatever the reason, they left him alone.

Following da Silva's advice to sketch without rest, he found that he could escape into the lines, shading, and contour. He lost track of time and forgot about his memories and nightmares as he sketched the rocky coastline, grove of distant trees, forbidding slope, and smoldering glimpse of lava.

"Sail, ho!" the lookout cried.

Emmet rubbed his eyes. In the distance a merchant ship headed south—perhaps from Acapulco. The bosun's warning whistle shrieked. Emmet quickly rolled up his drawing and stowed his supplies. The ship swarmed with activity as crew members unlashed guns, donned helmets and shields, and prepared to launch the pinnace for attack.

"All hands!"

The *Golden Hind* steered straight into the merchant ship's path.

"¡Cuidado! ¡Cuidado!" the Spanish helmsman warned. "¿Cómo se llama usted?"

Captain Drake, who had ordered Colchero on deck, prodded

the white-haired pilot with a pistol in the ribs and told him to shout that they were the ship of Miguel Angel from Peru. The *Golden Hind* drifted closer. Before the Spanish helmsman could respond, a line of archers and gunners rose from the deck of the *Golden Hind* and shot into the unsuspecting vessel.

The sleepy crew, numbering only a half-dozen Spaniards, stumbled into view, shouting, *"¡Piratas!"* The *Golden Hind* hoisted the special red flag that meant they would take no quarter. The signal meant only one thing: surrender or die.

The Spanish sailors waved their hands and kerchiefs in the air and begged, *"¡Pare! ¡Pare!"* Grappling hooks were thrown from the *Golden Hind* to the merchant ship. Armed men in the pinnace swarmed up the port side, while five mariners swung onto the deck of the surrendering ship.

A Spanish gentleman in a red velvet doublet and plumed hat protested loudly as he was dragged out of the captured ship's poop-deck cabin. He was shoved into the pinnace, which was rowed back to the *Golden Hind*. When the prisoner came aboard, he kneeled on the deck, bowed before Captain Drake, and kissed his hands. This seemed to please the captain very much. The crew, however, was not impressed.

"Look yonder!" jeered one sailor out of Drake's earshot.

"Fawning Spanish coward," another said, and spat.

"Rise, rise, rise, sir!" Captain Drake said. He motioned to Emmet to prepare the cabin for a special visitor. Emmet hurried to the captain's cabin to place a linen cloth on the table and set up a silver decanter of the best stolen wine. Before Emmet could finish wiping the silver goblets, the captain and the Spanish gentleman had arrived. The ashen-faced prisoner tugged his precise, pointed black beard. His dark eyes flitted about the sumptuously decorated cabin.

"Your name, sir?" the captain said, and paused to offer his guest his best chair with the thickest damask cushion. "I am sure you have already heard of me—El Draque."

"*¡Señor Draque!*" The gentleman sank with obvious discomfort into the chair. His gigantic, bombasted knee breeches, fashionably stuffed like wool sacks, made a creaking sound. Tremulously he plucked a lace handkerchief from his sleeve and dabbed his perspiring forehead. The air filled with the fragrance of violets. "I am," he continued in English with a heavy Spanish accent, "Don Francisco de Zarate, *caballero*, a knight of the Order of Santiago."

Captain Drake's eyebrows shot upward with obvious surprise and delight. "I am honored, sir." With a special flourish, he bowed low. "A *caballero* is always welcome on my ship."

"*Señor*, what are you . . . you going to do to me?" de Zarate's knobby knees shook so badly the fine silver rapier at his waist made a *jig-jig* noise.

Captain Drake gestured for Emmet to pour a goblet of wine for their trembling guest. "Let me assure you that I am a friend of those who tell the truth."

De Zarate coughed delicately. "I knew you were a gentleman."

Captain Drake took a seat at the table and raised his goblet. Not once did he take his eyes off his prey. "How much gold and silver do you carry?"

De Zarate sipped. "Excellent wine. Portuguese, isn't it?"

"I am glad you approve. How much gold and silver do you carry?"

"None," de Zarate said slowly. "Except for some plates and cups I use at table."

Captain Drake drained the goblet. Then he took his ballock knife from the sheath at his belt. "Sir, are there any relatives of the viceroy aboard your ship?"

De Zarate squirmed and stared at the ivory handle, the silver blade. "No, *señor.* Why should there be?"

"If there were, I would show you how a gentleman should keep his word." With a hollow *thunk* Drake stabbed the dagger through the fine linen cloth into the wooden table. The gleaming blade stood upright.

"Really that will not . . . will not be necessary, *señor.* Please tell me what you want. What I can do so that you will let me go with my life. I will do anything," he whimpered. "Anything at all. Please spare my life."

The captain grinned as if he were enjoying himself enormously. "Do not worry, sir. I have only to ask a few more questions. Please follow me." He replaced the dagger in its sheath at his belt and ushered de Zarate down into the hold of the ship. Emmet trailed behind them with a covered lantern.

Even though the pumps were manned nearly eight hours every day, the dark hold was ankle-deep in foul-smelling water. In some places the scummy water came nearly to their knees. With tremendous care de Zarate wrapped his short, fur-collared cape around himself and waded gingerly in his fine leather boots. "What is that sound, *señor?*" he whispered through the handkerchief he held to his nose.

"Rats." The captain gave a signal to the men who were guarding the treasure. The men held their guns at their sides. "Sit down, Señor de Zarate."

"Where?" de Zarate said, his voice quavering.

"Anywhere. You must stay here."

"Here?" de Zarate glanced toward the nearby iron cage that held miserable Colchero. Grimacing, de Zarate lowered himself onto a chest.

The captain stopped him. "Not just yet," he said and grinned. "First, tell me the identity of that man." He pointed to Colchero, who glared at them from between the bars.

"*Señor*, I am sure I do not know."

"That, sir, is the pilot the Spanish Viceroy was sending to Panama to take Don Gonzalo to China," the captain said with contempt.

De Zarate fidgeted with his handkerchief in front of his face and mumbled something in Spanish.

"What?" the captain demanded.

"Nothing, *señor*."

"Well, then," the captain announced in his most gracious manner, "I suppose you are hungry after your busy morning. Why don't you join me in my cabin for a simple meal, *señor*?"

De Zarate seemed to stagger with relief as he followed Emmet and the captain out of the hold. A feast of roast chine of beef, roast swan, candied fruit, and spiced wine stolen from de Zarate's ship was served in the captain's cabin. As usual, a small, select gathering of Drake's officers was invited: the chaplain, the master, the carpenter, and the master gunner. Stony-faced da Silva took his place at the far end of the table. Like the others, he remained silent, his cap removed.

Emmet and the other servants scurried with course after course. They toted bottles of wine, carried away trays, and scraped the silver plates with care.

"These dishes were a gift from the Queen herself," the captain boasted. "My coat of arms."

"Very handsome, *señor*," de Zarate said. He listened politely as the captain regaled him with exaggerated tales of his exploits.

The next morning de Zarate's bales of silk and linen and crates of fine china were expertly removed by the crew under the careful eye of the captain himself. No one dared touch a single item as the captain inspected delicate blue and yellow silk dresses decorated with bone lace and stiff ruff collars, and brilliant scarlet and bright green farthingales arrayed with small slashes, embroidery, and gold eyelet holes.

"My wife will appreciate these latest fashions!" declared the captain. Emmet was ordered to write down a detailed inventory as Drake carefully unpacked chests containing a dozen large-brimmed hats decorated with bands of jewels, one black velvet cap, a long string of pearls, a pair of soft leather slippers slashed to reveal exquisite yellow silk designs, three heavy spangled gold bracelets, and a pair of emerald earrings.

"Please be careful with my clothing, *señor*," de Zarate pleaded with Drake. "Do not let your men mangle my fine belongings."

"Sir, I shall treat them as my own," Captain Drake assured him.

After the last Spanish crate, barrel, and strongbox was transported to the *Golden Hind*, the crew appeared anxious to depart. By now the news of the fate of the Silver Ship must have reached the Viceroy, who would certainly dispatch Spanish warships in pursuit.

To Emmet's surprise, there was one more treasure that Captain Drake insisted on collecting before de Zarate would be given his freedom. Early on the morning that Drake had promised to take de Zarate back to his own ship, the two men were served a private breakfast in the *Golden Hind* cabin. Emmet had been told to make this an especially festive occasion. Sprigs of flowers and peacock feathers were arranged in bottles. As usual, the best silver plates were used. Emmet played sweet songs on the lute as accompaniment.

In exchange for the loss of his precious possessions, de Zarate was presented with a few of the captain's trinkets: a cutlass and a little silver brazier. "Of course, I stole them so long ago I can't remember who they once belonged to," the captain apologized.

"Thank you, *señor*," de Zarate said, although it seemed clear that the captain had made off with the better bargain.

"And one more thing, sir."

De Zarate sighed with impatience. "Anything, *señor*."

"You will do me the favor of leaving the pretty woman."

For a moment de Zarate did not speak.

With irritation Captain Drake glanced at Emmet. "Why did you stop playing? Play."

Emmet did as he was told, all the time straining to hear every word.

"What woman?" de Zarate replied.

"Come, come, sir," Captain Drake said, and chuckled. "You know the slave I mean. I saw her before she was locked up in your carpenter's cabin. Nearly bit off my mate's ear. Such a fiery temper for such an angelic face. Wherever did you find her?"

"I don't know what you mean, *señor*." de Zarate stared at the crumbled piece of white bread on his plate.

"The proper Negro wench. Her name is Maria. I keep a

careful inventory of every ship I board. How could I have missed her? She's quite a treasure. Surely you're a generous man. The crossing of the South Sea will take seventy, perhaps eighty days. I could use such attractive company."

De Zarate folded and unfolded his linen napkin with his long, elegant fingers. "How did you find her?"

"My men are clever. Luckily they know my rules about checking for false bottoms in floors, in walls. They never touch anything valuable, however. If they do, they lose a finger, a hand, another necessary body part perhaps."

De Zarate turned pale.

"I do not wish to bring up such ugly punishments in your delicate company."

De Zarate paused. "I am more than happy to give her to you, *señor,* if doing so will ensure my safe passage home."

"I knew we could agree. We are gentlemen, are we not?" Captain Drake said, and smiled.

Later that morning Emmet gazed in wonder at Maria as she was rowed in the pinnace from de Zarate's departing ship to the *Golden Hind.* For one brief moment in slanted light she looked up—a cloaked, hooded figure—the profile of her fine features unexpectedly illuminated. He could not help but think of the way dark gorse grass suddenly blazed red on certain early mornings, and how the whole moor seemed to glow as if on fire. No matter how hard he'd tried, he was never able to capture that radiance with his paints.

"O-weee!" the sailors hooted and waved from the deck rail. They shoved and elbowed each other.

"Look atter!"

"A real beauty!"

Maria seemed to ignore them, as if they were nothing more than squawking seabirds. In her lap she clutched a small satchel. Carefully she stood in the rocking pinnace, gathered her long, pale yellow skirt, and took a seat in a crude swing attached to a pulley. Slowly, she was hauled up onto the deck. Captain Drake waited at the rail with his gloved hand outstretched. He made a stiff courtly bow and helped her down to the deck.

"See if she kisses his hands!"

"She can kiss my hands!"

"Ow-wheeeeee!" somebody whooped. Reckless energy ricocheted through the ship. The men became louder, clumsier, more stupid trying to outdo each other with catcalls and lewd antics, until it seemed as if they'd all gone mad or been infected by rampant fever.

Crack!

"Belay it, boys!" Captain Drake bellowed. Smoke billowed from the pistol he held upright in the air.

Nobody moved. Nobody dared. They knew he'd shoot any one of them through the head without blinking an eye.

"Let this be a warning," the bosun called out in his loudest voice. "Nobody touches nothing what belongs to the captain. Any soger who breaks this rule answers with his life."

The deck rippled with grumbling. When the signal was given to weigh anchor, the sailors shoved their caps back on their heads and began hoisting anchor cable with the capstan.

"Page!" the captain announced to Emmet. "Take the young lady to my cabin and see that she is comfortable."

Emmet bowed and blushed. He glimpsed Maria's dark-eyed

glare. Unsmiling and defiant, she looked him up and down.

"Emmet is my servant," Captain Drake continued. "He will provide you with any food or comfort you desire. Take her satchel for her, boy. And keep her safe."

Shyly Emmet reached out to take her bag, but she shook her head and gripped the bag close to herself. He couldn't wrest it from her, could he?

He led her to the cabin and held the door open for her to go inside. His palms sweat so badly he had to wipe them on his tunic. Perhaps she'd noticed his gold chain. That was impressive, wasn't it? He cleared his throat.

She paid no attention to him. She was busy testing the cabin window, tugging on the lock on the chest, checking under the mattress. She quickly went through the drawers in the sideboard, one after the other. Emmet watched her, transfixed. She looked only a few years older than he was. Perhaps seventeen at the most. She was the most beautiful creature he'd ever laid eyes on in his life.

"*¡Maldito sea!*" She slammed the drawers shut, then began searching through the wardrobe, with her satchel still hanging from her shoulder.

Emmet cleared his throat nervously. "*¿Qué desea usted, señorita?*"

She yanked off her hood and turned toward him in disgust. Strands of long dark hair came loose from the bun at the back of her head. "The weapons. *Pronto.* Where are they?"

"You speak English!" Emmet said, amazed. "That is a relief. My Spanish is not yet very practiced. With my background in Latin and Greek I find I sometimes get everything confused. I have to concentrate—"

"*¡Silencio!*" She scowled. "I need them now. *¡Pronto!* Where does your captain keep them?"

Emmet studied her full mouth. It was beautiful even when she was frowning. And there was something so utterly charming about the dimple. Just in the left cheek. What had his grandmother called it? An angel's kiss.

"Are you deaf, boy?" she demanded. "Where are the weapons?"

Emmet blinked. *Weapons?* He could not believe she wanted a pistol. Perhaps her English was faulty. "Do you mean a glass of wine? Some cheese? A pitcher of—"

Suddenly there was a rap at the door. She jerked her head nervously in the door's direction. Emmet obediently yanked it open. Sky slunk inside, quietly locked the door behind himself, and slammed Emmet against the wall. Sky held him by the neck, twisting the gold chain so tightly that Emmet could only flail his arms and squeak, "I—don't—think—supposed—here."

"Aye, aye, sir!" Sky taunted. His breath smelled rank. "You'll keep your mouth shut, won't you? Just a dabble. That's all I mean, Cousin. Share and share alike, isn't that how kinfolk help each other?" He punched Emmet in the face.

Dizzily Emmet slouched onto the floor. Small white stars whirred past his closed eyelids. The captain must have told Sky they were related. With effort Emmet managed to open his eyes. He could see Sky's feet prowl around the table. Chairs, the globe, the bench tipped in his path. The gold chain! Emmet groaned and struggled to stand, wondering if Drake hoped to use Sky to steal back his gold chain.

"There, there, now, pet," Sky hissed, and lunged toward Maria. "Just a kiss. That's all we want. Just a kiss." Sky made a swipe to catch her but only grabbed a handful of cloak. She'd somehow unbuttoned the neck. "Such a pretty gown."

"¡*Puerco!*" She spat in his face and nimbly dashed around the table, out of his reach.

Sky flipped another chair. Closer he crept toward her, insolently smacking his lips. Something inside Emmet snapped. Months of humiliation ignited into rage. Emmet hurled himself toward Sky's back and grabbed him around the waist. There was a flash of yellow. Sky bellowed in pain and slumped forward. Something dripped down Emmet's face, his arms. Blood was everywhere.

"The wench cut me!" Sky cursed, holding his slashed face. Blood oozed between his fingers. The only thing that Emmet could think of was how he would explain the mess. How would he clean up before the furious captain saw what had happened and beat him?

Maria glared down at Sky, who sat crumpled on the floor. The small dagger in her hand was smeared with blood. Blood splattered down the front of her dress, across her cheek. She was breathing very hard, as if she were preparing to finish the job of killing him.

Suddenly the door rattled. "Open this!" Captain Drake's voice boomed.

"Oh, God—," Sky murmured. "God help me."

Maria's eyes narrowed. She kicked Sky squarely in the gut. The door rattled again. Expertly she wiped the dagger on the table carpet and slipped it inside her satchel. Emmet dashed about the cabin, trying to right the heavy furniture.

Maria unlocked the door and let the enraged captain inside.

Drake glanced around the room—at the overturned chairs, the scattered papers and maps, the blood—and his wounded brother hunched on the ground, then Maria, with her hair disheveled, stained dress, and terrified expression. "What happened?"

"Sky . . . Sky tried . . ." Emmet stammered. Every time he tried to speak, Maria interrupted in rapid, vehement Spanish punctuated by loud, heart-rending wails. Again and again she jabbed her finger at Sky, who looked as if he'd rather fling himself into the ocean than face the captain's wrath.

The captain leaned over and with one stout arm lifted his younger brother by the neck of his shirt. Drake kneed him in the stomach. As Sky hurtled forward the captain brought his fist down on the back of Sky's head. Then in one swift movement, he bent over, grasped Sky by the back of his shirt and the seat of his breeches, and hurled him out the door. "Bosun!" he shouted.

In only a few moments the bosun arrived to hustle Sky away to the hold for lockup. Meanwhile Maria combed her hair and dabbed her face from a basin of perfumed water Emmet had thoughtfully provided.

"There, there, now, my dear. You look as lovely as ever," the captain said approvingly.

"*Señor*, you are true hero," she said. Her words rolled like a melody. She appeared so tragic, so beautiful, that Emmet stopped mopping to watch her. "What I would have done without you?"

The captain shuffled his feet and bashfully stared at the floor. He appeared more like a schoolboy than a fierce pirate captain. "I promise you," he told her in a penitent voice, "this will never happen again."

She made a soft cooing noise and stroked the captain's rough, scarred cheek. Mouth agape, Emmet dropped the mop handle. The captain shot an irritable glance at Emmet, as if he'd forgotten he was still there. "Page, don't you have something to do on deck?"

"Certainly, sir," Emmet said, and headed for the door.

"Stop!" the captain commanded. "One more thing I need to discuss with you before you go."

Emmet took a deep breath. He pinched the gold links between his fingers until they hurt. He should have known he'd never get off this easily. He was supposed to have kept Maria safe and he'd failed. "Yes, sir? I'm sorry, sir, about what happened. I was completely taken by surprise. I—"

"The chain," the captain said. He held out his hand. "I think you should give it to me for safekeeping."

"The chain? But, sir, you said—"

"I'll take it now, thank you," the captain said. He gave a little wink in Maria's direction. She smiled sweetly.

Reluctantly Emmet took the chain from his neck and handed it to the captain. He knew his face burned with shame and humiliation. He could not bear to look at Maria, who had witnessed for a second time since her arrival how weak he was, how easily he could be betrayed.

Chapter Eighteen

13 April 1579

For past week we sail north along rugged coast with the small frigate captured off Caño Island 20 March. Sky remains chained in hold. Some sailors say his stab wound won't heal. We lack fresh water and food. The ship leaks badly. The captain has been seen on deck scarcely at all since the arrival of M. She does not speak to me except to ask for wine or food. Does she find life confining on ship where we are all prisoners? Crew speaks of nothing but her, how she nearly killed captain's brother and how unlucky it is to have a woman on a ship. I confess I find her welcome relief. The other day I heard her singing a sad song, and I sat outside the cabin window and listened a very long time.

At noon on 13 April, the *Golden Hind* and the thirty-eight-foot-long frigate of fifteen tons sailed into the small harbor at Guatulco, where one ship lay at anchor. The town did not appear promising—only a handful of buildings, a church, and a warehouse for about three hundred Indians and a dozen Spaniards. Dogs barked. A few children appeared to be gathering shellfish along the water's edge. The sun blazed. No one was seen on the dusty road. Captain Drake, however, emerged with great energy from his cabin. He was wearing his helmet and his rapier and immediately began ordering everyone about. The pinnace with Flea and two dozen other armed men was

lowered into the water and rowed to shore.

Emmet had been ordered to stay on board the ship to guard Maria. Captain Drake had left behind an old cutlass for him to use. Emmet felt rather foolish, but he leaned against the door of the cabin in attention. From his post he heard the sounds of shouting, ringing bells, and booming guns.

"What is happening?" Maria demanded from behind the door.

"They're ransacking the town." Emmet felt secretly delighted that she was speaking to him.

The door opened a crack and she peeked out. The men who had not been sent to the town were sleeping in the shade or playing dominoes. She looked pale and frightened.

"Don't worry, *señorita*," Emmet said. "If there's not much to steal, they'll just loot the church."

Maria made the sign of the cross. "And they will kill people?"

Emmet shrugged. He could feel her scowling at him, and it made him uncomfortable.

"You English pirates," she said with disgust, "you are devils, just as everyone say. You steal. You burn. You make sacrilege against holy church. You murder innocents."

"I don't— I'm not—" Emmet stammered just as she slammed the door in his face. He stared at the closed door. He wondered what she was doing on the other side. "Maria?" he said softly, desperate to hear her voice again. "*Por favor,* let me explain."

"Leave me alone," she replied with a muffled voice.

Emmet slumped against the cabin door, filled with deep loneliness and self-loathing. What could he possibly say to convince her that he was different from the crew members who, at this very moment, were probably stealing chalices and damask vestments, scattering and trampling altar bread, terrifying old women, shooting cats, and drinking stolen wine? Hadn't he done all these things too? He was no better than the worst pirate among them.

Until this moment he had not bothered to care.

Later Flea told Emmet how in Guatulco the children lingering in the plaza had scattered when the sailors fired shots into the air. Only the old, stubborn priest resisted the invasion. He had to be dragged from his church. A few other worshippers and visitors in town who had come for Holy Week were rounded up by Captain Drake and taken back to the ship for questioning. Moone and a handful of ruffians looted the biggest house they could find. The owner, who tried to flee from the pirates, was caught before he could run out the door with a sack filled with seven thousand pesos, a gold chain, and a few pieces of silver plate.

On board ship once again, Moone enjoyed telling everyone who would listen how he had torn a crucifix from the wall and smacked it against a table. "Nothing but a pagan idol!" he howled with laughter. "You should have seen that fool's face!"

That evening on board the *Golden Hind* the terrified prisoners from Guatulco were served a meal—in spite of the fact that it was Holy Week and they protested that they were fasting. The old priest, the richest man in town, and a few unlucky visitors who happened to be in Guatulco when the pirates arrived were hustled up to the deck for religious services with the crew. "I do not wish you to think," Captain Drake announced to his captives, "that I am a devil who robs by day and prays at night. Do you think I am a devil?"

"No, *señor*," the terrified priest mumbled.

"Do you think I am a common thief?"

"No, *señor.*"

The captain smiled, adjusted his fine velvet doublet, and motioned to Emmet to hand him his Bible. Ceremoniously the captain kneeled on a small bench, his elbows on a table. He appeared to be praying.

Meanwhile the reluctant crew assembled on the main deck. Among them was Sky, who had finally been released from the hold after a severe flogging. The zigzag scar on Sky's cheek was made by a woman—not by an enemy cutlass. Everyone knew. The fact seemed to be something of an embarrassment for Sky. He glowered at Maria, who stood demurely in a blue silk dress and dark cape. Around her neck glinted a string of pearls and three gold chains. From her ears hung the spectacular emerald earrings. On each gloved finger she wore silver rings with precious stones.

"Look at the plump witch!" one of the sailors grumbled.

"Better not be wearing my share of the treasure," another agreed.

Captain Drake, who seemed to have finished his silent prayer, glanced adoringly at bejeweled Maria. Her expression was as impassive as that of a ship's figurehead. Chaplain Fletcher had nothing to do now that the captain had taken over his job giving sermons. He fidgeted while the captain droned on and on from the *Book of Martyrs.* With great relish Captain Drake related the horrors of Spanish Catholics who burned English Protestants at the stake.

"And King Philip calls *us* bloody barbarians," Moone muttered.

"Amen," the captain intoned solemnly after the last psalm was read.

Da Silva, who wore his best doublet, lingered on the poop deck and chatted with Maria in Spanish. For once they both seemed animated. He leaned toward her and said something in a low voice. They looked at the captain, then they both laughed.

Captain Drake's face became florid. "Share your little jest, won't you, da Silva?"

"It was nothing, sir. Only a pleasantry," da Silva said, and bowed. Maria giggled.

Emmet gathered up the book and the Bible to take them back to the cabin. He sighed. He'd never be so lucky as to have Maria smile at and chat with him.

The next day as the prisoners were about to be rowed back to Guatulco in the pinnace, the captain ordered a last-minute change of plans. Also joining them would be stubborn Colchero and da Silva, who had served as pilot and navigator for almost eighteen months.

"You can't abandon me here, *señor!*" da Silva protested. "What of my wife, my children?"

"Thousands of miles mean nothing to an accomplished navigator like yourself," Captain Drake said. "I'm sure you'll find a way home."

"The Spanish authorities think I'm a traitor," da Silva pleaded. "They'll throw me in prison. They'll torture and kill me."

"It is not my problem that you have outlived your usefulness to me," Captain Drake said, and shrugged. "And when you fall into the hands of cruel Catholics from the Spanish Inquisition, I hope that you will tell them that your dear friend, El Draque the

Protestant, plans to sail home across the Pacific to the Moluccas and Spice Islands, around Africa and on to Europe. You can remember all that, can't you, da Silva?"

When Drake wasn't looking, Emmet waved desperately from the deck rail to da Silva, who was rowed with the others to the ransacked town. To Emmet's disappointment, not once did da Silva look up. He sat hunched forward in the pinnace like a doomed man. Emmet wished he could have said good-bye to him. He wished he could have offered some encouragement. No matter how hard Emmet tried, he could not ignore Drake's words. *Outlived your usefulness to me.* Deep down Emmet knew that da Silva's disastrous fate—like Doughty's, like Diego's—could happen to anyone on the *Golden Hind. We are all expendable,* Emmet thought miserably. *Even Maria.*

17 April 1579

After gathering fresh water and food, we set a southwest by west course with frigate. Farewell to New Spain. The captain intends to sail where none of our Spanish pursuers will guess—straight into South Sea. For hours he studies charts stolen from Colchero. What can he be thinking? I heard Colchero warn him that to leave New Spain in April is to court disaster. Something about arriving in the Spice Islands in time for typhoon season. After a long, mysterious absence, Flea's cat, Nipcheese, is found dead in the hold. Flea is beside himself with grief, certain that someone hexed the creature. We give the cat a proper burial at sea. None of us liked him much, but he was a good ratter.

On a late-April morning two dozen sleek, black-and-white porpoises sped about the heavily laden ship. Every so often they leaped high and cleared the water. No matter how quickly he sketched, Emmet could only create brief glimpses of the acrobatic creatures. Emmet and Maria sat in the roundhouse, a small enclosed area on the poop deck that was off-limits to anyone except the captain and his officers. Maria perched atop a barrel, with her cloak drawn tightly about herself. She was seldom seen outside the captain's cabin. When Emmet shot her a secretive glance, her eyes appeared closed.

"When the sea hog jumps, look to your pumps!" called one of the sailors from overhead in the rigging. Emmet could tell the fellow was showing off for Maria by the reckless way he bounded along the ratlines.

"No entiendo," she murmured, her eyes still closed. "What means he?"

Emmet cleared his throat, startled that she was bothering to talk to him. "When the sea creatures leap," he said, "the sailors say a storm's coming." He kept sketching, hoping she might continue the conversation.

She remained silent. She did not bother to open her eyes to look at the porpoises or at his drawing. Vaguely disappointed, he furtively peeked at her again. Her face was sallow and a bit puffy. Was she seasick? The only cure he knew was brisk activity in the fresh air. "A lovely day for a stroll about the deck," he suggested, then wondered if he sounded as stupid as the sailor showing off in the rigging.

"¡Siga! I would rather jump into the sea," she murmured.

"Do you swim?"

"Of course not."

"Oh," Emmet said, unwilling to admit that he too could not swim. Besides, what difference would such a connection make to her? Clearly she hated him. She hated all of them.

By late afternoon the mackerel sky revealed mares' tails, dark, ragged featherlike clouds on the horizon. The wind stopped blowing, then picked up again as a blunt headwind. Within the hour light winds began to play a kind of jinx on the *Golden Hind*. The growing swell turned a gray-green.

"What's coming?" Emmet asked Flea as they stood watch.

Flea shrugged. "Whilst she creaks she holds."

Emmet did not feel encouraged. Like Flea and the others, he had developed the knack of listening to the way the ship spoke in different weather, different seas. The urgency of thrumming rigging, creaking wood, complaining sail told of the ship's mood and how well or how poorly she was handling the action of wind and wave. Overburdened with Spanish treasure in the hold, the *Golden Hind* responded slower to the tiller and seemed to meet approaching waves with stubbornness. She rolled heavily and took in water through gaps between planks, the places where rotten caulking had washed away.

Through his bare feet, Emmet felt the ship shudder. Belowdecks, side planks shifted and beams moaned. Like a living creature, elastic but vulnerable, the ship plunged through the growing swells.

The wind began to blow hard and steady. The temperature dropped. And still the captain did not trim the sails. "I know the ship and what she can carry," Captain Drake shouted at the bosun when he appeared at his cabin door to report the shift in weather. Emmet, who ducked inside to turn the hourglass, spied Maria huddled in a corner of the room. Her dark eyes looked large and terrified.

"Aye, sir," the bosun replied. As he slunk out the door again, he grumbled under his breath. "Showing off for a woman. Letting her know how he can carry sail."

When Captain Drake finally stepped out onto the poop deck, he appeared to have changed his mind. "All hands!" came the cry from the bosun.

Emmet and every other available hand were needed to haul down and clew up every sail they had. Canvas flapped and rigging snapped in flying chaos as the men desperately attempted to reduce sail. The tack parted as one man struggled with the topgallant. In an instant the sail had torn and slatted itself to pieces. Icy rain pelted the men, who had to yell at the top of their lungs to be heard over the wind.

"Damn your eyes!"

"Lay aloft there and furl that main-royal!"

Emmet, Moone, and one of the mates scrambled up the ratlines. Salt stung Emmet's eyes. His leg and arm muscles trembled. In forty knots of wind a flick of canvas could knock a man off a yard. Yet he continued to climb. He had to clutch the shrouds, careful to pause every now and again as the ship rolled into the trough between waves. Each time the ship pitched and tossed, his stomach lurched. When he looked out to sea he could not spy the frigate. Had she gone under?

The keening wind pummeled him until he could barely breathe, as he climbed higher and higher. He heaved himself out around the foretop, drenched with spray. His knees braced against the yard, he and Moone and Hawkins reached out to pull in the sail. Canvas billowed up and back toward them. His mates grappled and leaned forward.

Emmet grabbed too. And at that moment he lost his balance and began to teeter backward into a fall as the foot rope swayed and sagged. Time slowed, stopped, and he felt as if he were watching himself, back arched, about to plummet, one arm flailing, when somehow someone reached out and snagged him by the shirt and yanked him toward the yard, back to safety. Half blinded by rain, Emmet tried to see who it was who had saved him. Was it Moone or Hawkins? No time to say thank you—to say anything. Only time to keep hauling sail.

As the wind increased, the ship corkscrewed and slammed against the waves. Aloft, Emmet and the others were whipsawed back and forth through the air as if on a bucking pendulum.

"There she goes, boys!"

"Hold steady."

"Put another bit of beef in soak!"

Moone mouthed curses none of them could hear. The wind was too ferocious, too deafening. Volleys of spray dashed as high as the topgallant. For a moment, once the sail was secure, Emmet looked between his feet and saw tons of water boil over the deck below. Waves tumbled over the windward rail and punished the deck, rushing in a devouring torrent that reminded him of the River Dart after a storm. Anything that had not been tied down was swept away in the blink of an eye. He thought he spied someone get hit chest-high by the rapids, sink beneath the current, and disappear.

From his strange remote height he panicked. *Maria!* If she were inside the captain's cabin with the door shut, she might be safe.

But if she'd been on deck when the last wave struck, she may have gone overboard.

Painfully Emmet and the others gripped the ratlines and lowered themselves down. Wind leached the heat out of their bodies. Emmet was too worried, too intent on making it down to notice. He could not hear Hawkins hollering next to him. The wind's roar stood like a barrier between Emmet and every other crew member.

"Flea, where's the girl?" Emmet screamed once he was back on deck.

"What?" Flea shouted, only inches away from Emmet's ear.

"The girl?"

Flea shook his head. Water streamed down his face, soaked his hair, his clothes. His lips were blue.

Emmet tried to scream his question again, but again the wind strangled his words. It was clear that Flea had no idea what he was talking about. This realization made Emmet suddenly feel lonely, isolated from all his shipmates. No one could hear. No one could understand him.

Desperately he clenched the rail and pulled himself toward the poop deck. Waist-high water rushed across the deck, nearly knocking him off his feet. When he opened his mouth, he was choked alternately by salt water and rainwater. He blinked hard and tried to keep his goal in mind: the captain's cabin. Punishing waves and wind had shaken his ability to think, to remember.

Another lurch, another dip. The ship groaned and rolled. How long would the ship hold? It seemed to take him hours, days, months to pull himself toward the poop deck, climb the steps. Finally with all his might he gripped the door and pulled it open.

The cabin was awash in knee-deep water. Papers floated

everywhere. Cushions, plates, linen coverings galloped in a tide from one side of the room to the other. All the captain's precious belongings. A soggy red velvet cap. A lone leather boot. Chairs were wedged under the table that had slammed against the wall. Overhead the unlit lamp swung in drunken arcs.

"Maria?" he called, even though he knew the wind drowned out his voice. "Maria?"

Terror-stricken and silent, she clung to the post of the soggy bed, the only piece of furniture still secured to the floor. In the dim light her face seemed to take on a greenish hue. Emmet ripped the table covering from the table and wrapped it around Maria's shoulders. He gestured for her to go out the door and down into the hold where she might be safer. He had heard of rogue waves large and powerful enough to rip decks clean of cabins, rails, masts.

"Go below!" he kept shouting. "¡Pronto!"

She refused to budge. She refused to leave the cabin. He pulled her arm to coax her out the door. She reached beneath the cushion. Her knife. Taut and alert, she gripped the blade. But it wasn't the knife that made Emmet let go of her arm and back away. It was the look in her eyes—fierce and deadly. She looked at him as if she did not know him. Did not remember who he was. Did not understand that he was trying to save her.

"Do as you please," he shouted. He knew she could only see him mouth the words, that she could not hear what he was saying as he backed toward the door. He opened it, exited, then shouldered against the door to shut it.

A wave plunged over the rail. Cold ankle-deep water rushed around his feet, under the door, then flowed back to the starboard side. In one last gesture he tested the latch on the wooden door that would be no match for a wave that might tower fifty, a hundred feet or more. And he was aware for the first time of the enormity of Maria's desperation. She would rather brave the waves, the plunge of sea, the possibility of being washed overboard, than go below with the crew.

Chapter Nineteen

For fifty days the crews on the *Golden Hind* and the frigate did not see land. For fifty days storms raged on and off again as the two ships were mercilessly blown west and northwest. The farther north they were blown, the farther the temperature plummeted. Snow coated the deck. Ice imprisoned the rigging. After brief lulls, just when it seemed as if they could not bear one more storm, the wind picked up. Again the ships were looted by waves and the awful destruction of the wind.

Some men aboard the *Golden Hind* had been so constantly exposed to wind and cold that they suffered from telltale black patches of frostbite on their hands, feet, and faces. While snow made work aloft or on deck cold, slippery, and dangerous, it was the rain that created the most misery.

Between watches Emmet and the others slumped on the hard wooden floor on the lower deck. Every pallet and blanket had been drenched. Rain and waves dripped through deck planks on men as they slept. No one owned a dry piece of clothing. It was too dangerous to build a fire to warm themselves or attempt to dry their clothing or bedding. Salt-soaked and chafing, their woolen breeches, shirts, and tunics offered little warmth.

Reduced to half-rations, Emmet gnawed a chunk of tough, putrid salt beef. He leaned against the damp wall and tried to close his eyes. The pumps were manned almost all day long—remorseless work for men so ill fed. And still the water poured into the ship. The cold and the constant dampness sapped their strength, their hope.

"That woman," one sailor grumbled. "She got a conjure spell on this ship."

"Never should take a woman on board," another agreed.

"Captain's bewitched."

"Only one thing to do—"

They stopped when they noticed Emmet. He tried to pretend he hadn't heard anything. He knew how quickly the firepower of such accusations might shift to him. They had all seen him use the Mosaical Wand. They knew he had access to the captain's cabin and that he served Maria food. He saw her more than anyone besides the captain. Sooner or later they might openly accuse him of conjuring.

It had become Emmet's custom to draw as little attention to himself as possible. Quietly he kept the captain's table and tried to mop water from the cabin floor as best he could. He pinned damp papers and parchment maps to lines that crisscrossed the cabin. He built small fires in the brazier and, like any trusted page, attempted to see to the needs of Maria and the captain.

Maria seldom spoke to him or even acted as if he or the captain were present. Perhaps it was the relentless storms. Perhaps it was the way the sea had broken their hearts. Whatever the reason, Maria had withdrawn into some other world.

"Can't tell what ails her," the captain grumbled one morning as Emmet poured him a sixth glass of wine. "Indian blood, maybe? Unpredictable. No way of knowing. Can't reason with her, threaten her. Tried beating her. Nothing works."

Emmet stood still, not certain what to say. What did he know of love or of women?

The captain kept talking as if Emmet were not in the room. "Power of some charm maybe. Some incantation." He stood unsteadily and blinked. "Where is it? Where?" He pawed through the papers dangling haphazardly from the lines. Then he began to fumble with the lock on the sea chest. Even in a drunken stupor, he knew exactly where his ring of keys were: around his waist. He never went anywhere without the ring. Awkwardly he tried to stick a key into the lock. "Boy!" he hollered.

Emmet tried his best to open the lock. After much effort, the key turned and the lock opened. The captain plunged his hands into the chest among the fine folded clothing, secret small boxes, and stolen bangles he'd set aside for himself. Finally he seemed to have found what he was looking for. "Here!" he declared triumphantly. In his hands he held a thick leather-bound book. "How to gain wealth, love, and power."

Emmet stared in dread. *The Key of Solomon.* "Sir, I don't really—"

"Land, ho!" came the cry from the deck.

The captain, suddenly sober, shoved past Emmet. He rushed out onto the deck, with the dangerous book under his arm. The gale blew out of the northwest. Emmet struggled out onto the deck to stare in the distance at a rugged, steeply mountainous coast. Between the parting of mist Emmet could make out rock-strewn beaches, pounding surf, and high bluffs that would tear the *Golden Hind* and frigate to pieces. Here and there along the coast appeared small inlets, if they could only find them long enough in the mist. Being driven ashore or stranding a ship was every sailor's nightmare.

The watch in the crow's nest shouted down, "To the north, a headland!"

The captain cupped one hand to his mouth and bellowed, "How many miles to seaward?"

"Three, maybe five," the watch called.

The captain ordered that the crews of the *Golden Hind* and the frigate make for the bay and anchor out of the wind. Guns were fired so that the frigate pilot knew of a change in direction. The crew went to work with a will to bring the *Golden Hind* safely around the point.

Once inside the bay their troubles did not cease. Wind gusts slammed against the two vessels. Anchor cables strained. Clearly the treacherous bay would serve only as a temporary shelter while the wind blasted from the northwest. If the wind shifted, the men knew they faced being driven ashore and wrecked. The weary, hungry sailors dubbed the place Cape of Worries.

The next day Captain Drake went ashore in the pinnace, with a small group of armed men, to oversee the gathering of fresh water and firewood. Nervous scouts watched the thick woods along the shore for menacing warriors.

Emmet had been left on board to clean the cabin. Maria sat stiffly in a chair beside the smoldering brazier. As usual, she clutched her satchel in her lap. "You prattle far too much this morning," he said.

As usual, she did not reply.

Desperately he rummaged through the drawers. He found the

wand, the crystal. None of these would help him. *Where had Drake hidden the book?* Emmet knew he did not have much time. With all his strength he yanked on the lock to the sea chest. The lock did not budge. The only way he'd be able to open the chest was to use the key. And how would he ever manage that when Drake kept it on his belt?

"Looking for something?"

Emmet jumped. Standing in the doorway was Sky. The scar on his face had darkened into a purplish welt. He carried a blanket and a rope under his arm. Behind him lurked two of his thugs, Moone and Edwards.

"Stand off," Emmet said in his bravest voice. He tried not to allow his eyes to shift to Maria. "If the captain catches you in here—"

"Step aside, little man. It's quick work to rid the ship of a witch."

Emmet clenched his fists. He took a step backward. "You're not to touch her," he said, louder this time.

Sky and the other sailors chuckled. "Dowse that now or we'll scupper you, too," Sky growled. He lunged toward Emmet and knocked him out of the way. Moone threw the blanket over Maria's head.

Edwards tied a rope around her waist, then hoisted her over his shoulder like a bale. "Heavier than she looks!" he said, and started out the door. "Ow!" He staggered forward and dropped her. His neck and arm were bleeding badly. Maria had stuck her dagger into him through the blanket.

Through the tear in the fabric, Sky grabbed Maria's wrist and knocked the knife away. "Grab the little demon!" Cursing, he grappled the struggling bundle. "Dowse that now!" he shouted when she began to scream.

Through the open cabin door Emmet saw a dozen sailors lurking near the starboard rail. They were grim and silent, as if they, too, were part of the plan. One held ballast weights from the hold. Another scanned the shore as if looking for signs of the captain and the returning pinnace.

Emmet knew he was outnumbered. In only a few seconds they'd tie the weights and cast her overboard. There was not a moment to lose.

"Lend a hand!" Sky barked to his henchmen.

"Captain's coming up the beach toward the pinnace," warned Edwards.

"Hurry, boys!"

Moone gasped. "What the devil?"

The sailors froze. They stared at Emmet in horror.

"Put her down in the name of vipers, slowworms, and adders," Emmet commanded in his loudest wizardly voice. He held the crystal high in the palm of his right hand. In his left hand he brandished the Mosaical Wand. "Three angels came from North, East, and West. One brought fire, another brought frost, and the third brought the Holy Ghost—"

Sky gulped. "We're not afraid."

"So out fire and in frost," Emmet chanted. "Bone to bone and vein to vein, and vein turn to thy rest again."

"What's he say?"

"Some curse maybe."

Wind flapped the sail. Neither Sky nor the other men spoke. They were so transfixed they did not notice the way fog began to creep stealthily across the bay.

"He know what he's doing?" Moone demanded.

Edwards shrugged. "You saw him after Callao."

"Belay all this," Sky barked. "We made a plan, remember?"

"Vipers, slowworms, and adders. And so shall thine," Emmet chanted, eyes half closed, as he began to call upon all demons, ghosts, conjurers, and spirits in the animal, vegetable, and mineral worlds.

"Sky," Moone whispered, "maybe you can't drown a witch so easy. If Captain finds out, he'll kill us."

"What use is treasure to a dead man?" Edwards agreed.

Emmet cleared his throat and repeated, "Bone to bone and vein to vein, and vein turn to thy rest again—"

"Captain's in the pinnace," the lookout called. "Pulling oars straightaway!"

Moone backed away from the kicking Maria. "No harm meant," he mumbled. He shot a nervous glance in the direction of the low scudding mist that had devoured the trees and the beach, and was now consuming the water.

Edwards looked over his shoulder at the ominous fog. "Curse our last breath, he will."

Moone pulled off his cap. "Was his idea." He coughed and pointed to Sky, who had been left to wrestle Maria by himself. "What's that stink?"

"Bone to bone and vein to vein," Emmet continued, "and vein turn to thy rest again."

Mist shrouded the ship. They could not see the shore, the horizon. They could not see the approaching pinnace. Their nostrils filled with the putrid smell of sulphur, dead fish, dead animals, and dead plants.

"Ahoy!" the captain bellowed. His disembodied voice sounded as if it were coming from the depths of hell.

"Lend a hand!" someone shouted in the distance. The lookout in the crow's nest blew the trumpet to indicate the ship's whereabouts.

The blaring trumpet and the awful sound of the captain's voice seemed to bring the men abruptly back to their senses. They retreated to the rail to lower the rope ladder over the side for the approaching pinnace.

Sky cowered for only a moment beside the kicking shape of Maria before he scurried out of sight. Meanwhile Emmet quickly untied and uncovered Maria.

Hair wild, eyes blazing, she stumbled to her feet. Ferociously she gave the blanket a kick. *"¡Maldito sea!"* she cursed. She retreated to the cabin without one word of thanks to Emmet, who had just saved her life.

Miserably Emmet hid the crystal and Mosaical Wand inside the bunched-up blanket. *I'm as good as dead now too.* Of course, Maria probably didn't care that he'd endangered himself by threatening Sky and his thugs with conjuring. What difference did it make to her that he'd broken Father Parfoothe's rule to absolutely never combine healing charms? If his memory had been better, he wouldn't have had to patch together chants for mending sprains, curing ague, soothing thorn pricks—not to mention healing snake bites and—

"What the devil?" the red-faced captain cursed as he clambered over the rail. "When I call, I expect an answer. Give way now, you scum of the earth. There's a fog and a contrary wind meant to drive us into the rocks. Look lively or I'll thrash the lot of you."

Chapter Twenty

17 June

Must write in haste of things right rare and strange.
Though this be the height of summer, cruel cold nips us.
So cloudy and foul for fourteen days together, we cannot
take height of sun with astrolabe or backstaff and know
not where we are. And yet the captain pushes on, prob-
ing for what? He will not say. He studies on his Great
Map some Secret Strait to take us back to the Atlantic. So
intent he does not hear how the People grumble we are
a cursed ship that will meet with some shrewd turn—lost
forever or dashed upon lonely shore. The men keep their
distance from me and from M, saying our magic caused
this distempered air. I live in fear night and day they
will kill me. Oh, that I had never played the part of
Cunning man.

The next morning clouds cleared enough so that the hulking
shapes of low hills could be seen above a rocky bay bordered
with treacherous white breakers. Beyond that a headland jutted
out nearly eight miles. With the prevailing northwest winds,
the *Golden Hind* and the frigate had to keep well out to sea to
avoid being driven ashore on the windward side of the point.

After safely rounding the headland, the main run of the coastline appeared nearly ten miles to the east. To find shelter in the
lee of this projecting point, the frigate was ordered in the lead to
sound the way. The *Golden Hind* followed. As they sailed east the

coast fell away to the north, and white cliffs jutted into view. To everyone's surprise, they discovered a broad protected bay.

"Looks like the chalky white cliffs at the mouth of the Axe River near Plymouth, don't it?" said Moone.

"Or Berry Head's high limestone headland west of Brixham," replied Edwards.

The battered ship and frigate came to anchor in a harbor out of reach of surf, swell, strong currents, or sudden storms—the perfect place to careen the leaking *Golden Hind*. Beyond the sandy beach somewhere among the dark, tree-covered hills there might be a river or spring where they could refill casks with fresh water and hunt for game.

Exhausted, scurvy-ridden, and hungry, the ragged crew stood upon the deck of the *Golden Hind* and looked out at the bay and the lush green hills beyond as if they were glimpsing paradise. After two continuous, harrowing months at sea, they seemed dazed by the possibility of stepping onto solid land and filling their empty stomachs with as much roasted meat, mussels, oysters, clams, and red crabs as they could eat.

"Maybe some women out there too?" Sky mumbled. He scanned the shoreline the way they all did—hopeful and anxious at the same time.

A few grunted lewd replies. None said aloud what they all secretly feared: ambush and death.

They had only just begun the long, arduous process of unloading the heavy cannon and treasure cargo from the *Golden Hind* when a lone canoe approached from across the bay.

"Who goes there?" shouted the captain. He ordered every man aboard to arm himself with pike, harquebus, or longbow.

The intrepid solo paddler came closer and lifted his hands to show he carried no weapon. His unseaworthy-looking vessel appeared to be made from bunches of reeds tied in bundles. His paddle had arrow-shaped blades at both ends. In spite of the chill air, he wore no clothing. Feathers festooned his long black hair.

Punctuating the air with his hands, he shouted a long speech no one aboard the *Golden Hind* understood. When he finally finished, he could not be convinced with sign language to come aboard or paddle any closer. The pinnace crew signaled to him in a friendly manner and tried to throw him a shirt and some bright cloth. The orator viewed these gifts with alarm and refused to retrieve them.

Before the visitor finally departed, he pitched into the pinnace his own offering: a mysterious bunch of black feathers tied in a round bundle, and a small, tightly woven basket filled with a strange dried herb fastened to a stick.

"Never saw a white man before, I'll wager," Captain Drake said as the native beat a hasty retreat across the bay. The captain handed Emmet the spyglass, then ordered the crew to arm itself and keep guard as the rest of the treasure was unloaded. They would take no chances of being unprepared for attack.

For the next four days the men worked quickly to transport gunpowder for safekeeping into the frigate's captain's cabin. Onshore fortifications were assembled from piles of rocks, canvas tarps, and ropes to house the men and store supplies. The captain seemed especially concerned about the safety of the treasure chests, which were kept under special protection, as much from light-fingered sailors as from the possibility of pilfering natives.

The air rang with the sound of hammers and axes as the men on the beach began to assemble pulleys to haul the tipped, empty

Golden Hind closer to the shore for careening. Meanwhile, for what the captain described as safekeeping, Maria had been transferred to the frigate and was not allowed onshore. Secretly Emmet felt glad not to have to worry about her whereabouts as he helped dig clams or net and clean fish. She had caused him enough trouble.

During the late afternoon of their fifth day in New Albion, as the captain insisted they call their haven, a shout of alarm went up. Emmet and the others grabbed their weapons. Instantly Emmet felt the back of his neck prickle with fear.

Down the beach came a crowd of two dozen native men and women. As they crept closer, their high-pitched lament and sobbing grew louder and louder. Emmet listened, amazed. If he did not have his eyes open he might have thought he was home again, listening to the heart-breaking keening of mourning women in black who followed coffins to the abbey cemetery.

The rest of the crew seemed equally shocked by the wailing. Throughout their long voyage they had encountered anger, derision, hatred, and—rarely—momentary delight. Not once had they been greeted with outright grief by native people.

"They's ravished in their minds," Flea said, aghast.

"Steady, scum," Captain Drake warned in a superior voice. "The savages have no weapons. Not even a stick."

Closer, closer the native men and women came, unarmed and carrying baskets of food. The sight of these simple offerings made Emmet relax a little his grip on his pistol.

Their dark-skinned visitors were short in stature, well built, and robust. The men wore no clothing. Their faces were painted black and red; their hair hung long about their shoulders. The women wore grass or skin skirts, and their upper bodies and arms were painted. Some had feathers in their hair. Others wore necklaces of shining white beads.

At a distance of ten feet, the approaching group suddenly stopped. Now Emmet could see their tears and how the paint on their cheeks had smeared to their chins, to their necks. The visitors' dark eyes searched the crew members' faces with what appeared to be curiosity and sorrow. The more they stared the louder they wailed, until their sobbing reached an ear-wrenching pitch. The women clawed their skin with their fingernails until it bled. They tore out handfuls of their hair, and in anguish hurled themselves on the stony ground as if they did not care how much they were bruised or injured.

"Stop them!" Chaplain Fletcher begged the captain. "Can't you make these infidels stop?"

Captain Drake did not reply. He seemed mesmerized by the way the visitors sobbed and pointed to the *Golden Hind* and then west out to sea, in the direction they'd come. "Who," he muttered, "do they think we are?"

"Maybe gods," Sky said.

Chaplain Fletcher scowled. "Blasphemy!"

The captain smiled as if pleased by his brother's suggestion. "We are not gods," Captain Drake declared in a loud voice none of their visitors seemed to understand. "We are simply mortal men!" The captain stretched out his arm in a gesture to include his crew. He seemed careful not to point directly to himself.

The visitors only wailed more loudly.

"This isn't working," Chaplain Fletcher said. "Look at them. They're like animals, the way they hurt themselves. Give them some clothing. Cover their nakedness."

Shirts and linen cloth were offered. The natives refused to touch anything. They filed past one by one to lay before the captain's feet beautiful woven baskets heaped with herbs and nuts. They presented gifts of feather caps, soft animal skins, and a doe-skin quiver for arrows.

Emboldened, Sky reached out to pinch a woman in dangling ear ornaments made from beads and feathers. *"Nocáto mu! Nocáto mu!"* she screamed and scrambled away, as if his touch might kill her. *"Nocáto mu!"*

"Guess she don't like you, ijeet!" one of the men hooted.

"Try me!" another hollered. The crew laughed nervously.

"Belay it!" Captain Drake ordered.

Suddenly the crowd of natives retreated. They hurried up the beach. Every so often one of them would turn and look again at the crew. Emmet watched, fascinated. Where before had he seen that backward glance, that look of terror and sorrow? Then he remembered. Once long ago he and Father Parfoothe had been invited to a farm near Milemead to perform a special spirit-ridding ceremony. Although Emmet could not remember anything about the chant or the herb they'd burned, he recalled clearly the farmer's face. He had the same tormented expression as these natives. The desperate look of men haunted by ghosts.

Two days passed. Only one side of the *Golden Hind* had been scraped clean, in spite of the fact that the crew worked in shifts during all available daylight. Captain Drake bullied his men. He threatened them. Yet somehow the work proceeded as slowly as ever.

Late one afternoon, the trumpeter gave the alarm signal. When

Emmet looked up from the sail he was mending, he saw the silhouettes of hundreds of giants coming over the nearest hill.

"To arms! To arms!"

The crew rushed about to retrieve their weapons, helmets, and shields. They fumbled and nearly fell upon one another in their rush to dive inside their crude fort.

"Steady, now!" the captain ordered. Emmet handed him his rapier and gleaming silver helmet. They were clearly outnumbered, and yet the captain seemed full of enthusiasm. Drake was never as happy, Emmet thought, as when he was about to engage in a battle with impossible odds.

The rest of the crew, however, did not appear to share the captain's delight. Grim-faced, they watched as the natives poured down from atop the hill. Some were dressed in tall black feathered headdresses. Some carried bows and spears. Behind them marched women and children. The crowd paused. A lone individual stepped forward and shouted a long speech delivered with violent gestures.

"God's wounds," Flea grumbled after the men finished. "That fellow's as noisy as Davy putting on the coppers for the parson."

"Quiet, Butter Box!" Moone warned. "Want your head on a spike?"

Finally, when the native orator appeared to have finished, the men, women, and children reverently bowed and called out their approval in unison. "Oh!" they shouted. "Oh!"

The men, whose tall black headdresses had made them appear much larger than they really were, came forward unarmed to deliver presents of food, feathers, and necklaces. The women piteously shrieked and cried.

"Please, please, Captain, let us show them how to pray!" Chaplain Fletcher declared. He leaped to his feet and waved his arms to encourage the reluctant crew members to bellow a prayer.

The native visitors listened politely. "Oh!" they shouted with approbation.

Chaplain Fletcher's face glowed. "I think these savages could be saved!"

"Gnaah! Gnaah!" the visitors boomed.

"They want more," Chaplain Fletcher announced. "Let us give them Psalms!"

With warlike gusto, the captain and crew recited prayers and Bible chapters—those they knew by heart and those they simply pretended they knew.

"Oh! Oh!" the visitors called. *"Gnaah! Gnaah!"*

"Hymns now. Ready? Sing!" Chaplain Fletcher looked out over the crowd with the same kind of joy Captain Drake showed when he counted piles of doubloons.

The crew members roared hymns off-key. "Oh! Oh!" The crowd went wild with delight. In spite of Captain Drake's entreaties, they refused to take any of the gifts offered by the crew before they departed.

Three days later the largest crowd yet assembled on the hills and along the beach. Completely outnumbered, the crew members watched nervously as a man approached carrying a tall black pole tied at the end with long looped strings decorated with shell disk beads and colored feathers. Behind him marched nearly one hundred guards, and tall men wearing fur capes, dozens of disk-bead necklaces, and net caps decorated with feathers. They surrounded the man who appeared to be their leader. He wore a waist-length coat of white fur, and on his head he wore a black feather crown.

In the rear followed men and women and children. The adults, painted in black and white, were adorned with feathers tufted like horns in their hair. Each woman carried an ornate basket filled with a kind of bread made from ground roots, broiled fish, and the seed and down of milkweed. After chanting and singing, the native leader's retinue hung shell necklaces around the neck of Captain Drake. They crowned him with a bunch of feathers and called him "Hióh!"

"A comely name," the captain told Emmet, who stood beside him in the throng. "I suppose it means 'God.' How do I look?"

"Very well, sir," said Emmet, who turned away to hide his smile.

"I think they've given up their kingdom to you, your grace," Chaplain Fletcher said, bowing low. "They wish to be your vassals."

The captain beamed. "Vassals! Tut-tut. They are my devoted subjects here in New Albion, nothing less."

"Gnaah! Gnaah!" the crowd shouted.

Captain Drake ordered his crew to sing. Emmet played his lute, and another sailor beat upon the tabor to much acclaim. As soon as the music ended, the rest of the native people presented gifts. While keeping a certain distance, they swarmed around crew members and wailed with sadness.

"Nocáto mu! Nocáto mu!" they warned as Emmet tried to wriggle past them.

Before Emmet could extricate himself a new mob of moaning, weeping men and women surrounded him with beseeching tears.

They called to him as if they knew him. No matter how hard he attempted to avoid them, they followed him, calling out names, tearing their faces. "I'm sorry. I'm sorry," he insisted. Sweat poured down his arms. "I don't know who you are."

"Shove off!" Flea shouted, and tried to break away from the wailing circle. "I ain't your long-lost relation."

Frantically Emmet gazed at the swirling mass of humanity. The sailors—wan, disheveled, dirty, grizzled—appeared as insubstantial as ghosts as they bobbed among the robust natives.

"Ain't dead yet!" Flea complained. "Let a fellow breathe."

Emmet too struggled beyond the web of arms and legs. *They think I'm a ghost.* The thought was chilling. *Perhaps they're right. Perhaps we're all dead.*

For what seemed hours, Emmet and the crew members were besieged by distraught natives. The most youthful crew members seemed to be the most frequently targeted. And then slowly the noise lessened to a dull roar. The native men and women pushed around Emmet now with new demands. "What is it? What do you want?" Emmet asked. They held out gnarled hands and twisted, sore feet. They displayed ulcers on their necks and pointed to scars on their ribs.

"I ain't no barber-surgeon!" Flea called.

Every so often an ancient man or woman would make a desperate demonstration. They would press their lips against their own wounds or broken bones and make a little blowing noise with their mouths, as if to show how they might be cured.

Emmet shrank back in horror. He was no cunning man. He was a fake, a fraud. *Can they not tell?*

Still the blur of suffering swam around him. In the dizzy

flood of begging voices and maimed bodies Emmet heard Father Parfoothe's voice. "They cannot heal such as do not believe in them."

"Easy, easy, mate!" Flea shouted in desperation. He made a little puff of breath on a man's twisted wrist. "Here's your touch. Now you're whole. Who's next?"

Besieged by so much suffering, Emmet did not know what to do. A stubborn young man pointed to the pussy boil on his shoulder.

"Sorry," Emmet said in a low voice.

The insistent man pointed and gestured.

"Sorry. I really can't help you."

The man refused to move from Emmet's path.

Emmet sighed. He closed his eyes and mumbled the chant he knew best:

> "*Adder, adder, adder, lay under a stone or hole*
> *he hath done this man wrong. I fold, two fold, three fold,*
> *in the name of the Father and of the Son.*
> *So let this sting pass away from this wretched man if the*
> *Lord please. Amen.*"

The man still would not budge. "All right, then," Emmet said. Reluctantly he whistled a puff of air onto the man's boil. His patient smiled and walked away.

"Think you're the only one who can conjure among us!" Flea shouted to Emmet. He made an elaborate motion over the head of a woman.

We are all conjurers now.

Chapter Twenty-One

15 July

M not allowed to step ashore from frigate. This vexes
her. When I bring her fresh broiled fish to eat, I
describe the People of the Country and their lamentable
manner, how they treat us as if we are dead men. She
only laughs at me saying, "Such wise folk!" The Sailors
ignore her now that there is freedom onshore. Empty
bellies, cold, wetness, hopelessness on board ship
forgotten, and the sailor does what he does best: being
happy by the month.

Out in the harbor, the *Golden Hind* and the frigate stood at
anchor. Barrels of dried fish and meat, mended sail and rigging
had been stowed below in preparation for departure. To make
certain there would be enough provisions, Emmet was among
a dozen crew members sent inland into the forested hills to
hunt for what the natives called *tante*, a creature with hooves
and horns they described in exaggerated sign language. "Some
kind of stag, perhaps," Moone announced.

The captain, clearly impatient to begin their South Sea
crossing, ordered the hunters to bring back as much fresh game
as they could carry.

Emmet had little experience as a bowhunter but felt delighted
to be included in the overland expedition led by one of the native
men. This was Emmet's first chance to see what lay beyond the
dark ridge of trees.

The hunting party left early in the morning with bows, nets, quivers of arrows, harquebus, and swords. Their native guide, whom the mariners nicknamed Shellback, wore no clothing. He laughed when he saw how much equipment the sailors had packed upon their backs. The only thing Shellback carried was his small, light bow and a quiver of arrows. Minutes after beginning to trudge up the hilly trail, the swift guide was already out of sight.

"Our pilot's marooned us," grumbled Moone. Like the rest of the able seamen, he was no great hiker.

"Quit your growling," replied Sky, who had begun to limp. "You came aboard willingly. You can only blame yourself for selling a farm and going to sea."

Emmet brought up the rear of the line so that he did not have to worry about having Sky or Moone at his back. Although they had not bothered him since the foggy-harbor incident, he was taking no chances. Slowly the crash of surf behind them became fainter. A raven croaked overhead. Hidden birds called from low bushes. As the path zigzagged along a ridge, the trees became taller. The cool air smelled fragrant with pine and madrone. Branches creaked in the wind.

Stepping inside the shade of woods seemed to Emmet strange and familiar at the same time. When was the last time he had been able to look up and watch the shift of sunlight-dappled leaves? Before the voyage. A lifetime away. He could hardly remember that boy he used to be. In spite of the beauty around him, he felt a lump in his throat.

"Tumble up!" Sky shouted.

Emmet hurried to catch up with the others. A cloud of mist

had settled along the ridge. They seemed to hike for miles as the trail meandered among laurel, willow, and bay trees dripping with moisture. When they reached a cluster of oaks, they saw a meadow in the distance. Children's shouts, singing, and voices echoed. There was the steady *clink-click-clink* that reminded Emmet of the Tavistock blacksmith. The air smelled of cooking fires and something nutty and sweet, like the roasted chestnuts he recalled peddlers selling on market days.

The sailors stepped from the darkness of the trees into the bright sunlight and discovered a village of about a dozen rounded houses that seemed to Emmet to be haystacks with door flaps. The walls were made from overlapped bunches of reeds tied in bundles. In the center was a low dirt-covered house with smoke curling from a hole in the roof.

"There's Shellback," Moone said, pointing. He leaned wearily on his bow.

Their guide spoke to another native man, who seemed to find the sight of the exhausted hunting party amusing. Curious villagers, some carrying baskets of acorns or bundles of dried fish, wandered past. Under a nearby canopy made from leaves and sticks an old woman sat cross-legged on a mat, weaving a basket with red feathers and grass. She looked up and smiled a toothless smile at them. A child dodged past. Then another. Beside a camp-fire a woman lifted a stone pestle and brought it down heavily on something white inside a stone bowl. *Thud, thud, thud.*

No one in the village seemed surprised to see the sailors. Unlike at the first encounter, the native people did not appear alarmed or mournful. They kept their distance, however, and appeared shy. For some reason only the children were truly fearless in the men's presence, as if they alone understood that their white visitors were not ghosts.

While Shellback appeared to be busy gossiping and Moone and the others were nursing their sore feet, Emmet strolled among the houses. A woman stirred the ashes of a fire. She poked a rock from the ashes and dumped it into a basket bubbling with something that looked like porridge. An old man squatted on his haunches and flaked an arrow-shaped point from a shining black rock.

Everywhere Emmet went he saw that the people had no metal. They owned no iron cauldrons or knives or spoons. No cloth, no pottery, no books. There was no gold here, no silver. No guns. No churches. No bells to ring the time. No prisons, no gallows, no government. And yet they seemed happy. They seemed peaceful. No one fought. No one argued. No one threatened each other.

The more Emmet wandered, the more amazed he felt. Here was a people who seemed, at first glance, to be of a tractable, free, and loving nature. *Without guile or treachery.*

He paused and watched a young boy blowing a whistle made from what looked like two short white bones tied together. The boy grinned. He hid the whistle behind his back. Emmet pointed to his left arm. The boy shook his head. Emmet pointed to his right arm. The boy laughed and gave Emmet the whistle to try. He put it to his lips, placed his fingers over the holes, and tried to make a little melody. The boy clapped his hands. "Oh!" he shouted.

Emmet smiled, returned the whistle. *"Gnaah!"*

The boy exclaimed with delight, as if surprised that this

stranger might know a familiar word. With gusto he played another tune. Then he stood and took Emmet by the wrist. He led him to one of the haystack houses and lifted the flap.

Emmet had to bend over to peer inside into the darkness. Not wishing to be rude, he crawled in and the little boy followed. A small smoky fire burned in the middle of the dirt floor that had been strewn with rushes. It took a few moments for Emmet's eyes to become accustomed to the lack of light.

Sitting on the other side of the fire, cross-legged on a mat, was a woman with a kind of cape around her shoulders. Her dark matted hair hung about her face. When she saw Emmet and the little boy enter, she looked up and said a word that Emmet could barely hear. The little boy turned to Emmet and tugged on his wrist and said, *"Huchee kecharoh."* The boy motioned for Emmet to take a seat.

"I really should be going," Emmet said shyly. He knew the others would wonder where he was and what had happened to him. But the woman was insistent, and she handed him a small round basket containing what looked like a piece of bread. Not wishing to offend her, he sat down and nibbled the bitter bread. "Delicious," he said. "Thank you so much."

The woman watched him eat and began to cry. Nervously Emmet scooped up the last of the crumbs. Had he done something wrong? He could not tell. What should he say? What should he do?

"Tcipa. Tcipa," she repeated, wiping her eyes with the heel of her hand. The little boy broke off another chunk of bread from a big basket and waved away the flies. He smiled at Emmet and handed it to him.

Gingerly Emmet kept eating. The woman cried and murmured. She was telling Emmet something. A story perhaps. He listened carefully, trying to see her face in the darkness. Every so often she would sob and pull on her hair. She glanced up at him as if he must understand.

Emmet anxiously cleared his throat. After so many similar encounters, he sensed that she too was speaking to him as if he were the ghost of someone beloved. A lost relative perhaps. He tried to remember how Father Parfoothe had listened when a homeless widow or the desperate father of an ailing child came to him to tell their stories. Father Parfoothe never interrupted. He never turned them away. He sat very still, Emmet remembered, and he focused on their faces. Quietly, carefully, he listened to their words and to their silence. Emmet tried his best to do the same.

Finally the native woman was finished.

"I am so sorry. I am so sorry," he murmured. What else could he do? He shot a glance at the little boy, who was lacing a kind of string around his dirty toes. In the half-light the boy's profile reminded him of something he had tried so hard to forget. The boy beneath the bell tower. A fly buzzed. In the smoky darkness Emmet spoke. She looked at him expectantly.

"I am so sorry. I am so sorry," he began. And then without meaning to really, he began to tell his own story. The story of who he had once been back in Tavistock. He told her of his voyage to this place. He spoke of Doughty's betrayal, Diego's death, and da Silva's banishment. He told her what he had done, and how ashamed he felt. He described his participation in the stealing, fires, shooting, and death of the innocent boy beneath the bell tower. He spoke of his guilt, his fears, his sorrows, his loneliness, and how he could never go home again.

And when he was finished, she looked at him intently, as if she were still listening. She wiped her tears from her cheeks. *"Hodeli oh heigh oh heigh ho hodali oh,"* she sang softly in a mournful voice.

Emmet was glad it was dark and she could not see the tears streaming down his face. "Thank you," he said, and quickly wiped his eyes with his shirt. He wished he could stay in this peaceful place forever. But he knew that the others were outside waiting for him. "Thank you," he said again. He stood, opened the flap, and crawled back into the bright sunlight. He had lost track of time. How long had he been gone? He staggered to pick up his bow.

"Up keeleg!" Sky hollered.

Two of the others hooted and waved.

"Hope you had a pleasant time with that woman!" Moone said, and gave Emmet a hard jab in the ribs with his elbow.

Emmet blushed, not willing to explain. *Let them think what they like.* He followed the others trekking behind their guide. The trail zigzagged among trees up a ridge, then skirted another meadow. Exhausted and discouraged, the men slumped onto fallen logs beside the clearing. Suddenly Emmet was aware of a terrible shaking beneath his feet. The ground trembled as if it might explode.

A great blur of enormous brown bodies thundered through the meadow. The huge animals leaped and jostled. The tips of their antlers loomed twice as tall as man. Never before had any of the hunters seen anything like these beasts.

"God's wounds!" Moone whispered. "Nothing like the puny stags back home."

Moone and the others strung their bows and aimed. Even as

the arrows zipped through the air and thudded into their targets, more beasts poured through the woods. A river of thundering, snorting animals, eyes flashing, antlers clattering against each other. Emmet stared, openmouthed, unable to move. And after what seemed like hours, the herd vanished.

Moone and the others whooped with delight. They hurried out into the meadow to examine their kills. "Come along, soger," Moone said to Emmet.

Emmet stood transfixed, barely breathing. His bow hung at his side. Not once had he shot an arrow. At that moment he could not imagine killing any creature ever again.

Transporting the carcasses required several trips back and forth from the clearing to the harbor. The crew members enlisted the help of several strong native men, who lashed together long branches and dragged one end to haul the game.

After the last carcass had been carted down the trail, Emmet was given the task of carrying four bows back to the fortification on the beach. Each bow weighed nearly thirty pounds. The other mariners had been too preoccupied with their hunting triumph to warn him not to dawdle. Emmet paused every so often along the trail. He was in no hurry to return. This was the most peaceful day he'd known since he'd left Tavistock. For a moment he closed his eyes and listened to the whispering of the trees.

Something flickered atop his hand. A white moth perched on his knuckle, opening and shutting its delicate wings. "Good morrow, pysgy," Emmet whispered. Back home white moths were said to transform themselves into small, trooping fairies at twilight. Emmet had never seen such a thing with his own eyes.

Perhaps if he were very quiet, very attentive, he'd have his chance.

He watched carefully as the moth flitted to a nearby tree branch. Abandoning the bows in a heap, he crept toward the moth. The white winged shape flew atop a low hill, then vanished. When Emmet came closer he saw that vines and ferns concealed a hole as big as a barrel top. Protruding from this hole was the end of a stout log stripped of bark and carved with a large notch. Emmet moved his hand farther down the log and felt another evenly spaced notch. Then another. *Odd.* This carving was clearly the work of someone who knew how to use an adze, or perhaps an ax. He studied the log and decided it must be a kind of ladder. Where did it lead?

He pulled more leaves away from the mouth of the hole. Poking out in a pattern were the butt ends of logs—none very old or decayed—that seemed to have been arranged and then covered with dirt. Perhaps this had once been the sturdy roof of someone's home—similar to the earth-covered dwelling he'd seen earlier in the village.

"Hello?" Emmet called down.

No one answered.

He stuck his head into the entrance. Six or seven feet below, he glimpsed what looked like a hard-packed dirt floor. The only way he was going to find out what was down there was to climb below. What was so difficult about that? The place didn't appear any darker than the hold of the ship. Inspired, he sat on the edge of the opening and stuck his feet and legs into the roof entrance. Slowly he lowered himself down the log ladder.

The damp earth around him had the same pungent odor as Grandmother's cellar. When he reached the bottom he held the ladder with one hand and extended the other outward as far as he could reach to try to feel any solid walls. He could reach nothing in any direction. The underground house was much bigger than he'd expected. How many families once lived, cooked, and slept here? He sniffed the faint scent of wood smoke.

In the darkness he heard what sounded like dribbling bits of loose dirt shifting and falling. He wished he had a torch so that he could see better. There was only a small circle of light coming through the roof entrance. The walls, he suspected, were like the roof—made of logs lined with packed dirt. An ideal location for snakes to nap. His pet adder would have loved this house, he thought. *The perfect place to hide.*

He took a deep breath and considered a new and startling idea. What if he hid here? No search party would ever find him in this underground place. After the ships left without him, he'd emerge into the light—a new beginning in a peaceful new world. He'd make a go of it, alive—himself again. Free-willed again.

His heart beat in his throat. It might work. What did he have to lose? The risks of an unknown shore had to be better than continued hardships of a voyage with a madman captain and a cutthroat crew.

Confidently he pulled himself up the ladder. As he scrambled to gather the bows and head back to the beach, he looked around to memorize landmarks so that he would be able to find this place again. Three pines beside a boulder, a toppled chestnut limb, a—

Crack! A branch broke.

Emmet froze. He scanned nearby shadows for movement, for

the flash of eyes. He was sure it was nothing more than one of those bold coneys with long tails they had seen everywhere. He listened intently for scurrying but heard nothing.

Just my imagination. He swung two bows over each shoulder and headed down the path.

Chapter Twenty-Two

On the beach Emmet immediately sensed that something was wrong. Over and over again the trumpeter blasted an alert. The pinnace had been rowed out into the bay. Natives in a battalion of reed canoes patrolled the shoreline. As Emmet hurried to the fortifications where he saw the other crew members assembling, he spied the gleam of the captain's distinctive silver helmet.

"All hands!" the bosun shouted.

"Flea, what's happened?" Emmet asked, out of breath.

"Runaways," Flea replied somberly. "Captain's going to hold their chief hostage till the deserters are found and brought back."

Anxiously Emmet scanned the crowd to see who might be missing. Somehow he felt he'd been cheated. *Lucky fellows. I should be gone too.*

The captain thumped the side of a barrel to get the crew's attention. "We need every hand to make it back to England, so that you scum can enjoy your treasure," Captain Drake announced.

"Aye, aye, sir!" the men replied in uneasy unison. For once the mention of reward did not seem to have its usual energizing effect.

"July is well advanced. Sailing season for the Spice Islands is upon us now. Every day wasted here," the captain continued, "means we run the risk of being trapped in typhoon season on the other side. The deserters must be found by nightfall. There'll be no holding on to the slack. No idlers here. Do I make myself clear?"

"Aye, aye, sir!" Slowly the crew went back to work loading the ship and bark with supplies.

"Typhoon, says he?" one sailor grumbled in a low voice.

"First we have to survive crossing the South Sea," another replied. "That's danger enough."

Emmet helped Flea roll barrels of dried salted fish to the water's edge. "Who's run off?" he asked, trying to sound as if he did not much care.

"They say the wench is among the ones that got away. That's the rumor."

"Maria?" Emmet asked in disbelief. "How?"

Flea shrugged. "A couple of gunner's mates stole a canoe before sunrise. Perhaps she bribed them. All three's gone."

Emmet felt too stunned to speak. Who would have guessed? *Maria!* Never before had he so admired her cleverness. If she could run away, why couldn't he?

"It's a big country, ain't it?" Flea squinted in the direction of the fog-covered hills. "Easy to get lost in such a place."

"Not if you keep your wits about you," Emmet replied slowly. Maybe Maria and the other runaways had the right idea. By leaving together they could help each other. "Plenty of game up there. I've seen the herds myself. A fellow could live like a king."

Flea glanced nervously over his shoulder. The rest of the men were too far away to hear their conversation. Even so, Flea made a great pretense of checking a barrel stave. "What about a fellow's treasure share?"

"Who's to say the ship will make it back? Even if it does, who's to say the captain will keep his word about dividing the spoils?"

Flea nodded. Clearly these ideas had crossed his mind too. "When would a fellow make a run for it, if he were to be so bold to try?"

Emmet searched Flea's broad, expectant face. He could be trusted, couldn't he? He was a loyal friend, a steady worker, and handy with tools. Not much of a shot, but he could build almost anything with wood. He had good reason to risk a venture that might mean his own freedom—away from the torment of Sky and the others. If anyone was going to join him, he thought, it would be Flea. "Tomorrow at dawn," Emmet said in a low voice. "Meet at the path on the way up into the hills. You know the place?"

Flea nodded.

"You must swear on your mother's life you will not tell a soul."

"I swear," Flea said in a solemn voice. He promised to filch a few tools and perhaps a weapon if he could manage to open the carpenter's chest unnoticed.

Emmet felt a surge of hope. Perhaps his scheme would work. Perhaps they would escape.

Suddenly from across the beach came a chilling bellow. "Page!" Captain Drake shouted.

"Tomorrow, then," Emmet murmured to Flea, and hurried to the captain.

"Can you not see this needs polishing?" Captain Drake angrily thrust the silver helmet in Emmet's direction. Emmet could barely look at the captain's face for fear he might be able to read his mind. "And I have other tasks for you as well. Walk with me up the beach, away from the others."

Emmet reluctantly followed the limping captain along the water's edge, where there were no sailors within earshot. Emmet felt a rising sense of dread.

"I am," Captain Drake began slowly, "an earnest man who has never been lucky enough to enjoy an easy life. I've been through the mill, ground, and bolted."

"Yes, sir."

"My father abandoned my brothers and me when we were very young. 'The priest's bastards'—that's what they called us when we were driven from our home. Do you know how much shame there was in that? I can hardly tell you." He paused and glanced out to sea.

Emmet squirmed and tried to imagine the captain as a boy, homeless and humiliated. *Not so different from me.* He wondered if he had ever overheard Grandmother tell the unsavory story of Uncle Edmund's children—"the priest's bastards."

"After my father vanished," the captain continued, "a rider came to Tavistock. He carried in a sack the remains of a charred leg. I was eight years old that summer. We all had to look at the thing swinging on a rope from a tree in the middle of the village. The lord's men made everyone in Tavistock file past. It was, they said, a kind of warning. What remained of a Catholic rebel who had been drawn and quartered after the uprising against the Crown's church." Captain Drake paused and chuckled. "I wasn't afraid to look upon that foot. I was glad to see such a thing. Do you know why?"

"No, sir."

"I believed it belonged to my father."

"Yes, sir." Emmet gulped.

"I have never flinched from the use of power to best grieve my enemies."

"Yes, sir."

Captain Drake turned and placed a heavy hand on Emmet's shoulder. "And that is why I am commanding you to your duty."

"Yes, sir?" Emmet asked weakly.

The captain motioned at the scene on the beach. Sailors and native people mingled around a cooking fire. Boxes and barrels were piled haphazardly in heaps. "You can see that the men are growing comfortable here. They are stiff-necked as stubborn horses and must be broken to put back on their harnesses again. As for these simple people, they will one day be the Queen's subjects and must also learn to work profitably to earn her protection." He paused and motioned toward the bark bobbing in the harbor. "And there are other stubborn creatures that must be brought to an understanding as well. An understanding of who is in control."

"I'm afraid, sir," Emmet said in confusion, "I do not know who you mean."

"I mean," the captain said impatiently, "the wench."

"Yes, sir." Emmet winced.

"I'll speak plain. Tomorrow morning before we sail I will assemble the crew and the people. I want you to use *The Key of Solomon* to do my bidding."

"But, sir—"

"I am master here. And I'll suffer no mutiny from crew or subjects or that woman, when I am so close to my goal of returning to England richer than any nobleman in the realm."

"Sir, I—"

Captain Drake gripped his shoulder until it ached. "You have the skills to gain wealth, love, and power, do you not? I have seen you perform in the past with remarkable results."

"The truth is, sir, I—"

"Do you fancy your legs?"

"My legs, sir?" Emmet spoke in barely a whisper.

"I pray you fancy your legs strong and healthy and attached to your body, do you not? Not dangling charred from a tree. Not swinging from a rope. Answer me: Do you fancy your legs?"

Emmet nodded.

"Then you will do as I command."

Before sundown the native searchers brought back to the fortifications the runaways, who had been easily discovered a mile inland in one of the villages. The two gunner's mates' hands were tied to a long vine, and they were led along the path to the beach. Maria, who had apparently convinced the two men to secretly take her by canoe to shore, seemed as unrepentant and indomitable as ever.

Her hair stood up in wild tufts, and her clothing was torn and dirty. She moved heavily, wrapped in a large piece of old sail draped around her shoulders. As she approached the captain she spat. In one swift movement he slapped her face. "Take her to the frigate and bind her well so that she does not escape again,"

Captain Drake ordered. His voice shook with anger.

The crew was ordered to stand at attention on the beach and watch the two gunner's mates as they were severely flogged.

"Changed my mind," Flea hissed at Emmet, as they watched the two bloody mates herded onto the pinnace. They were to be rowed across the harbor to be locked up in the hold of the *Golden Hind.*

"You won't even try?" Emmet whispered.

Flea shook his head. "Look what happened to them."

Emmet sighed. Their escape seemed impossible now. He could not argue with Flea. Emmet had not told him about the assembly tomorrow on the beach, or mentioned what the captain meant to do with the book. Captain Drake would be watching Emmet like a hawk until then. How could he ever slip away unnoticed?

That evening Emmet rowed to the frigate to deliver the sailing instructions from the captain for the master. He crossed the harbor, pulling hard against the oars. Once, long ago, he would not have been able to row alone this far without pausing and resting. Now he pushed against the splintered oar handles with strengthened muscles in his back and arms. He did not notice any exhaustion. His hands were so calloused they no longer blistered.

To move was a relief for him. He could not stand to be trapped another moment on the *Golden Hind* as he waited for his own execution in the morning. On deck he knew the captain was watching him with his spyglass. Emmet felt as trapped as one of the deer stampeding through the woods into the hunters' ambush.

The air felt cool against his flushed face. He tucked the rolled parchment in his belt and climbed aboard the frigate, which appeared strangely empty. A swivel gun had been lashed to the deck. Emmet pulled on the door of what had once been the modest captain's cabin.

"Who do you seek, Horse Marine?" Hawkins demanded in a slurred voice. He waved a pistol in the air. "Nobody in there. That's powder magazine now. Captain's orders. Keep out. State your business."

"I've come for the master to give him sailing instructions from Captain."

Hawkins chuckled. "He's busy. Last minute farewells onshore. Leave the writing with me. I'll give it to him."

Emmet shook his head. "I was told by Captain Drake to give it to the master directly. I'll wait."

"Suit yourself," Hawkins replied. He replaced his pistol in his belt and took a seat in the bow. He uncorked a leather bottle. "Drink?"

To be friendly Emmet took a swig, wiped his mouth with the back of his hand, and handed the bottle back to Hawkins. The shore had turned so dark with shadows that only the outline of hills was visible in the distance.

"I'm going below," Emmet said in as casual a voice as he could muster. Quickly he lowered himself down the hatchway. A covered lantern hung from the low ceiling. The frigate seemed so small it looked as if it might only hold two dozen people at the most. He wondered how it might make the long crossing ahead. If anything happened to the *Golden Hind*, the frigate would be their only means of rescue.

"Maria?" Emmet called softly. He searched the dark shadows of the hold. The covered candle threw off faint flickering light. He found a pile of boxes and bales, and three or four chests with stout iron locks. The hold was crammed with what Emmet immediately recognized as some of the choice treasure Captain Drake had reserved for himself.

Among the loot was the fancy carved chest from the cabin, which had been moved into the frigate after the careening of the *Golden Hind.* Emmet fingered the carving on the chest, wondering how anxious and fearful the captain had become. Perhaps he intended to move the chest back to the bigger ship in the morning. He yanked on the lock. The last place he'd seen *The Key of Solomon* was in this chest. Of course, it was possible the captain may have moved it, too. He seemed obsessed with arranging and rearranging his treasure, counting and recounting doubloons as if he were certain someone may have stolen something.

"Won't open without a key."

Startled, Emmet saw Maria peering at him from the shadows. Had anyone bothered to give her any food or drink since she'd been captured in the woods?

"Do you have your knife?" she demanded.

Emmet knew her tricks. "I can get you some water. Maybe some meat."

"*Ayúdame, por favor.* I'll make bargain with you." She sounded desperate.

Emmet sighed, glad that he had not told her of his plan to escape. To involve her in any way would only mean disaster. "What kind of bargain?"

"I'll give you key to that chest if you cut me free."

The key! If he could open the chest, perhaps he could throw over-board the book, the wand, and the crystal. They'd be gone forever. He might be blamed for their disappearance. He might be punished. But even two dozen lashes would be preferable to spending the rest of the voyage forced by the captain to do the impossible.

"There's not much time. *¡Pronto!*" She held out her hands, which had been tied to a thick rope. He took his knife and sliced the knot that held her prisoner. She handed him the key that she'd hidden inside her dress, around her neck on a string.

Desperately he turned the key back and forth in the lock. "Doesn't work."

"Let me try," she said. She too struggled with the lock. "Perhaps I stole the wrong key."

Emmet kicked the chest in frustration. "I am supposed to perform a ceremony in the morning before we set sail. The captain wants me to use the book of magic to conjure demons and give him powers over the crew, over the people. Over you."

Maria laughed bitterly. "What you fear most? Being humiliated for not making magic, or doing something you know is wrong?"

Emmet kicked the chest harder this time. He wished she would stop making fun of him.

"We are alike, you and I," she said. "We are both shams. You are no conjurer. And I am no pirate *puta*. Perhaps, *amigo*, we should help each other."

"Will you keep your voice down?" Emmet whispered. "Why should I help you? Look what happened to the two fellows who risked their lives for you. They were nearly beaten to death. Trouble, that's what you are. Stay away from me, Maria. I don't need your help."

Maria made a spitting noise. "Those men, they had no heart for freedom. They were cowards," she whispered. "Not like me. I'll do anything. Anything at all to get my freedom."

"Anything?" Emmet studied her nervously. Didn't she realize she might be killed? He couldn't bear to think of that.

"The captain believes he can carry me to sea again by force. I will never go. Soon I shall be mother of the child of *caballero*," she said with pride in her voice. "My baby will be free."

Emmet was too stunned to speak. *De Zarate's child.*

"Will you help me?" she whispered. *"Ayúdame, por favor."*

Above them on deck came the sound of muffled greetings, footsteps, and the clunk of a paddle. The master had returned in a native's canoe. If Emmet were identified as the person who set Maria free, he'd be hung for certain. "The captain awaits my return," Emmet said, and averted his eyes from her desperate face. "I must go."

Before she could bewitch him with another word—another impossible, dangerous demand—he hurried up the ladder. He had done all that he could do to save her. Besides, what was she to him? A great weight around his neck. She made him feel guilty with her honesty, her accusations, her story about being with child. How did he know that what she'd said wasn't another one of her tricks?

After presenting the master with his sailing instructions, Emmet hurried into the longboat. As soon as he pulled the oars and felt himself gliding away from the frigate and from Maria, he made up his mind. Tonight, he decided, he would flee. Alone. He'd never see her again. He'd never have to feel guilty again. He was going. She was nothing to him. Nothing.

He paused as a dozen natives in canoes cruised past on their way between the beach and the *Golden Hind.* Some transported mariners, who waved and sang drunkenly. Others carried gifts of fish and furs. In so much confusion back and forth across the bay, who would notice the disappearance of one canoe? Emmet would simply wait for a native to moor beside the ship and come aboard. Then Emmet would borrow his canoe, paddle across the harbor in the darkness, and take his chances onshore.

Chapter Twenty-Three

Constellations climbed the sky. Emmet ducked inside the darkness of pines along the shore. He had abandoned the canoe along the beach, past the place where the bonfires burned and the sailors drank and celebrated their last evening in New Albion. The late-summer night was filled with moonlight and laughter and singing and the stink of burned feathers—some kind of native offering for their departure. Canoes continued to shuttle back and forth between the ship and the beach. In the chaos it had been surprisingly easy to slip away unnoticed. Especially after the captain passed out at the table from drinking too much wine.

After so many hours of anxious anticipation and preparation, Emmet felt calm. He did not know why. In the distance he could hear the rush and crash and hiss of waves. Farther out in the harbor bobbed the *Golden Hind*, his home for almost two years, and his last contact with England. He was never going back.

Emmet regretted not being able to say good-bye to Flea. *Too dangerous.* He shifted the satchel containing a flint to build a fire, an extra shirt, a leather bottle of water, a few salted fish wrapped in a piece of cloth. Everything else he had left behind: his precious lute, his drawings. Even his secret journal. Those were part of his past life, he told himself. Where he was going he had to travel without any encumbrances.

He turned and entered the woods.

While the moonlight allowed him to see his way, the illumination also made his detection by others a distinct possibility. He broke into a steady run. With all his might he tried to move as silently as possible.

Wind moaned. He slunk into a shadow and held perfectly still. When his heart stopped pounding, he noticed that the woods seemed alive with twitters, rustles, and thumps. He held perfectly still and listened to the footsteps of a large creature. Was it a prowling bear or a hungry wolf? He'd heard of such things from the other sailors. What would he do if he met such a beast? He had no gun, no sword. Only the dagger in his belt.

Without meaning to, he softly chanted the protection against rats and vermin. "As I will, so mote it be." As he said these final words, he heard Father Parfoothe's voice telling him, "No animal falters but knows what it must do."

"Such advice does me no good here, sir," Emmet whispered. "Defenseless and alone." He wished he'd brought along a pistol. He wished Flea were here with him. Another's voice would surely calm his wild heart.

A howl pierced the air.

Emmet started. The high-pitched cry sounded almost human. Was someone following him?

Cautiously he stepped out of the shadows and bolted up the trail. Another curve, another hill, another boulder. He had to remember where his hiding place was, but everything looked so different in the moonlight. Trees seemed larger, thicker, more menacing. What if he could not find the deserted dwelling again?

Another hill, another dip in the trail. He thought he recalled this stretch. Yes, there was the boulder, green-gray and glinting in the moonlight. And the three trees.

Voices! Emmet froze. In the distance rumbled the sound of men speaking. They seemed to be coming this way.

"Aye . . . and what of it?"

"Your share, man. Don't forget—"

Any moment the mariners would see him. He'd be dragged back to the ship and punished as a deserter.

Overhead a startling pale motion luffed like a topgallant. *Whoosh. Whoosh.* An enormous bird with riveting golden eyes stared at Emmet, then vanished in a graceful swoop of wings.

There!

Emmet spied the small low hill that resembled a sleeping animal. Desperately he scrambled up the side, grasped the carved log ladder, and nearly fell most of the way inside into the darkness.

He crouched, listening, as the voices grew louder, louder. He kept one hand on the ladder, one hand on the soft, damp ground. A pool of exquisite moonlight illuminated his hands. Never before had he felt quite so alive. *Any moment, any moment,* he told himself, *I'll be found.*

But the voices began to fade now. And soon he could hear nothing except the rasping rhythm of his own breathing. *Safe!* The very ground, the shadows, the smell of dirt seemed intoxicating. He was still alive!

Delighted by his good fortune, he curled into a contented ball, with his satchel as a pillow. He closed his eyes. And just as he was about to drift into sleep he heard a sneeze.

It was small and muffled, but the sneeze was most certainly human. And it had come only a few feet from his head.

Within an instant Emmet was on his feet. He whirled, knife in hand. "Who's there?" he hissed. Something rustled. In the far dark recesses of the house he thought he heard someone whimper, as if in pain.

"Be quiet, *por favor,*" a voice begged.

"Maria?" A terrible chill clutched Emmet. All his plans for freedom—all dashed. He was doomed. For several moments he did not speak. What should he do? "Who else knows about this place?" he finally managed.

"No one," she said. Her breathing sounded ragged. Every so often she made a low groan.

"Are you sick?"

"No. *Estoy bien.*"

"Did anyone see you on the path? Did anyone from the ship follow you?"

"No se," she mumbled. "I came in the water, kicking beside an empty canoe."

"Take this dry shirt." Emmet pulled a shirt from the satchel and threw it in the direction of her voice. "You're ruining everything," he said bitterly. "How did you find this place?"

"The gunner's mates abandon me on shore. On my own I follow you."

Of course. The noise in the woods. Now what was he going to do? He crouched, shivering. *Think!*

The ground rumbled. In the distance an explosion boomed like thunder.

"Bueno!" Maria said in a low voice. "It is done."

"What?" Emmet whispered, certain the sound must be from a Spanish ship's cannon.

"Frigate exploded," she said softly. "I set slow fuse."

"You?" he said with disbelief.

"By now Captain must notice missing key to powder magazine." She chuckled, then made another wincing groan.

Emmet scurried up the ladder, then climbed a tree to see for himself. The tree was not tall enough. The harbor was too far away. He climbed down and crept through the woods as close as he dared to a high ridge. He climbed another, taller tree. As the pine bent in the wind, he saw in the distance flames shooting up from what had once been the frigate.

There was another loud blast as the rest of the gunpowder must have been ignited. Everything stored aboard would be destroyed—including the book, wand, crystal, and the rest of the captain's private treasure.

Emmet smiled and wished he could see the *Golden Hind* with a spyglass. He imagined the furious captain on deck bellowing orders. Calling all hands—

Emmet had a chilling thought. Once the men shouted out their names for the bosun, it wouldn't take Captain Drake much time to realize that his page—his archconjurer—was missing. How long, Emmet wondered, before a search party would be sent into the woods to look for him and any other deserters?

Emmet scrambled down the tree, then froze. Right now he knew he could save himself. There was still time. If he kept running alone, he could be miles inland before sunrise. He still had a chance. When he went to inspect the explosion, he'd left Maria the satchel with the water and food and flint. If she knew how to set a ship's gunpowder magazine afire with a slow fuse, she'd certainly be able to work a flint to start a cooking fire, wouldn't she? She was a resourceful woman.

Guns boomed to the west. Swiftly Emmet hiked the way he'd come. The sky was beginning to brighten. Nervously he broke into a run. He scurried along the ridge, then up another, past the boulder, past the three trees.

After running for a stretch he slowed to a trot, then to a walk. Then he stopped. He stood there, unable to move—unable to run away. Deep down, he knew, he could not leave Maria. If he did, for the rest of his life he'd be cursed by her haunting face, her anguished voice pleading for him to help her.

Emmet turned. He made his way along the trail again back to the hiding place, reworking his plan as he went. He'd have to find more water. They would have to remain completely silent. Perhaps the captain and the crew would not find them. Perhaps they'd give up. Emmet didn't feel as hopeful as he once had, but what could he do? If he abandoned her, he knew he would never feel truly free.

Gunfire echoed in the distance.

Emmet slipped down the ladder, careful to position the leaves and vines over the roof entrance. "Maria?" he called softly. He wished he had a candle, a torch. "Maria?"

No answer.

Emmet wondered if she might be sleeping. He moved slowly across the floor to the place where he had heard her voice.

"Maria?" He felt a foot, a leg. She was still here. *Good.*

Something mewled like a cat. "Maria?"

No answer.

Frantically Emmet scrambled up the ladder and found a small branch. He wrapped it with pine needles and moss and scrambled back down into the hiding place. His hands were shaking so badly that he could barely strike the flint properly to light the dried moss. Once, twice, three times he tried. Finally a spark jumped into the moss and began to burn. The pine needles curled and turned orange.

By the weak light he peered at Maria and saw that she seemed to be resting peacefully. Something squirmed beside her. Tiny arms flailed the air. The thing whimpered piteously. The terrible noise pierced Emmet's ears and his brain and filled him with dread.

"Maria!" Emmet said desperately. *God's eyes!* Why didn't she cover the thing? Why didn't she do something?

Guns grumbled again.

The torch began to smoke. The light and the terrible noise of the infant would surely give them away. He had to work quickly. Emmet held the flame aloft, just for a moment. "Maria!" he said urgently. He shook her arm.

Still she did not respond, even though she stared at him. Stared through him, her eyes glassy and faraway. He did not know how much time passed. A minute, an hour, a week. He felt numbness, then sorrow. He should have been here. He should have helped her. Instead she had been alone.

Gently he reached down the way he'd seen Father Parfoothe do a hundred times and closed her eyes. He said a small prayer.

All the while the baby, no bigger than Nipcheese, kept wailing. The little boy's skin was blotched and covered with blood from its birth. Somehow Maria had managed to cut the cord connecting her to her baby with her knife. Now what should he do? He felt paralyzed.

Emergency signal guns crackled three times in rapid succession. The familiar sound suddenly jolted Emmet into action. He was certain that at this very moment aboard the *Golden Hind* all hands were assembling under the hawklike eyes of the captain.

"Cousin," Emmet declared, and snuffed out the torch's flame, "don't look for me among your pirates." Even though Drake was too far away to hear him, saying the words gave Emmet a surprising pleasure. He felt as lightheaded and grateful as a man unexpectedly cured of a life-threatening snake bite. For the first time he felt truly free.

Now he knew what he must do.

Gently he picked up the slippery baby. The thing was so small that he worried it might wriggle from his hands and smash to pieces. "How you do squall with the fury of your mother!" Emmet whispered. To get a better grip he wrapped the bawling child in his extra shirt, still damp. Somehow the swaddling seemed to calm the infant. "Hush. There, now."

The newborn needed food, didn't he? Perhaps that was why he howled. Where would he find food a baby could eat? He was going to have to make a run for it. There was no time to linger here any longer. Not in the tomblike darkness, trapped with Maria's lifeless body. He'd rather try his chances aboveground.

He enfolded the baby in Maria's shawl and tenderly tucked him inside the satchel. "Do not cry, wee soger. You are free."

Emmet hung the satchel around his neck. "I will take good care of him," he whispered to Maria. Then he clambered up the ladder into the early dawn. The mist had begun to dwindle. Holding the precious satchel under one arm, he set out running into the wilderness of New Albion.

Afterword

After leaving New Albion the *Golden Hind* crossed the Pacific in sixty-eight days and arrived in the Indonesian archipelago, where Drake bargained for spices and silks. In spite of several near disasters with dangerous reefs and local political riots, the *Golden Hind* managed to successfully transport its heavy treasure westward across the Indian Ocean, around the Cape of Good Hope, and north along the coast of Africa.

When the *Golden Hind* and its surviving crew of fifty-nine men finally sailed into Plymouth harbor on 26 September 1580, Captain Drake had only one question for the first two Englishmen he met: "Is the queen still alive?"

Fortunately for Drake, the answer was yes.

Queen Elizabeth refused to press any criminal charges for the fortune that Drake had stolen from the Spanish, nearly causing an international incident. Instead she knighted him. Heralded as a national hero, fabulously wealthy Sir Francis Drake was praised in poetry, paintings, sermons, and ballads for his three-year, forty-thousand-mile voyage. He was considered not only the first Englishman to circumnavigate the globe, but he was also hailed as the first from his country to sail into the Pacific. The plunder from the *Golden Hind* filled Drake's pockets and the Queen's treasury.

Meanwhile all of the expedition's journals and charts were confiscated and kept as state secrets. The *Golden Hind*'s crew was forbidden on pain of death to describe the journey or their visit to New Albion.

In 1588 Sir Francis Drake had another chance at greatness when he helped lead a motley fleet of English ships in a stunning defeat of the invading Spanish Armada. But though he was rich and famous enough to afford a manor, a beautiful new wife, and a coat of arms, uneducated and often boorish Sir Francis Drake was never accepted as a gentleman among the closed ranks of the queen's court and the landed aristocracy.

He exemplified a quality that the English of the sixteenth century called "bottom," a virtually untranslatable characteristic that meant stoicism and enthusiasm, histrionics with conviction, foppery with toughness. He followed his own rules in an era that mandated that everyone know his or her place and act accordingly. One historian wrote that he often behaved "like an overgrown, if divine juvenile delinquent more suitable for house of correction than hall of fame." He traveled and took risks more for profit than for service—not even to the queen, whose orders he regularly disregarded.

Proud, undisciplined, and extravagant, Sir Francis Drake was always on the lookout for honor and plunder. After his voyage to New Albion he eagerly led several more government-sponsored pirate fleets into the Caribbean. Unfortunately storms, sunken ships, and enemy gunfire helped bankrupt every subsequent expedition. His luck had run out.

In 1596 Sir Francis Drake died of dysentery while aboard a foundering ship near the West Indies. Childless, he left his fortune to his unscrupulous younger brother, Thomas.

Acknowledgments and Author's Note

This historical novel is based on the true story of the 1577–1580 voyage of the *Pelican*, renamed the *Golden Hind*. The characters featured in the novel are recorded to have taken part in this remarkable adventure. They include Sir Francis Drake's teenage cousin, John Drake—whom I have nicknamed Emmet—and Drake's brother, Thomas Drake—whom I call Sky.

Many mysteries surround the voyage. Because the expedition was secret and officially "forbidden" by the queen (although secretly supported with her own monetary investment), most of the surviving charts and firsthand journals, and Captain Drake's own log were heavily edited, lost, or destroyed years after the ship's return. One of Sir Francis Drake's nephews used Chaplain Francis Fletcher's notes to create a somewhat glorified version of the journey in *The World Encompassed* (1628). Captain John Cooke was believed to have written *Narrative*, printed in 1855 and housed as a handwritten manuscript in the British Museum. Captain John Wynter, also in the novel, wrote *The Report* in 1579 to explain how he managed to bring the *Elizabeth* to safety back in England before the *Pelican*'s return.

Ironically, the Spanish Inquisition depositions of captured Spanish and Portuguese pilots and other kidnapped travelers provide much of what we know about Captain Drake's exploits in the Pacific. These too are not always accurate.

Conflicting reports of secret landfalls, especially in North America, further complicate research. Some of the most fascinating debates rage around the *Golden Hind*'s "lost harbor" in what is now the West Coast. Countless maritime historians, Native American authorities, and others have tried to pinpoint exactly where the *Golden Hind* moored during its attempt to locate the fabled Northwest Passage. As yet, no one has conclusively identified these ports.

I investigated the folk tales, early customs, medical beliefs and superstitions, and early history of Drake's native Tavistock in Devon. This information is amply recorded in early letters, plat maps, and court records that portray a time of intense political and religious violence and economic upheaval—not unlike our own.

Contemporary portraits, songs, poetry, and diaries provided me with insightful glimpses into the sixteenth-century English maritime experience. To gain an understanding of a sailor's life aboard a galleon, I found especially helpful the archeological research done in England in retrieving another, larger warship, the *Mary Rose.* This well-preserved ship and its contents, housed in a museum in Portsmouth, England, have revealed clues about sailors' clothing, food, weapons, and pastimes. Skeletal remains provide forensic insights into the life and death of boys and men in the early Tudor navy.

Unfortunately the *Golden Hind,* which had been beached in Deptford around 1580 as a permanent monument to the expedition, quickly rotted away. In 1618, nearly forty years after the ship had been brought ashore, a secretary to a Venetian ambassador visiting England wrote that the "ship of the famous Captain Drake looked exactly like the bleached ribs and bare skull of a dead horse." Souvenirs from the hull's timbers were made into a chair housed at the Bodeleian Library, Oxford, and a table, which can be seen at Middle Temple Hall, London. After eighty years of neglect the site was eventually cleaned up, and what remained was burned or hauled away. No other trace of the famous ship remains.